26

W9-BNP-667

DEATH AND THE
CROSSED WIRES

A TRUDY ROUNDTREE MYSTERY

DEATH AND THE
CROSSED WIRES

LINDA BERRY

FIVE STAR
A part of Gale, Cengage Learning

GALE
CENGAGE Learning

Detroit • New York • San Francisco • New Haven, Conn • Waterville, Maine • London

GALE
CENGAGE Learning

LIBRARY OF CONGRESS CATALOGING-IN-PUBLICATION DATA

Berry, Linda, 1940–
    Death and the crossed wires : a Trudy Roundtree mystery / by Linda Berry. — 1st ed.
       p. cm.
    ISBN-13: 978-1-59414-747-0 (alk. paper)
    ISBN-10: 1-59414-747-7 (alk. paper)
    1. Murder—Investigation—Fiction. 2. Police—Georgia—Fiction. 3. Policewomen—Fiction. 4. Georgia—Fiction. I. Title.
PS3552.E7475D4 2009
813'.54—dc22   2008049397

First Edition. First Printing: March 2009.
Published in 2009 in conjunction with Tekno Books and Ed Gorman.

Printed in the United States of America
1 2 3 4 5 6 7 13 12 11 10 09

DEATH AND THE CROSSED WIRES

CHAPTER 1

Methodists and Baptists have different opinions about whether a person has to be completely submerged in water for a baptism to be scriptural, or, since it's pretty much symbolic anyway—not involving the River Jordan, John the Baptist, or Jesus in his human form—if it's okay to get by with a sprinkling of water.

I'm not a theologian, but I will say this: I've never heard of a Methodist minister being electrocuted in the process, which is what had happened to Josh Easterling, part-time youth pastor at the Ogeechee Baptist Church, in front of all two hundred or so people who had come that beautiful hot June Sunday morning intending to see Crys Cleary baptized, hear a rousing but not too accusatory sermon, and then adjourn to the fellowship hall for a potluck dinner and ice cream social.

I was on the scene shortly after the electrocution, not because I'm a Baptist—I'm not—but because I'm a police officer. I'm Trudy Roundtree, the first and still the only female on the Ogeechee police force. The reason I broke the barrier is that the police chief's mother (my aunt Lulu) and our mutual grandmother (Jessie Roundtree) had brought pressure to bear on my cousin (Henry Huckabee), who is the Chief of Police. They threatened to quit making banana pudding and cornbread for Hen. Under this pressure, he overcame his instinctive feeling that as a female relative I should be under his protection, and caved in, even though it would mean he'd be required to expose me to the seamier elements of life and send me into danger.

Not that the streets of Ogeechee are especially mean most days, but you never know.

The police had been summoned to the church, along with an ambulance, by a quick-thinking deacon, Bobby Turner, who was an ex-Marine and knew an emergency when he saw one. He saw one when poor Josh Easterling started twitching, fell backwards into the water-filled baptistry, and didn't come back up.

The sanctuary had been decorated with peace and tranquility in mind—dark pews, forest green carpeting down the aisles, enormous brass chandelier over the dais, and tall stained-glass windows along both sides depicting scenes from the life of Christ—but confusion was in control. It would be a while before peace would reclaim the space.

Showing admirable presence of mind—or possibly an equally admirable knee-jerk impulse to do something devout in the paralyzingly horrible situation—Branch Harden, the senior pastor, had moved everybody to the back of the sanctuary, away from the baptistry, for intense and heartfelt prayer for divine aid while Bobby Turner administered CPR and they all waited for earthly help.

Now, an hour or so later, Hen was at the front of the church with deacon and hero Bobby Turner, Mrs. Harden, and the EMT squad, watching over the removal of Josh Easterling and surveying the scene, forming his opinions as to what could have lead to the "accident." The horrified witnesses had the privilege of calling it an accident. A good policeman—and Hen is a very good policeman—has to treat any unattended death (that is, unattended by a doctor—two hundred worshipful witnesses don't qualify) as a homicide until it is proved otherwise. It does no good to decide after a scene has been sanitized that it would have been a good idea to go over it and look for evidence.

Notwithstanding the officially neutral police attitude regarding what had happened and why, only the nearsighted or most blindly optimistic had any doubt that they had witnessed the death of their young youth pastor.

Officer Jerome Sharpe and I had finished taking names and trying to decide who among the congregation might have something useful to tell us about what had happened, something more useful than: "I couldn't believe my eyes," "It's the aw-fullest thing I ever saw," and the ever-popular "He was so young! He had his whole life in front of him."

Officer Jerome Sharpe has all the size and authority of a freight train. People take one look and decide there's no point in arguing with him about whatever it is he wants them to do. He had used his deep, rumbling, freight-train voice to calm the masses and cut loose the ones who had nothing to contribute but hysteria, encouraging them to do their weeping and wailing in private, or at least in smaller groups, away from the church. We'd narrowed the crowd considerably and retreated to a quieter, less emotionally charged part of the church complex.

So, instead of being in the midst of a hysterical crowd or a happy bunch of casserole-filled connoisseurs who, bypassing commercial products, would have been rolling spoonfuls of homemade ice cream on their tongues and trying to guess whether this was the recipe that used sweetened condensed milk, or whether Agnesanne Porter had used freezer peaches instead of some of the new crop, or if Harl Edwards had gone a little too heavy on the vanilla this time, there were only five of us in the fellowship hall, a large room at the back of the main building: Jerome Sharpe, Evan Saddler, Crys Cleary, Howard Cleary, and me.

In times of stress, people are easily confused. It's good procedure to interview witnesses while the event is fresh in their minds. Given a little time, purely innocently, they will begin making up reasonable, logical things to fill in the gaps in what they actually did see or hear, trying to impose some sense onto a senseless event. It's even worse when they've had a chance to talk to other witnesses, who've done the same thing. They can all be swayed by what other people say into thinking they saw something they didn't see.

So we divided them up. Jerome led Evan Saddler to one corner of the room and was overwhelming one of the folding chairs that had been set out for the ice cream social. Evan was the person in charge of the sound system for the First Baptist Church of Ogeechee, Georgia. Like Crys, he was a high school student. It would take Jerome at his relaxed, friendly best to calm Evan down enough to find out if he had any ideas about what had happened.

I sat across the room from Jerome and Evan, with Crys Cleary, the girl whose baptism had been so brutally interrupted, and Howard Cleary, her grandfather and guardian.

A pretty girl, slim, brown-haired, she looked a bit like a medieval peasant or a mystic in the white robe she was wearing for the baptism. She seemed bewildered and unfocused, understandable in the circumstances. Crys had been the person standing nearest to Josh Easterling when he picked up the microphone and underwent the shock that killed him.

Howard Cleary had broken with his well-known pagan tradition and shown up to witness this important event in Crys's life. Howard, also known as "How Come?," or "Howcum," because of his habit of questioning established truths and customs—as in "How come those fat cats in Washington can't . . . ?" writes a weekly column for *The Ogeechee Beacon*. The *Beacon*'s publisher and guiding light—my own guiding light, if you want to know—Phil Pittman, refers (but not in print) to Howard's column as "Howcum's Rant," since Howard can generate five hundred words of off-the-wall opinion, at the drop of a hat, on subjects as wide-ranging as leash laws, UFOs, tattoos, and the best time to spray for soybean rust. Usually he manages to take a position nobody else would have thought of. Phil's attitude toward Howard is amusement. Phil says Howard's column is popular because readers like getting mad with Howard over issues that take their minds off really big problems or things they could actually do something about. Howard seems to thrive on stirring things up, and the column gives him plenty of that kind of affirmation, but today all that blustery, edgy cantankerousness was absent. He'd pulled his chair close to Crys's, put his arm around her, and was doing a good job of keeping his mouth shut.

Crys was nearly as white as her robe, her brown eyes the size of silver dollars darting here and there as if in an effort to find answers to the questions that had only now quit tumbling out of her mouth: "What happened?" (It looks like Josh Easterling got electrocuted.) "Is Pastor Josh okay?" (No.) "If he's not okay, why am I okay?" (Because you weren't in the water.) "Am I okay?" (I expect you will be.)

Like Jerome's job with Evan, my job with Crys was to settle her down and see if she had anything useful to say. It was tempting to ask leading questions, based on cartoon depictions of electric shock. Did she see sparks? Did his hair stand on end? Did his eyes bug out? I controlled the impulse.

"How are you doing?" I asked her.

"How do you think she's doing?" Howard asked.

"I didn't get shocked or anything," Crys answered, but she looked like she was *in* shock. Even as she spoke to me in a soft, hesitant voice, her gaze wandered, her fingers plucked at her robe. "Can I go get dressed now?"

"Not yet," I said quickly, glaring at Howard to keep him from weighing in again. I don't usually have a lot of luck at the intimidation game, partly because I'm female and several inches short of six feet tall, and partly because people like Howard

Cleary, who have lived in Ogeechee all my life, if not all their lives, remember me as a child. No, for intimidation, Jerome Sharpe, five foot eighteen or so, is much more effective. But this time Howard merely nodded at me, patted Crys's shoulder, and subsided. I took that as evidence that he was as shaken up over what had happened as everybody else.

"I'll make this as quick as I can," I said, "but I need to try to find out what happened while it's fresh in your mind. Just tell me what happened the best you can."

She shivered, and her unfocused eyes might have been looking backward, or inward, or through the far wall as she spoke. She grabbed a handful of white robe and clenched it. "I was watching him so I'd know when to go to down into the water. I was nervous, so I was watching him. And he . . . he reached for the mike . . . it wasn't pointed right, or something, and he reached for it and . . ."

"And what?" I prompted.

She jerked, as if surprised to see me. "I don't know. All of a sudden he started . . . twitching. Twitching." She shivered again and leaned against her grandfather. "He . . ."

I waited.

When she spoke, it was so softly I had to lean closer in order to hear. "First I thought he was maybe like kidding around, and then I realized he wouldn't kid around about something like that, solemn and sacred, I mean. I mean right there in the baptistry and all and in front of . . ."

Howard cleared his throat and squeezed her shoulder.

Crys took a deep breath and sat up straight again before continuing. "I didn't know what was happening. And he just sort of slipped under the water . . ."

I was getting used to her pauses, so I waited.

"And then Mr. Turner was yelling and then the lights went out." She let her breath out in a whoosh and closed her eyes.

"Bobby Turner took charge," Howard explained. "He was pretty quick on the uptake. Yelled for the kid to unplug the mike and somebody to pull the breakers, and he made sure nobody went in after Josh before that happened. Told me to call nine-one-one, which I did."

"And then what?" I asked.

Again it was Howard who answered, which was fine. He was likely to be a better witness to this part than Crys would have been.

"Bobby got him out of the water and started CPR. Kept at it till the ambulance got here. Pretty obvious it wasn't doing any good, but he kept at it."

"What about you?" I asked Crys. "What did you do?"

"Nothing, I guess. I was like frozen or something. I stayed there on the steps down to the baptistry, waiting for somebody to tell me what to do. I kept thinking things would get back to normal, I guess."

"The preacher's wife brought her to me," Howard said.

"Oh, yeah. Mrs. Harden was helping me get ready," Crys said. "She was waiting with me, with a towel for after." She managed a weak smile. "I was nervous. People probably get nervous, and then with Pastor Josh . . . I was scared and didn't know what to do. Do people usually get scared? Is it part of her job to calm people down?"

I thought that was a rhetorical question, but Howard answered. "Lots of people probably want to back out at the last minute, and she's there to keep 'em from it." It sounded like he was recovering from shock and was getting back to his normal irascible self.

Howard's comment had the effect of calming Crys, or at least re-directing her thoughts. "Gramp didn't really want me to do it," she explained, "so maybe I was extra nervous because of that. Anyway, Mrs. Harden grabbed me when Pastor Josh started . . . when he. . . . She grabbed me."

"Kept Crys out of the water. Probably saved her life," Howard said. "Raynell Harden had more of a job today than she bargained for."

Crys gave him a little smile and grabbed another handful of the white fabric in her lap.

"Okay," I said. "I guess that's all for now. Thanks, Crys. You go on home now. This was a terrible experience. I'm sorry. Let your granddaddy pamper you a little bit."

"Yes, ma'am," she said.

"That's my best reason for living," Howard said, taking hold of her arm to help her up. For once, I didn't get the faintest whiff of sarcasm or irony in what Howard said. Howard was widowed—and childless, since the death of Crys's father. He'd probably been speaking the plain truth.

Howard kept a firm grip on Crys as they walked out. I joined Jerome and Evan, noticing that Evan was paying more attention to Crys's departing form than he was to Jerome or me. He was probably wishing he was leaving with her, that the last hour had never happened, that all he had to worry about was how to get the attention of a girl he liked.

"Evan and I were talking about what passes for a sound system here," Jerome said, "and Evan was trying to help me understand how it works. You got any questions for him?"

"I'm not big on electronics," I said.

"Give him a try," Jerome invited.

"Well, for starters, I thought most microphones these days weren't really electric, just little portable things, that wouldn't— couldn't—carry a charge. Certainly not enough of a charge to do what was done to your pastor," I said.

"Yes, ma'am, you're right, they are. Most of 'em are, but that's not the kind we have, except for the clip-on one Reverend Harden uses. There's a hardwired microphone up where the pastor stands when he's giving the sermon, the kind you're talking about, but you can't move it around, so then we have this one on a cord for when people want to talk from someplace else."

"And it's your job to . . . what?"

"It's not much of a job. I sort of try to adjust the volume for like the choir and the pastor. And when we need the other mike, the one with the cord, like we did today, I get it out and put it in the holder there in front of the baptistry."

"When was the last time you used this particular mike?" I asked.

"I don't know for sure. We don't use it much."

"Not havin' a lot of baptisms?" Jerome asked leaning back and causing a protest from his chair.

"Not a lot, no."

"Tell her about the amplifier," Jerome prompted.

Evan had been doing pretty well so far, which I attributed to Jerome's calming influence and the fact that they'd probably already been over most of what I'd asked. His hair was sticking out in all directions, but I knew that was the style, caused by gel, not stress or electricity. Now he squirmed and dropped his gaze to the floor. He didn't want to talk about the amplifier.

"Oh. Yeah. Okay. When we use that mike, I'm supposed to put it where whoever wants it can reach it. It just kind of sits there in the holder until we're ready for it, and then I plug it into the amplifier." He looked up as if to see if we were understanding. I nodded. "You don't want it hot all the time," he continued, "because it picks up all kinds of noise, people coughing and papers rattling and that kind of stuff."

"Got it," I said. "So you're saying the mike was dead until you plugged it in?"

Evan started picking at the skin around his right thumbnail. He looked miserable. "Dead. Yes, ma'am." After a pause, "It's really old? Maybe that's what caused it? Something got old or something?"

"We'll try to find out," Jerome said. He caught my eye and I nodded.

"We're through here, Evan," Jerome said. "We'll get back to you if we need anything else. Thanks for your help."

"You're welcome," Evan said, and wasted no time getting out of there.

"Anything else?" I asked.

"Says he was watching the preacher for the signal to plug in the mike, which he did, then he wasn't looking at the preacher any more. Which I believe. If he'd been looking in that direction at all, he'd've been looking at the girl, or looking for her, to see when she came into sight going down the steps into the baptistry. Not exactly a space case, but he is a teenager. He says there was some kind of static in the amplifier and a burning smell, but he didn't think about that until later. What I think is he wasn't paying much attention to anything till the sparks started flying and the amp started sputtering."

"Did he have anything else to say about the equipment?"

"He's a kid. Knows everything. Says the church keeps putting off getting new equipment. Wants to spend the money on less important things like a new roof and helping foreign missionaries take the gospel to southeast Asia."

"This is a church, after all, not a big corporation," I said. "We might have guessed the equipment would not be state of the art."

"Be a miracle if it was," Jerome agreed. "Patched up and worn out, if I know anything. Rotten shame."

We found Hen, Bobby Turner, and the Rev. Branch Harden and his wife, Raynell, standing in the parking lot watching as Josh Easterling's body—bagged, tagged, and wrapped up for its trip to Atlanta and the requisite autopsy—was sliding into the hearse.

Hen, Jerome, and I were in our short-sleeved summer uniforms, but the heat and humidity of the June weather made me wish for something even lighter. Bobby Turner, in a golf shirt still damp from his efforts to save Easterling, was probably the most comfortable person in the group.

Harden, the "regular pastor," had shucked out of his suit coat, revealing a white short-sleeved shirt. With his customary bow tie in place, and with his usual air of confidence replaced by stark confusion, he looked more like an old-timey general store clerk who'd found a rat in the cracker barrel than a pastor. As Jerome and I approached, he was running his hand back and forth through his sparse curly brown hair and saying, "Lord knows, this is just about the worst thing I've had to deal with in all my years in the ministry. Don't know where to start."

Mrs. Harden was holding his coat and shivering in spite of the heat and the fact that she was wearing a lightweight dress and sandals that revealed toes with pale pink nails showing through her pantyhose. Even with the hose, which I'd have skipped in the heat, she had to be cooler than he was. Women do have the best of some things. Maybe the shivering had more to do with shock than temperature. She brushed tears from her red-rimmed eyes and reached for her husband's hand. The pastor was pale, not teary, but clearly shaken.

"Start with yourself," Hen advised. He's never short of advice. If he'd been around, he'd probably have felt comfortable advising the Lord God on creation. Comes of being an only son of an adoring mother, not to mention the Big Chief of Po-lice. "Preach yourself a sermon about trusting the Lord and serving your fellow man, and it'll all come together for you," Hen said. "In the meantime, you got a lot of work to do. And you better call off your services for this evening. We're gonna make sure your church is locked up, and I don't want anybody in there till I say so. Don't want anybody else getting hurt."

Mrs. Harden made an odd gurgling sound.

The idea of doing his job, which was surely to comfort and counsel his stricken congregation, seemed to brace the distraught minister. He shook hands with Bobby Turner. "Don't know how to thank you for taking charge, Bobby. If you hadn't kept your head, we'd probably still be in there trying to think of the phone number for nine-one-one."

"That's my training kicking in," Turner said, shaking his head and offering a weak smile to acknowledge the pastor's attempt to lighten things up. "Just wish it had made a difference."

Turner left. The pastor shook hands with the rest of us and then, taking his wife's hand, ambled off toward his home at the far side of the lot where the church stood. Mrs. Harden's voice faded away as they walked. "I'll get us some dinner first. Then we can figure out what to do. Probably get the phone tree going to cancel . . ."

"Mmm, mmm," Hen said, watching them go. He handed Jerome a bag. "Get somebody to look at this microphone."

"Yes, sir, Chief. You think we're goin' to have to arrest the First Baptist Church for criminally negligent microphone maintenance resulting in death?"

"Never hear the end of it if we do," Hen said. "We'll probably just settle for tragic accident. Miz Harden says she'll see the poor man twitching every time she closes her eyes for the rest of her life. The reverend says Josh was a real spark plug."

"He did not," I protested.

Hen grinned. "No, come to think of it, what he said was that young Josh was well-beloved and had brought a lot of energy to the youth program here. He will be sorely missed."

"That's more like it."

"Y'all learn anything?" Hen asked.

"All I learned is that Howard Cleary isn't all crust. He's a softie where Crys is concerned," I told him. "What about you?"

"Our would-be hero of the day, Bobby Turner, says the boy, Evan, didn't have the sense to unplug the thing, just stood there goggling."

"One of the older women said it took everybody a while to realize what had happened," Jerome said. "She said she saw him, the victim, waving his arms and everything, but thought it was probably one of his dramatizations about the electrifying power of Jesus or something. Sounded to me like she thought he was a little too much of a sparkplug for First Baptist Church of Ogeechee."

"Good Lord Almighty! Bobby Turner deserves more credit than I'd been givin' him," Hen said. "I hope somebody buys him dinner today. You learn anything from talking to the boy?"

"Evan Saddler," Jerome said. "Gave us a rundown on the equipment. Kid's a mess. Took me a while to get him settled down. Nervous, wasn't he, Trudy?"

"I can understand that," I answered. "Probably thinks we're going to blame him. Nervous, yes."

"We'll have to see about that," Hen said. "You think it was guilty nervous?"

I looked at Jerome and shrugged.

"Guilty of something," Jerome said. "Maybe lusting after that angel girl, Crys, right there in the church."

"Oh, good Lord!" Hen said

CHAPTER 2

By Monday morning when I got to the stationhouse, Jerome Sharpe already had a report on the microphone.

"Somebody messed with this thing," he said, bypassing official language as he placed the offending microphone on Hen's desk.

"That was quick," Hen said.

"Took it to my cousin Waddell over in Glennville. He does electrical contractin'. Made him wear gloves, so he wouldn't forget this was official po-lice business."

"How'd he like that?" Hen asked.

"Seemed impressed, just like he was s'posed to."

"And he found something wrong?"

"Uh-huh. It's the kind of thing you never would see if you weren't looking for it, but Waddell's a Baptist and he doesn't like the idea of people being afraid to be baptized, so he wanted to find some reason to explain what happened, something besides the Lord passing judgment on First Baptist Ogeechee. And he found it. Look here."

We all bent closer. Jerome pointed with a pencil.

"This little wire here ought to be connected over here instead of where it is. This thing's been what you call cross-wired. Guaranteed to short out."

"Lordy, lordy," Hen said.

"Any way it could have got that way by accident?" I asked.

"No way," Jerome said. "See, the wire's not loose and wobbly, where it might have got jiggled around and touched the wrong thing on its own. Uh-uh. It's been soldered that way on purpose."

Hen looked at Jerome through narrowed eyes. "What do you make of that, Officer Sharpe?"

The look didn't rattle Jerome. He knows that's Hen's way of making sure thought processes are engaged. "Well, Chief, what it says to me is somebody was up to no good with this." He paused before adding, "Maybe they didn't mean to kill anybody, but they meant some kind of no good."

Hen smiled. The analysis of the situation was under way, complete with putting his officers on the defensive. "You're suggesting that poor man's death might have been more or less accidental?"

Jerome straightened up and smiled back at Hen and took up the challenge. "Yeah, Chief, I am suggesting whoever did it might've just wanted to cause some mischief. Might not have set out to kill anybody."

"Somebody smart enough to tamper with the thing but dumb enough not to see the consequences?" Hen asked.

"A random act of malice?" I suggested.

Hen turned his smile on me. "I don't see where that'd be much fun. Vandals like to see results."

"What would have happened if Easterling had grabbed it when he wasn't standing in the water?" I asked.

Jerome nodded as though he'd expected the question. "I asked Waddell that. Thought maybe whoever it was had a grudge against the choir director or one of the choir members, or somebody like that. What he said was you'd probably get a shock but not a big one."

"Like when you shuffle across a carpet in cold weather and then touch somebody?" I asked.

"Maybe bigger than that," Jerome said. "Waddell said some

of the old guys used to brag about how they'd check to see if a line was hot by touching it. He said they claimed they could tell what the voltage was by how big a shock they got. A little buzz was one-twenty, you'd get a pretty good jump out of two-twenty, and if it was four-forty, it would knock you down."

"Sounds pretty stupid to me," I said.

He laughed. "Uh-huh, but you'd learn pretty quick to use the back of your hand."

"Why's that?"

"The way electric current works, your muscles go into a spasm, and if you're holding on, you can't let go. Not many people make that mistake more than one time." He shook his fingers and grimaced as though he'd received a shock.

"I'll try to remember not to do that," I said. "Could this mike have gotten like this because somebody was trying to fix it and didn't know what they were doing?" It was far-fetched but possible.

Hen nodded. "That would point to Evan Saddler, wouldn't it?"

Jerome shrugged.

"Could be," I said. "Irresponsible. I hate to say it, but it sounds like typical adolescent behavior to me."

"Officer Roundtree!" Hen pretended to be shocked. "You sure got a dim view of young people! Haven't you heard stereotyping is bad practice? Are you due for some sensitivity training?"

I mimicked Jerome's shrug.

Hen continued. "Maybe it was somebody who could foresee the consequences but didn't care."

"Still sounds like a teenager to me," I insisted. "As a group they aren't known for long-range planning. And it's possible that Josh Easterling really was meant to die. Maybe somebody did just what he set out to do. Or she." Sometimes I forget to be an equal opportunity blamer.

Hen was no longer smiling. "Our Monday morning just got one whole heckuva lot more interesting. It's up to us to find out which of all those possibilities is the truth. Instead of sitting around like we usually do, drinking coffee and eating donuts and telling jokes, we're gonna have to find out who messed with this thing."

"And why," Jerome contributed.

"And what whoever it was had in mind," I added.

"And if Easterling was the intended target," Jerome said.

Hen sighed and got to his feet. "I've got to get my charmin' self over to a meeting with the mayor to talk about our budget. Got to convince him I'm not making up all these things I tell him I need money for, so I don't want to irritate him any more than I have to. Meanwhile, Trudy, you go talk with the Reverend Mister Branch Harden in light of this new development. See if you can find out who had access to that microphone. Jerome, you go find that boy and talk to him again. Ask him if it had been broken, if he or somebody else tried to fix it. And thank your cousin Waddell. Buy him a catfish dinner on me."

Jerome grinned. "He'll go for that."

Hen sighed. "And I'd better get the crime scene boys—and girls," he added with a look at me, "—over there to that church before we let the Baptists loose, just in case there's anything for us to find."

Hen reached for the phone. As Jerome and I left, I heard him yelling, "Dawn, call the mayor and tell him I'm on my way."

Sometimes it's nice not to be the boss.

Chapter 3

On my way to visit the Hardens, I stopped at the First Baptist Church and was gratified to see the police tape still firmly in place around the entrances to the sanctuary, the main doors locked. At the side, I found a locked door next to a sign that read "Office, Ring Bell." I gave the button a firm push, and a moment later Louella Purcell, the church secretary, bustled into view. She peered through the small window in the door and, recognizing me, opened the door, waving a welcome as she turned back to answer the telephone. She was obviously not having a routine Monday morning, the kind of day when she could count on the pastor not bothering her too much and she could update the attendance and offering figures from Sunday over a leisurely cup or two of coffee.

Mrs. Purcell looks exactly like you'd want your church secretary to look: mature, moderately but not aggressively stylish (wouldn't want to suggest an excessive interest in material things, after all, instead of wholehearted financial support of God's agenda), businesslike, plump, kind. She was wearing a matching knit shirt and slacks—Lane Bryant, not Saks Fifth Avenue, I judged—in a shade of blue that went well with her blue eyes and stiff gray curls. She was having a hard time not being frazzled.

"Phone's been ringing off the hook." She swiped her glasses off with an abrupt, impatient motion, and let them drop dramatically to dangle off her bosom—there's no other word for it—from a beaded cord necklace. "People just can't get over it."

Between phone calls, during which I lost track of how many times I heard her repeat that she didn't know yet about a memorial service, I told her there'd be some police lab technicians coming to go over the scene, and she told me the pastor usually didn't come in on Monday mornings and I'd probably find him at home and those young people would all need to have grief counseling and maybe everybody else in the church, too, and wasn't it awful. . . . The ringing telephone interrupted her again, and I made my escape.

I've always imagined Monday as kind of like a pastor's Saturday, the easiest day of his week, breathing space before he starts feeling the pressure to perform again the next Sunday. Even if that's how it usually is, this wasn't a routine Monday morning for Pastor Branch Harden, any more than for Louella Purcell.

Rev. and Mrs. Harden couldn't have been happy to see me, but they're pros—professional enough to have themselves and their house in order by ten o'clock on a summer Monday morning, knowing there's no telling when somebody will drop by the preacher's house for a visit. No, it's not fair, but people *will* expect the clergy to be better than average, even in non-spiritual matters. They smiled and invited me into their living room, an attractive, not especially modern room, a comfortable blend of old wood and modern upholstered pieces. I have an eye for old things, since my house and most of what's in it used to belong to my grandmother, and the Hardens had some nice old pieces.

"Y'all holding up okay?" I asked. They both looked much more composed than when I'd last seen them, in the church parking lot. Raynell was wearing slacks, a blouse, and open-toed sandals without pantyhose. She looked more like her usual self, an attractive fortyish woman, than the red-eyed, haggard woman she'd been the day before. The pastor, too, in a sports shirt instead of dress shirt and suit coat, the strain missing from his face, was his usual smooth, good-looking self.

"Lots of strain," the reverend answered. "People want to do something and there's nothing to do. Want to understand it, and there's no way to do that, either, except to say it was in some mysterious way the will of God." He didn't look like that platitude gave him much comfort.

The telephone rang in the kitchen, but neither Harden made a move to answer it, merely exchanging resigned glances. "We'll let the machine get it," Mrs. Harden said. "That'll separate the ones with something to say from the ones that just want to talk. I've already got a crick in my neck from bein' on the phone so much this mornin'." Then, briskly, "Josh's family's from Brunswick. They'll have the funeral down there, but we'll have a memorial service here, too, when we can get it arranged, probably next Sunday, we think. When can we get back in the church?"

"Next Sunday will probably be all right, but you'll have to talk to Hen about that," I said. "We'll need to keep people out till we find out exactly what happened. I've told Miz Purcell some people will be coming in to go over the church and see what they can find."

"Thanks for coming by to let us know," Reverend Harden said.

"That's not all I came for," I said. "We're trying to get a picture of what happened. Miz Harden, you had a good view of the baptistry. Did you notice anything wrong?"

She shuddered. "Of course I did."

"Before Josh grabbed the microphone," I said. "Did you see anything wrong with it? The position? Anything?"

"No, but I wouldn't. I was giving my attention to Crys and trying to make sure we didn't miss her cue to step down into the water."

"Did you see anybody messing with the microphone?"

"When?" She began to look alarmed.

"Any time. Sunday or any other time?"

"No, but I don't know why I would."

"What are you getting at?" her husband asked.

"It's early yet, but our initial investigation" (I imagined Jerome's cousin Waddell puffing up over being called "our initial investigation") "indicates there was something wrong with that microphone—"

"Of course there was!" Mrs. Harden said. If she'd been thirty years younger, she'd have no doubt said, "Well, duh!"

"—and that somebody tampered with it," I finished.

"What? What do you mean?" Both of them looked at me in shock. "But . . . Branch, that means . . . it means somebody meant to hurt you!" Mrs. Harden clapped her hands over her mouth, eyes wide.

"Not necessarily," I said. "Do you know of anybody who'd want to hurt you?"

"Nobody but Foy Lynch over at the Methodist Church," the pastor said in what even he obviously recognized as a weak attempt at humor. He shook his head as if to erase it.

"Of course not!" his wife said. "Not everybody thinks he's infallible, like the Pope, but nobody would. . . ." She trailed off, apparently unsure what nobody would.

"Okay," I said. "If you think of anybody who might have wanted to hurt you, or embarrass you, let me know. What about your music director or somebody in the choir? Any enemies there?"

They consulted with a glance and both shook their heads.

"Well, if you think of anybody with enemies, let me know."

"Of course," Reverend Harden said.

"For now," I continued, "let's talk about who could have tampered with it."

They looked at me blankly. I tried again. "Who had access to the microphone?"

"Access? You mean who could have gotten to it? For all I could say for sure, it could have been anybody in town," Reverend Harden said. He looked to his wife, and she grabbed the lifeline and swam with it.

"That's right, anybody in town. Not just our congregation," she said. "We serve the community in a lot of different ways. There's the senior citizens' luncheon every month and a blood drive once in a while, and the clothes closet for the needy. All kinds of people come in."

"That's right," Branch Harden contributed. "Anybody at all. And nobody would necessarily notice if somebody was foolin' around with the sound equipment, or think anything about it if they did. You know how it is. Everybody's doing whatever they came to do. And if somebody was up to no good—which sounds like what you're talking about—they'd make sure nobody noticed them, wouldn't they? But why would anybody do something like that?"

Now it was my turn to shake my head, offering no answer. "Okay. I get it that it doesn't have to be somebody in your congregation. But it was somebody, and we need to find out who and why. Let's go at it this way. You keep the church locked during the day?"

"Yes," he answered. "I have office hours over there, but I'm out and around a lot, too, with hospital visits and different things, so we just automatically keep it locked. Louella'd quit on us otherwise, and we don't want to lose her. She's skittish ever since she walked into her kitchen one day and found a man going through her pocketbook. You'll remember that, that rascal had quite a run before y'all caught him, didn't he?"

"He's repenting at leisure," I said, not responding to the implied criticism over the OPD's sloth in capturing the man.

"Y'all have a jailhouse ministry?" I asked, knowing they didn't. Tit for tat.

The pastor got back on track. "We leave the doors at the church set where they lock automatically when they close."

"Okay." I made some notes so they wouldn't forget this was a police interview. "What about keys?"

"Oh, my goodness! You're seriously thinking this is police business, aren't you?" Mrs. Harden looked scandalized.

I gave her my own version of a "well, duh" look. "Yes, ma'am. I'm afraid so, and the more I find out today, the sooner we can get this cleared up and the less likely I am to have to bother you again. Who has keys?"

"I do," the pastor said. "Louella. Irene Todd and her daughter, who come in to clean for us . . ."

"Stan," Mrs. Harden said, when he ran down.

"Yes, Stan Smith. He takes care of the building and grounds."

"Calvin," Mrs. Harden prompted.

"Yes, Calvin Hall. He's the Sunday School superintendent. He's the first one here on Sunday mornings." He stopped again.

"Annie."

This struck me like a game they'd perfected—tag-team conversation. Did he really need prompting, or was it that she couldn't wait for his thought processes to process—or didn't trust him to say the right thing?

"Annie Hicks has a key so she can come in and practice on the organ when she wants to," he explained.

"A lot of keys out there, then," I said.

"But they're all good people, responsible people, people who need them," Harden protested. "You can't be thinking—"

"Just collecting information at this point, Reverend Harden. What about Evan Saddler?"

"No. Evan doesn't have a key. He doesn't need to be there when it's not open for some other reason. I wouldn't feel comfortable trusting a key to somebody like him."

"Somebody like Evan? What do you mean? Don't you trust him?"

"He means Evan's a teenager, that's all," Raynell offered, proving I was in good Christian company if I occasionally stereotyped teenagers. "He's not saying he thinks Evan would have done anything wrong. It's just that he's that age. There's no reason to think Evan is any more irresponsible than any other young person, is there, Branch?"

"No, of course not, or we wouldn't be letting him work for us." On his own time, without pay, most likely. "But you ought to talk to Evan. He might know something about it."

"We've talked to Evan," I said, on his side now that somebody else was being unfairly and unreasonably critical of teenagers as a group. "Now, about that microphone. Do you use it every week?"

"No," Reverend Harden said. "We don't. It's sort of a backup. I have a little one that clips on to my lapel. Cordless. Unless there's something special going on, we don't need another one. Maybe it just got old."

"Why didn't Easterling use a clip-on?"

"They're expensive and we just have the one."

"Branch is real careful with it. He doesn't use it in the baptistry, so it won't get wet and ruined," Raynell explained.

"When we use that one, the one Josh was using, we put it in a holder, kind of a stand, attached to the ledge in front of the baptistry, so my hands will be free," her husband continued, nodding to acknowledge her point. "Normally I'd be the one doing the baptizing," he went on. "It's a real privilege to baptize somebody and celebrate their entry into the Kingdom, but since Josh and Crys had a special relationship—no, not what you're thinking, just that he'd helped her make her decision—I didn't see any reason not to let him do it. It meant a lot to her, and I was willing to go along with it, even though some of the more traditional—I don't want to say hide-bound—members didn't like it."

"Why is that?"

"Josh wasn't ordained, and some people choke over that, but I didn't see the harm in this special case."

"I sided with the ones who didn't want Branch to let him do it," Raynell said. "I don't think it's a good idea to downplay the status of the pastor and let people get the idea that just anybody can do what he does."

"Well, honey, I did let him, and he died for it, so you must have been right," the pastor said, a trifle sharply. Then, with obvious condescension, he explained to both of us, "It's a church matter, a spiritual matter, not a legal matter, so it was up to me when you got right down to it, and I . . . well, maybe I wanted to make a point. Raynell knows that."

"What kind of a point?" I asked.

He looked surprised, as though unused to being asked to explain himself. "That some people don't understand the fine points of how our denomination works as well as they think they do. I made the point that letting him do it didn't break any rules and I'm the one who gets to decide things like that in my own church."

"It was bound to upset some people, and I didn't think Branch should have let him," Raynell said. "They talked about it a lot, Branch and Josh, about whether Josh could do it. He was so full of ideas! That's why the young people liked him so much. In fact—remember, Branch?—he wanted to baptize Crys in the Ohoopee. Well, it's not the River Jordan, of course, but he wanted to make his first baptism as symbolic and memorable as possible."

"But I couldn't go along with that," her husband said.

"Why not?" I could see why the young people would have loved it.

"I had a lot of reasons," he said, and an obstinate look came into his eyes that made me wonder if he had simply felt the need to make another point, that he could pull rank over a popular young threat to his authority for any reason he wanted to.

"The river's low right now, and it's so hot, and we have a lot of old people who couldn't get down there," Raynell said, coming to his defense.

"So," I said, (not saying, "Instead, you had the baptism inside, and let Easterling officiate, and he got electrocuted." Could Harden have been jealous enough of the popular young man to do something like that?) "Was anybody upset enough over his ideas to want to kill him?"

They both just stared at me. The pastor's wife recovered first.

"If you're looking for some kind of a controversy, that's one," Raynell said, "but not the kind of thing people would try to hurt anybody over. You can't blame us! Josh should have known better than to grab that thing while he was in the water! It's like using a hair dryer while you're in the bathtub. Everybody knows that's dangerous!"

"It was just like him, though," her husband picked up. "Josh was full of energy, full of jokes, impulsive, and he was nervous, too, over his first baptism. He wouldn't have thought about that. When he saw the mike wasn't pointing the right way, he'd have just reached out and—"

What had Crys said? Something about the mike not being pointed right. "The mike wasn't in the right position?"

"It was pointed down, wasn't it, Branch? I forgot that. Yes, it was. Naturally, he'd have wanted to straighten it out. I guess he doesn't have—didn't have—much experience with using a hair dryer."

Maybe we'd gotten to something useful. "And everybody knew the plan—that the baptism would be inside and Easterling would do it and that he'd be using that microphone?"

"Oh, yes," Raynell said. "Well, we didn't put an ad in *The Beacon,* but there was no secret about it. Everybody who was involved would have known."

"Josh. Crys. Evan. That's all, really," the pastor said. "But I wouldn't think most people would have known about, or even thought about, the microphone, if that's what you're getting at."

"That's one of the things I'm trying to get at," I said. I consulted my notepad, the essential tool to keep me from getting so far off track I can't find my way back. "I'd like to try to narrow down a time when somebody could have tampered with the microphone. Can either one of you remember the last time it was used?"

"I'll have to think about it," Raynell said.

"You could ask Evan. He'd know," Branch suggested.

"Yes." I folded my notebook closed—a ploy to suggest we were through with the hard stuff and were just relaxing now. "Tell me about Josh Easterling," I said, doing all I could to suggest neighborly, not official, interest.

"We all thought he was an answer to prayer," Mrs. Harden said. "It's hard to keep young people interested in church. Even the good ones have a lot of choices to make, and we'd been worried about our youth program. Josh was an answer to prayer."

Her husband took up the song of praise. "He's . . . was . . . still in school, over at Brewton-Parker, so he was just part time with us, but the young people were really responding to him."

"Was there anybody in particular who didn't like him?"

"No," the pastor said.

"Not as far as I know," said his helpmate.

"And you can't think of anybody who might have wanted to

33

hurt him? Maybe not kill him, but hurt him?"

They looked at each other and shook their heads. "I can't believe anybody would have wanted to kill him," he said. "He was a little too modern for some of our people, too free and easy. Some people thought he was too irreverent. But—"

"Nevertheless." I waited.

"It must have been a joke," Raynell said. "Meant as a joke. Josh was always joking. Joshing around, is what Branch called it." A brief smile, inviting me to appreciate her husband's wit. "That's one reason people liked him, the young people especially. Made him a lot more fun than their parents."

"Would it have been somebody's idea of a practical joke?"

"I don't know about that, but you know how teenagers are," the pastor said. "Their enthusiasms sometimes get ahead of their judgment. I don't know. Maybe somebody . . . maybe somebody thought it would be funny to give him a shock."

"So you're suggesting it was one of the kids?" I asked.

"Branch! That's horrible! You can't mean it!"

"No, I don't mean that. I don't think that. I'm not suggesting anything. But . . . it had to be something like that, didn't it? If you're right and it wasn't just an accident, it had to be somebody who didn't know how dangerous something like that could be."

I smiled a kindly police-officer smile. "This doesn't look like an accident. Somebody was trying to hurt somebody, and if nobody really had anything against the actual victim, well . . ."

I trailed off suggestively and stood. Let them chew on that.

Mrs. Harden saw me to the door but didn't open it.

"I think you're looking in the wrong direction, looking for people who wanted to hurt Josh. It had to be aimed at Branch, not Josh," she said in a low voice.

"Oh? You're saying you think your husband is less likeable than Josh?"

"Of course that's not what I'm saying." She flushed with embarrassment or suppressed anger before she got control of herself and tried to answer my unreasonable question reasonably. "Josh hadn't been here very long."

"And Reverend Harden has been here long enough to make enemies? Anybody in particular."

"No. You're twisting what I say."

"Oh? I thought you said—"

"I know what I said," she snapped, and then immediately took a softer tone. "But Josh was so good at what he did, making connections with the kids, so warm and kind and loving. I just can't imagine anybody wanting to hurt him." She paused to take a delicate swipe at the corner of her eyes and moderate her voice.

We seemed to be in a loop, conversationally, and she must have realized it. She put her hand on the doorknob and resumed her pastor's wife persona. "Poor Crys. I know she's taking this hard. Feels like it's her fault. She's had a sad life, you know. Her mother died about three years ago, not long after she got out of jail. You remember all that?"

"Some of it," I said.

She lost no time reminding me. "Her mother and daddy tried to hold up a liquor store. That was several years back, now, and her daddy got shot in the process and her mother went to jail. That's when Crys came to stay with Howard. Crys was supposed to go back with her mother when she got out of jail, but she was going to finish out the school year here, and before the year was out, her mother, Sandra, had died."

"I don't remember much about that," I said. "Where was she living?"

"Over in Macon, in a sad little apartment. I went to see her once, tried to witness to her, help her turn her life around, but she didn't seem to appreciate it, so I never went back."

35

"How did she die? Some kind of an accident?" I asked.

"Slipped in the bathtub while she was drunk and drowned. Something like that. No telling what kind of life she was leading, and her with a daughter. We've been trying to do what we can for poor Crys. Orphaned at thirteen, an age when all she ought to have on her mind is school and boys."

"That's tough," I agreed.

Raynell Harden flashed a daintily catty smile. "Don't tell anybody I said so, but living with Howard Cleary might not be a bed of roses, either, even if he does think she hung the moon. She'll probably never be baptized now, the way Howard is about religion, and her everlasting soul will be on his head."

I nodded, struck by the image, and moved toward my car. As soon as Mrs. Harden had closed the door behind me, I called Jerome's cell phone to see if he'd solved the case yet.

CHAPTER 4

Petty crime isn't something we in the OPD usually welcome, but I was glad for the fact that Jerome had been delayed in getting to Evan by the more pressing need to interrupt a couple of little boys who were building a fire in the weedy vacant lot behind the post office and deliver them to their parents along with a stern lecture. I could join him in interviewing Evan, and after my talk with the Hardens, I had some questions we hadn't asked when we talked to him on Sunday.

Evan Saddler had a summer job at the hardware store, and that's where I headed. I found Jerome inside, talking to the cashier, who turned out to be Bettye Saddler, Evan's mother. As I approached, she abruptly came from behind the counter. She slapped the counter top, getting the attention of George Berkeley, who'd been working in another part of the store, and gestured for George to watch the register.

"Back here," she said, including me in the invitation.

Jerome and I followed her toward the back of the store, where she summoned Evan, who'd been opening boxes in the cramped hallway, and led the way to a room that was probably an office, judging from the desk, papers, and filing cabinets. It was a good-sized room but so filled with miscellany that our knees were practically touching when we sat, even with Evan sitting on the desk instead of on one of the grimy chrome-and-vinyl chairs that blocked access to a low-slung couch that was useless anyway because of the boxes stacked on it. A narrow path led to a doorway through which I could see a sink.

"So?" Bettye said, once we were settled. She was a small, stringy woman with a worried look that seemed at home on her pinched face. Her right hand massaged her left arm, and she sat straight and stiff, both feet, in sporty leather athletic shoes, planted firmly on the floor.

"You know about what happened to Josh Easterling," Jerome said.

"It's all over town," Bettye said. "I don't know any more than anybody else, and neither does Evan."

"Well, ma'am, that's where I think you're wrong. Maybe you weren't on the spot, but Evan was."

"I know that."

"Yes, ma'am, then you also know Evan's one of our best sources of information, him being the one in charge of the church's sound system." Jerome smiled at her, which usually melts icy women into warm puddles. It didn't seem to have any effect on Mrs. Saddler. She looked at him without expression as he continued. "Didn't see you yesterday. You don't go to church there?"

"No." She made an obvious effort to relax, abandoning the grip on her forearm and clasping her hands together. "Evan told me what happened. And he said he told you what little he had to tell, so why don't you leave him alone?"

"Does Evan get in trouble a lot?" Jerome asked.

Evan, squirming in miserable embarrassment, looked like someone who wished he was somewhere else.

"He does not. Whatever happened, he didn't have anything to do with it." Bettye Saddler made up in feisty loyalty what she lacked in size.

Jerome leaned toward Mrs. Saddler. She leaned back, even though he spoke softly, gently. He'd given up on the smile.

"Well, see, he's the one takes care of that electrical equipment, and he's the one that plugged in the microphone and then stood and watched while the poor man got electrocuted."

"Mom, I didn't—"

"You don't scare me," Bettye Saddler said. She sat up a little straighter. "We know our rights, and we know about police harassment, police brutality. We'll get a lawyer—"

"Mom—"

"Miz Saddler!" I raised my voice. In that tiny space, it sounded surprisingly forceful. Everybody shut up.

"Let's start over," I said. "Miz Saddler, we just need to ask Evan some more questions. We have to find out what happened to Josh Easterling. We aren't accusing Evan of anything."

Good cop, bad cop—but usually in our duet, I get to be the bad cop. It confuses people.

"Ask me," Evan said, a little shakily, I thought, but trying to take responsibility. Good for him. "It's okay, Mom."

"Did you know Josh Easterling pretty well, Evan?" I asked.

"What's that got to do with the price of birdseed?" Bettye asked. First Raynell Harden, now Bettye Saddler. This was a great day for interfering, overprotective women.

I tried to smother her fire with a heavy blanket of words.

"We have evidence that what happened to Josh Easterling wasn't entirely an accident," I said. "And it would help if we had a sense of the kind of person he was, how people felt about him. Different kinds of people. Pastor Harden, now, he said Josh Easterling was well liked, that he was friendly, that he liked to joke around. Is that how you saw him, Evan?"

Darting a glance at his mother, Evan answered, "Well, yeah, pretty much. Everybody liked him."

"Everybody? Somebody else told me people didn't like him, thought he wasn't a good influence on the kids." That was my paraphrase of Raynell Harden's comments.

Evan threaded his fingers through his wild hairdo and gripped his head, giving the impression he was trying to keep the whole thing from exploding. "I don't know about that."

"Did you like him?"

Again, that nervous gesture. "Sure, I liked him okay. He had different ideas for things for us to do, field trips, like that. Not the same old sh . . . the same old stuff. He wasn't narrow-minded like. . . ."

"Like the parents," Bettye said. "It's okay, Evan." She turned to me, ignoring Jerome. "I liked Josh, too, if you want to know. With Evan's daddy gone, I appreciate a man who'll take time for kids. He wasn't all that much older than they are, so he knew how to talk to them, knew what they were interested in. He might have tried a little too hard sometimes to act like he was one of the group, but he was somebody they could respect and trust and look up to and talk to about things they might not want to talk to their parents about. He wasn't stuffy and holier-than-thou. Isn't that right, Evan?"

Evan nodded. I wondered if there were things he talked to Josh Easterling about that he didn't want his mother to know.

"He was fun," Evan said. "If you're looking for somebody who didn't like him, some of the older people complained about some of the things he did with us."

"Anybody in particular come to mind?" Jerome asked.

"There was some complaining when he took the youth group to the arcade in Statesboro," Bettye said, a good mother, help-fully directing police attention away from her son. "You know that place where they have all kinds of games? Some people thought that wasn't a good atmosphere for them to be running around in. They think they're doing their kids a favor by protect-ing them—trying to protect them—from the world, from anything and everything that doesn't go on at church."

"He was fun, you said. Funny? Jokey?" I was thinking of what Raynell Harden had said, something about jokes, joshing.

"Yeah." Evan looked puzzled.

"What kind of jokes? Telling jokes? Playing jokes on people?"

"Well, yeah, both, I guess. He was just funny. He played jokes on people. Like when Harley and Ted weren't back at the bus when they were supposed to be, he drove off without 'em. Just went around the corner, but . . . Well, maybe that's not a joke. Anyway, he didn't do mean jokes. Harley and Ted had it coming. He wouldn't let us pick on people."

I followed up. "If he liked to play jokes, did people think they could play jokes on him?"

"Sure. I guess."

"Did the jokes ever get out of hand?"

"You mean, like, could somebody have thought it would be funny to give him a shock?"

"Yes, Evan, that's exactly what I was getting at. Can you think of anybody who might have thought that would be funny?"

His headshake was firm and decisive. I glanced at Jerome, signaling it was his turn.

"You remember when was the last time you used that mike?" he asked.

"I'd have to think about it." Evan had quit messing with his hair, and now had his hands flat on the desk, supporting him as he rocked and thought. "Or maybe I could look it up. I didn't have things set up right for a special music thing one time, and Miz Hicks got mad at me even when I said nobody had told me, and Reverend Harden said we needed to start keeping a notebook where people would write down what they wanted me to do if it was anything special. I always check the notebook. Unless somebody forgot to write it down, it'll be in there. Maybe when the women's trio sang three or four Sundays ago, or when that little girl was baptized. I don't remember which came last, but I could look it up."

"Where's that notebook?" Jerome asked.

"Miz Purcell keeps it in the office."

"We'll take a look at it," Jerome said.

"Are you and Crys . . ." I paused, trying to find a phrase that would say what I meant without marking me as hopelessly adult or prudish. Evan rescued me.

"Is she my girlfriend? Not a chance."

"She'd be a lot better off with Evan than that boy she used to go with," Bettye Saddler said, patting her son on the knee.

"Dixon was okay," Evan said.

"He was a big jock, and his daddy bought him that flashy car," his mother said. "That's all he had you don't have. Crys'll come around, once she gets over him."

"Dixon?" I asked. "Dixon Tatum?"

"Yes, Dixon Tatum," Bettye Saddler said. "Football player. Supposed to go off to college on a scholarship for playing ball, when they don't have enough sense to give money to smart kids, kids who might amount to something sometime if they could get a little help."

"Mom!"

"I'm just saying, Evan. Evan's a good boy, a smart boy. Took honors at the science fair. Ask anybody. Why don't y'all leave him alone?"

"Mom." Evan looked uncomfortable. "It's not helping anything for you to tell them how smart I am. A smart science student could have done whatever was done to that mike."

"Oh." She looked from Jerome to me without finding the reassurance she was looking for, then back to Evan. "I was just trying to help," she mumbled.

"Should we be talking to the boyfriend?" I asked, wondering if a boyfriend who didn't like Crys's friendship with an attractive young minister—a jock, who might not have known how dangerous his actions were—was the explanation for the malfunctioning microphone.

"Good luck," Evan said.

His mother made a sound between a snort and a choke. "He's not in the picture any more. Got killed in a hunting accident last year. You remember." I did remember, then. Hunting accidents aren't uncommon, but the whole community was shaken at losing such a popular young man. I was especially shaken at the similarity to the way my husband had died. I've almost quit having nightmares about that.

Bettye turned back to Evan. "You're fighting a ghost right now, son. Hold on. She'll see you when her vision clears."

Evan blushed. "It's not like that with me and Crys, Mom. I keep telling you."

"But you like Crys. Would you play a joke to get her attention?" I asked.

While his mother was drawing an affronted breath, Evan answered calmly.

"Sure, I'd do that. Once I rigged a . . . oh. You're still talking about Pastor Josh. No, I know better than to mess with electronics. For one thing, it would ruin the mike, and I'd get in trouble."

"If anybody found out you were the one who'd done it," Jerome amended.

"Well, yeah, but I'd be the obvious one, if it had something to do with the mike, wouldn't I?"

"Yes," I said. "You're smart enough to know that's why we're talking to you. So, if you didn't do it, who did? Who do you think could have?"

"Isn't that your job to figure out?" Bettye asked, not as aggressive as she'd been earlier, but reminding us that she was there to look out for her son.

"Yes, ma'am," Jerome said, smiling at her again. I think he'd been hurt when she hadn't fallen under his spell immediately, and he was determined to charm her. "But the way we figure things out is by paying attention to what people tell us. Different people know different things, and they tell us different parts of different things, and we put it all together. Let me tell you, Chief Huckabee is one smart policeman, and when he listens to me and Officer Roundtree, and we're pretty smart, too, we usually get to the truth. We're not out to get your boy. We're out to get the truth."

She nodded, still wary, but coming around.

"Evan," I asked. "Who could have gotten to the mike to tamper with it?"

The sight of his mother nodding at Jerome must have assured Evan that it would be all right to cooperate with the police.

"We keep it in a sort of a cabinet at the back of the church," he volunteered.

"Does the cabinet have a lock?" I asked.

Evan smiled. "I guess you can call it a lock, but it's lame, just a kind of a lever thing that comes down and fits into a slot and keeps the doors from opening. All you have to do if you want to open it and don't have the key is slide a credit card in the crack and push the lever up."

"You ever done that?" Jerome asked, risking his status as good cop.

Evan grinned. "I don't have any credit cards." The smile widened. "I used my pocketknife."

"Evan!" Bettye Saddler protested.

"It's okay, Mom. I have a right to get in there. I have a key, remember? But one time I didn't have the key with me. No big deal."

"No big deal," I agreed. "But it's good to know it wouldn't be hard for somebody to get to it, even if it was locked up. Evan, whoever tampered with it knew where to find it. Any ideas?"

"It could have been somebody looking for something else," his mother offered.

"It's usually kept locked?" Jerome asked.

"That's right. Usually. Mostly to keep the little kids from getting in there and messin' around, I think."

Jerome nodded and continued. "But if somebody opened it with a credit card, they wouldn't be able to lock it back, would they? If I'm picturing this thing, you could put the lever up with a credit card, but not back down. That right?"

"Right," Evan said.

"So if that happened, it would have been left unlocked. Would you notice if it wasn't locked sometime?"

This answer didn't come quite so quickly. "Yeah. I would."

"That happen sometime lately?"

"Maybe. Maybe it was unlocked, but I wouldn't remember exactly when. It's not a big deal."

Maybe not to Evan.

"There's just one other thing I wanted to ask about, Evan," I said.

Evan turned to me.

"On Sunday morning, you put the mike out."

"That's right."

"In that holder on the ledge in front of the baptistry?"

"That's right. Brother Harden—he's usually the one baptizing people—likes it there so he can talk into it while his hands are busy."

"And it's your job to position it where he can talk into it?"

"Well, yeah." He was uncomfortable now, and I thought I knew why.

"So why did Josh Easterling reach out and grab it?"

"How could Evan know that?" Bettye asked.

"I think he does know that. Evan?"

"It was pointing down, Mom. That's why. But that's not how I put it." He turned from me to Jerome, to his mother, and back to me, looking for understanding, messing with his hair

45

again. "Sure, if it was pointing down he'd want to straighten it up, but if it was—"

"If?" I asked.

"Okay, yeah, it was. But it wasn't my fault. I know I put it in the right position."

"Maybe the holder is loose and wouldn't hold it?" Jerome suggested.

Evan didn't jump at that way out. "No. It would be my job to fix it, if that's how it was. I don't know what happened. Maybe somebody from the choir jiggled it or something like that. An accident."

Except for the crossed wires in the microphone, I could have believed that.

I caught Jerome's eye and we both stood.

"Thanks for your help, Evan, Miz Saddler," Jerome said. "We'll get to the bottom of this. Don't you worry."

"What've we got?" Jerome asked as we walked to our cars.

"Not much."

"You like the idea it was a joke that got out of hand?" Jerome asked.

"Not much," I repeated. "I thought for a minute we might have had a jealous boyfriend."

"Jealous of the preacher?"

"It happens, Jerome."

He sighed. "Well, it looks like if that's what was going on, the jealous boyfriend would have to be Evan. Even if it was a joke, Evan is still our number one suspect. Keeps coming back to him."

"But I don't think he did it," I said, based solely on the fact that Evan had looked relieved when I promised we'd get to the bottom of things. His mother had looked worried.

"I don't think so, either," Jerome said, without giving his reasons.

"What does that leave us with?" I asked.

"Let's go see what the Chief has to say."

Right. Like he's the fount of all wisdom.

CHAPTER 5

Jerome and I weren't able to hear what the chief would have to say about our interviews with the Warners and the Saddlers because when we got back to the stationhouse, Hen wasn't there.

Dawn, the dispatcher, said Hen had come back from his meeting with the mayor without visible wounds and had gone over to the Baptist church to get in the way of the crime scene techs from the GBI field office in Statesboro. "Want to make sure the heathen among 'em don't hurt themselves too bad laughing over jokes about the preacher dying in the baptistry," she said, in a poor but recognizable imitation of Hen. In her own voice she told us Hen expected to be there the rest of the day. Then, in a better imitation, "Got a date with the high sheriff in the morning. Wants me to go with him and his boys to see about a meth lab, help him make sure the excitable ones don't rush in like a pack of wild hogs and do irreparable damage to themselves and our case."

"Good goin', Dawn," I said. Seeing skinny little twenty-one-year-old Dawn trying to bulk up and lower her voice to suggest Hen was a treat. Ever since I've been on the force, I've been trying to cure her of the unwholesome reverence she has for him. I took it as a good sign that she'd mimic him, and especially that she'd make him sound arrogant, like he thinks he's the only one who knows anything. One of the reasons Hen is so good at his job is that he knows how important it is to play nicely with others. With the lamentable exception of his one female cousin on the Roundtree side, he's generous with praise and appreciation for what others contribute to law and order.

"Probably be tomorrow afternoon before he comes back in," Dawn said in her own voice. "Said he expects to have the autopsy report on Josh Easterling and maybe something from the GBI by then and he'll want to talk to you and Jerome. Said he hopes y'all can entertain yourselves till then."

"Got it."

For a while, I entertained myself with police matters less absorbing than a murder, or an accidental murder, or whatever we were dealing with. Then I decided to break for lunch. It was well past noon. I punched the speed dial for *The Ogeechee Beacon,* hoping Phil hadn't already eaten. Since he's the boss at *The Beacon,* Phil can break for lunch whenever he feels like it, and he usually feels like it whenever I do. In spite of the story of Josh Easterling's spectacular death, Phil wasn't under particular stress. He'd already written the short factual report. Most people in Ogeechee read *The Beacon* to confirm whatever they already know, and maybe to see what the County Extension Coordinator has to say about the perils of putting too much nitrogen on your cotton (boll rot, delayed maturity, and defoliation), the relative merits of Sioux, Desirable, Caddo, Oconee, and Cape Fear pecans, or reduced spray programs for peanuts. They do not read *The Beacon* to keep up with the news. The Easterling story would be all over town before the paper came out on Thursday, so, although *The Beacon* had to cover it, the story didn't have to be a long one. Unlike big newspapers in a brutally competitive market, *The Beacon* has a steady reader-ship, which means it can respect its readers and their privacy and does not have to go out of its way to exploit the sensational and prurient aspects of whatever is going on in town. This policy extends even to the obituaries, so formulaic the reader usually can't even guess the cause of death.

"I'm glad you called," Phil said. "I'm ready to get out of here. Home Cookin'?"

No, he wasn't hinting that I should cook for him. Home Cookin' is a new lunch buffet place near the *Beacon* office. Restaurants have a rough time in Ogeechee—too basic and they can't compete with the amateur good cooks, too experimental and customers can't make the stretch. Phil and I have been trying to give Home Cookin' a fair chance instead of sticking with our old favorites. Even late in the lunch hour, the steam table held zipper peas, crowder peas, baby lima beans, fresh tomatoes, fried sweet potatoes, creamed corn, fried okra, pork chops, pot roast, fried chicken, biscuits, cornbread sticks, and peach cobbler. At our table, Phil looked at his loaded plate, smiled, and sighed. "You're a lifesaver, Trudy. Maybe not my life, but somebody's. Saved me from having at temper fit right there in the office. Nobody's getting anything done. All anybody wants to talk about is what happened at the Baptist church. We may have to do a whole edition on the dangers of out-of-date wiring."

"Not for publication, of course, but we don't think it's that simple," I said. "In fact, Hen's over at the church now with. . . ."

"The word around the water cooler is that First Baptist Church is a hotbed of hypocrisy and this tragic event is the modern equivalent of a thunderbolt from heaven, designed to scare them back on the straight and narrow."

"You got all that around the water cooler? I didn't even know you had a water cooler."

"That was literary license. I meant the computer terminals. Anyway, that's what's on everybody's mind, and there's strong consensus that God was smiting the Baptists for getting too fundamental and narrow and un-Christian."

"Consensus? Really?"

"Well, no. You're right, consensus is not the right word, but there wasn't anybody who was willing to face Howcum—and, anyway, to argue that with him would be to assume his major point, that the accident was an Act of God. Poor Gwendy Mitchell was just about in tears. She never has learned how to take him with a handful of salt. She nearly fainted when he tried to claim that buncha Baptists wouldn't let anybody go ahead and call nine-one-one till after they'd taken up the collection."

Phil paused to calm himself with a spoon full of peas, rich with the unmistakable flavor of pork drippings. As Hen has said more than once in my hearing, "If it cain't be made better with bacon fat, it probably wasn't fit to eat in the first place."

"Howard sees himself as the star in the drama at the Baptist church yesterday?" I asked, scattering sugar as I waved a spear of fried sweet potato.

"I think it's safe to say he considers himself the star of whatever movie he's in," Phil answered, brushing sugar off the back of his hand. "Howcum being like he is, the accident suggested several columns to him."

"You don't look happy about that." I scattered more sugar, just to see how much attention Phil was paying to me.

"I'm too mature to get into a food fight with you right here in public," he said, "no matter how I'm provoked."

"Just trying to take your mind off Howard," I said.

"By being as irritating as he is?" Phil asked.

"Have some artery-clogging food," I suggested. "It'll make you feel better."

He grinned and picked up his knife.

Somebody or other has said that the only time you really see a person is the first time. After that, what you see is prejudiced by whatever happened in that first encounter. If that's even partly true, there's no chance I could describe Phil Pittman in

51

any objective way. I've known him so long I don't even remember the first time I saw him. It would have been in grade school, I think, sometime along in there. Or maybe even earlier. He's a few years older than I am, closer to Hen's age, so I might have known him as Hen's friend. I know I knew him in high school, or knew who he was, casually, the way you know everybody in a school, or in a small town, for that matter.

When I say Phil is stocky, freckle-faced, with reddish tones in his brownish hair, that's probably true, or was once true. When I say he has a studious air and an impish twinkle in his eye, that's probably not what someone meeting him for the first time would see. That person might see some gray—distinguished sandy gray—in the hair, might notice the neat shirt, trim slacks, friendly smile that I no longer see because they're always there. I do still notice the way he has of fiddling with his glasses when he's embarrassed or stalling for time. I used to think that was irritating; now I think it's endearing. That's how familiarity changes the way we see people. When I came back to Ogeechee after a time in Atlanta that left me widowed and emotionally battered, Phil and I took a new look at each other and became friends. Now we're "more than friends" as the phrase goes, and I can't imagine not having him in my life. Which obviously doesn't mean we're always lovey-dovey (as another phrase goes).

I wonder if, when he looks at me, he sees a slim brown-haired, blue-eyed girl with a smart mouth, or something else. I'll have to ask him some time.

Unlike me, Phil has never married. He says the pressures of taking over the family business, and his father's failing health, which put more and more of a burden on him, not to mention the small pool of eligible women in Ogeechee, kept him from finding the right woman. I think he was waiting for me and just didn't know it. I'll ask him about that sometime, too, but not when he's in a bad mood and not in a public restaurant.

Phil neatly cut a piece of pork chop away from the bone and continued in a calmer tone, but still on the subject of Howard Cleary. "You know I usually leave him alone and let him rant."

"It's a tribute to your heroic self-control and superior strength of character," I said, smiling sweetly.

He saluted me with his fork, but gently so the pork didn't fall off. "Right. And this morning was a real test of that self-control and strength of character. The things he was suggesting were too far out, even for Howcum."

"He was probably baiting you," I said.

"Maybe. He asked me if I'd like to have a column on how the Baptists have got so full of themselves and so sure they're the only ones in the world with a direct line to God that it's about time for God to take them down a peg."

"Let me guess. If God liked Baptists as much as they think He does, why did He—or would Howard say 'She' to rile people up even more?—why did God let this good Baptist preacher-boy die in the baptistry?"

"Close. At the very least, according to Howard, it was an act of God, at least passively. If it wasn't, then why didn't God stop it?" Phil said.

"That's very close to what Reverend Harden said, Phil. Maybe Howard's onto something."

"He did offer to find Scripture to back it up. I'll bet he could, at that. He also offered, if it would suit me better, to do a column lambasting liberalism in modern religion. I'm not sure where he stands, except that it sounds like he's against whatever the religious establishment is in favor of. Maybe it's even simpler than that. Maybe he's willing to take whichever side he thinks will rile his audience."

"Which did you choose?" I asked, batting my eyelashes at him.

My batting was wasted. Phil was seeing only Howard Cleary.

"I told him it didn't make any difference to me whether he figured the Baptists were in the middle of a conservative resurgence or a fundamental takeover or a flaming liberal sell-out, I wouldn't run it." Phil paused for a swallow of tea. "So he suggested one about sexual predators."

"He really suggested that? That's kind of strong medicine for *The Beacon*." Considering the timing, I wondered if that idea was connected with Josh Easterling in Howard Cleary's mind. And, if so, if there was any justification for it. I'd have to look into that.

"That's what I told him, and he put on a totally unconvincing hurt look and tried to act like he thought we aren't doing our duty to the newspaper-reading public if we insist on dodging serious issues."

"He thinks people take him seriously?"

Phil shrugged.

"So what will you run?"

"He was a bit put out with me by then—you know I don't usually rein him in—so he offered to do an exposé on how the FDA and the National Institutes of Health are in a conspiracy to ruin Southern cuisine with their unholy jihads against pork drippings. I told him we'd go with that one, but only the usual five hundred words. Not one of his two-parters."

"People will probably get a kick out of that."

"Uh-huh. And some of them will believe him, but that shouldn't do any real harm. I think he's setting me up for next week. He's been wanting to sound off about beauty pageants."

"What's his angle?" I can't speak for other readers of *The Beacon*, of course, but I am usually entertained by Howard's columns.

"Something along the lines of how wrong it is to spend all that money and energy training those girls for something that won't do them any good, teaching them to think beauty is only as deep as the skin and the beaded gown and tiara you can get your daddy to buy for you, instead of getting them to join the Army and get some useful training."

"I cannot for one second believe he's in favor of women in the military," I said, "but the attack on beauty pageants will go down well." Of course it would not. There's a thriving beauty pageants industry here. Hardly a week goes by without a Miss, Teen Miss, Little Miss, Little Mister, or Baby Miss This or That—Ogeechee, Sweet Onion, Georgia Peach. "Will it cost you advertisers?"

"No. They don't advertise much, and I always run plenty of pictures for them. Anyway, most of the time people think he's kidding."

"Do you?"

"Do I what?"

"Think he's kidding?"

"I'm never sure where he is. If he's not kidding about these last two ideas—the church and the beauty pageants—he's a heretic and a feminist."

"Heretic sounds right to me."

"So that's my Monday," Phil said, turning back to his vegetables. "How's yours going?"

"Not as interesting as yours, even counting the fact that it looks like somebody tampered with the microphone that electrocuted Josh Easterling. God had a human helper."

"No kidding!"

"No kidding. Hen's over at the church now with the GBI guys, trying to find out what happened."

"You're saying murder." Phil still looked stunned.

"They're trying to find out," I repeated.

"I hope Howcum never finds out. The next thing would be a veiled, or not so veiled, attack on the victim's character."

"He must have had it coming?"

"Sounds like Howcum logic, doesn't it?"

"We don't know anything about Josh Easterling that would make that credible," I said. I'd definitely have to check into that sexual predator angle.

"That's irrelevant," Phil said. "What do you know about Easterling?"

"Not much, but he was a college student, after all."

"He's had time to make enemies. Maybe a lurid past caught up with him—gang connections, bad companions who couldn't stand it when he went straight."

"Give me a break!" I gulped iced tea.

"Think about it."

"I don't want to think about it—or about what kind of things you've been reading to give you such ideas."

Untroubled by my comment, Phil continued in the same vein. "Or maybe he had a wife with three small children who's been suffering from postpartum depression who cracked under the strain of childcare and murdered him because he was off having a good time."

"He was a single twenty-three-year-old student who planned to be a minister, Phil, but go on. I'm fascinated."

Now he pointed at me with a spoon full of peas. "Ah, yes. That's what you think, of course, and you may be right. But even that kind of person can have enemies. I remember one of my college friends, no, make that one of my acquaintances; no, one of the campus legends of my college days, who got three different girls pregnant his senior year. Think of all the people who might have wanted to murder him!"

"I see your point. But a seminary student?"

"Even they can fall, Trudy."

"You're right. We'll be looking into it."

He nodded. "I should hope so."

To change the subject from poor Josh Easterling's character, we critiqued the food—in low tones, since the owners were *Beacon* advertisers and probably somewhere on the premises. The cooks at Home Cookin' were doing a lot of things right. The peas and beans were excellent, not overcooked. The fried sweet potatoes with the sprinkling of sugar and cinnamon were crisp on the outside, soft on the inside, and scrumptious. The corn was a little too sweet, the chicken a little too greasy. Phil and I both skipped the cornbread. Once you've had Aunt Lu-lu's version, you don't want anybody else's. Late as we were, it might not have been their fault that there wasn't a choice of desserts. A solid B+ for Home Cookin'. Good enough to stay on our list. We were into our cobbler—a shame not to stand over the sink and eat the peaches fresh, instead of cooking them, but this was a good cobbler—when Phil said, "I ran into Digger DeLoach the other day."

Uh-oh. "You getting some yard work done?" I asked.

"No, and from what he told me, you aren't, either."

"I've been meaning to talk to you about that," I said. "He was backed up. Couldn't get to me for a while. Anyway, don't jump to conclusions. Digger's not the only one around here who does yard work." I knew I was babbling. "Maybe I need more of a landscaper, a landscape architect or something, not just somebody who does yard work."

Phil waited, a spoon full of cobber halfway to his mouth. I didn't like the expression on his face, but I had no choice but to talk. "I realized that the whole project wasn't as clear in my mind as I thought it was," I said.

"The project." Phil's voice was flat.

I found I couldn't take another bite of cobbler. I couldn't look at Phil, either.

"I thought what you're referring to as the project was pretty well defined," Phil said.

"I did, too, when we were talking about it," I said.

"You said you'd get the house and the garden fixed up by the end of the summer, and—"

"I know I did, Phil. I know I did. But there's a lot to think about. It's hard to know where to stop. I keep getting overwhelmed. And whatever I do, I want to do it right."

"And you've been thinking," he said.

"Haven't you?"

"Haven't had any new thoughts," he said.

"Well, I haven't either, not really."

"Okay, then. What's going on?"

"We'll talk, but not here," I said.

Taking me literally, he didn't say another word as he slowly finished his cobbler and went back to *The Beacon*.

It was probably my guilty imagination that made me think he stalked off in anger. I'd been tactless, at the very least. I may be too self-centered, too self-absorbed, for my own good.

We'd been talking in code, of course. In what I was beginning to be afraid was a fit of temporary insanity a few months back, we'd started talking about a wedding. The logical place for a late summer—or maybe autumn—ceremony was at my house, which I've known even longer than I've known Phil. I have no more objectivity about the house than I do about Phil. It's old and needs work, but I love it like it is and have a hard time thinking of making changes. There could be a reception on my grounds, where the plants have had their own way about things for too long.

Anyway, I'd been too busy to devote my every waking thought to thinking about a wedding, like some starry-eyed eighteen-year-old who thought worrying herself sick over each detail to ensure the perfect wedding would mean happily-ever-after. What did Phil think, anyway? That that was all I had to do?

We would have to talk. Definitely. Soon and seriously.

CHAPTER 6

Hen thrives on interactions with other law enforcement agencies and personnel. He believes the relationships are important and that observing others at work helps keep him up to date on procedures and technology as well as aware of current issues and emerging problems.

Monday had been a rich day for him, and he was so full of himself, and stories, that he started spilling over as soon as he had an audience, in the form of Dawn, Jerome, and me.

First, he told us about his outing with the county sheriff.

Meth has been around for a good many years. For the longest, cheapest high, this ice is hard to beat, and it's so easy to manufacture there's a whole "come watch me make it" subculture among those with short sight, weak minds, and a death wish. This industry is especially prevalent in rural areas in the Midwest and South, which puts a new spin on the usual notion of home cookin'. Lately, cheap imported crystal meth has been undercutting the homegrown mom and pop industry, but there are still enough local entrepreneurs to keep things cooking right here at home. The sheriff's crew Hen went out with had found the meth lab they'd gone looking for and absolutely connected the operation to a couple of Ogeechee men. This last part was easy since they found the men, sitting in their truck half a mile from the lab. Sitting there dead.

"Some farmer shoot 'em?" Jerome asked, slouching against the door of the break room with a coffee mug in his hand. He likes to encourage Hen when he's in a story-telling mood.

"Nah. Being the geniuses they were, they'd done the customary thing and helped themselves to a supply of anhydrous ammonia from an unsupervised farm tank," Hen answered. "Where they went wrong and paid the ultimate price was using their propane cylinder one time too many. You know how that stuff corrodes the valves. Looks like it leaked into the cab with 'em. We found 'em both sitting there looking surprised at how fast that unfiltered jolt of anhydrous ammonia quick-cooked their innards. Did us all a favor by helping get some sludge out of the gene pool."

I shuddered. "A bad way to go."

"But quick," Hen said. "You'd think even the kind of low-functioning specimens who'd mess with that stuff would have enough sense to know how dangerous it is."

"Brains didn't come into it much," Jerome reminded him. "Even before they got fried."

Hen nodded his agreement. "So we got that place roped off and called the GBI HAZMAT crew and got ourselves out of there like our shirt tails were on fire."

He looked at his audience—the adoring Dawn, the encouraging Jerome, and me—with satisfaction. "Y'all get this Easterling thing wrapped up while I was off helping the sheriff protect the people of the town, the county, the state, the world, the universe, and man-and-woman-kind in general?"

"Not quite, Your Excellency," I said, drowning out Jerome's more respectful, "No, sir." Since Jerome and Hen do not share a grandmother, Jerome can't afford to be as mouthy as I am, even if he were inclined that way.

"We thought we might be getting ahead of ourselves if we didn't wait for the autopsy and the report from the crime scene techs," I said, frowning at Jerome to suggest he shouldn't contradict me.

"Got that here somewhere," Hen said. "Came while I was gone. Come on back to my office and let's see what we've got."

Luckily for us, although Ogeechee is so small and rural that we can't afford a lot of expensive high-tech equipment, we're also small enough that we don't have much of a backlog of cases. If we were a suburb of Los Angeles, for instance, there's no telling how long we'd have to wait for attention to our needs. The three of us crowded into Hen's office, and he consulted some papers.

"Autopsy first," he said. "Nothing we didn't expect. Not like he had a weak heart and died of surprise instead of electrocution. No medical conditions that would have contributed, no drugs. The poor fella died just like everybody thought he did. Got short-circuited and had his blood boiled right there in the baptistry. Maybe not as quick as our methamphetamine geniuses, but quick enough."

I shivered. Somehow Hen's description gave me the most vivid picture so far of what had actually happened.

"The CSI team come up with anything?" Jerome asked.

"Spent a lot of time for not much result," Hen said.

"Nothing?"

"Lots of something, just not much result. So far, anyway. Found forty million fingerprints on the microphone and stand and the ledge at the front of the baptistry where the stand is screwed down. It's a public place. People crawling all over it all the time. They may not be inclined to take all those fingerprints seriously."

"But they'll check them out, won't they?" I asked.

"That's their job, Officer Roundtree, but keepin' us happy isn't their only job. Might take 'em a while to run 'em all down."

That would have to do.

"Did they check the cabinet where the mike was kept?" I asked.

"They know their business, Officer Roundtree."

"I'll take that as a yes, then."

"They found some scratches that make it look like somebody slipped a knife blade between the doors of that cabinet to unhitch what passes for a lock. Nothing much useful there. No helpful distinctive little nick in the knife blade. Don't know where that leaves us."

"We got a good list of suspects, though, Chief," Jerome said, giving me a wink.

Hen turned to Jerome. "Tell me."

"Well, maybe not a good list. More like a list of everybody concerned, the likely suspects."

"Who all you consider likely?" Hen asked, suspicion in every syllable.

"We got that Evan Saddler, who mighta wanted to kill anybody he thought of as competition for that girl's attention. He's got it all—motive, means, opportunity, everything."

"Hmm," said Hen.

"Evan is the most obvious one to have messed with that microphone," I contributed. "And he knew Easterling would be using it. But even Delcie could probably break into the cabinet where the microphone is usually kept, so Evan's not the only one who could have gotten to it, and neither one of us really thinks he did it."

"Noted," Hen said, without making a note. "Who else?"

This rundown of suspects was Jerome's idea. I waited to see who he'd finger next.

"Evan's mama, Bettye-with-an-e Saddler," Jerome said. "That's a mama hen acts more like a mama rooster. She mighta killed the preacher that had so much influence with Crys so her boy could have a clear shot."

"Really?" Hen said. "I'm impressed with your imagination, son, but not with the rest of it. That's what you've got for motive. She got means? Opportunity?"

"Probably not," I said, "but she works at the hardware store. She probably knows how to do all kinds of handyman things. What happened to Evan's daddy, by the way?"

"I don't know, but I'll bet my mama does."

I smiled at Jerome. "As long as we're making a complete list of suspects, I want to put Raynell Harden on it."

"Hold on a minute," Hen said, proving he doesn't have to make written notes to keep up. "You got anything to suggest Crys and the preacher boy had something going on, to support your jealousy motive?"

We had to admit we didn't.

"Okay," Hen said. "You got anything real that points to Raynell Harden, or is that more of the same?"

"More of the same," I admitted. "Wild speculation is all we have so far. Miz Harden's just as protective of her husband as Bettye Saddler is of her son. Maybe she did it to keep the young upstart from putting the real preacher in the shade."

Hen took a deep breath and tried to touch his elbows behind his back, a relaxing stretch I assumed he needed because of his stressful day with the sheriff and not because of Jerome and me.

"She's got motive, then," Hen said.

"And opportunity," Jerome said, supportively. "Can't deny opportunity."

"If she'd have the know-how," Hen said. "So we got the preacher's wife, the kid who takes care of the sound system at the church, and his mother," he said. "Good work, men!"

Jerome grinned at me. "Might be one of those women knows something she didn't tell us, Chief."

"I'd bet on it," Hen said.

"There's the preacher, too," Jerome said. "Maybe he was jealous of this other guy, being so popular and all. He'd have opportunity, and be more likely than Miz Harden to know how to do it. Yeah, Trudy, I know that's sexist stereotypin', profilin', whatever you want to call it, and I'm against profilin' on general principles, even of teenagers, but it's still the truth."

Hen relaxed his stretch. "Y'all might as well include Crys and Howard Cleary, as long as you're at it," he said.

"Right," I said. "Sure. I like that. Anybody could tell you it was suspicious that Howard showed up at a church. And he'd probably tell you he knows how to do all kinds of things—even cross-wire a microphone."

"That Crys, now, that's harder to see," Jerome said. "But did y'all notice she didn't get into the water with the preacher? Maybe she was waiting for her cue, like she was supposed to, or maybe she knew what was going to happen."

"Motive?" I asked.

"No telling," Jerome said. "Teenage girls are worse than teenage boys for bein' squirrely." Nobody will admit they like profiling, but it was beginning to look like everybody does it.

"Maybe Crys Cleary and Evan Saddler were in it together," I suggested.

"You two having a good time?" Hen asked. "You seriously telling me this is the best you could do while I was out putting my life on the line looking for a meth lab?"

"Jerome didn't say they were likely suspects," I reminded him.

"And we might have to scratch off the preacher and his wife," Jerome said. "Good Christians like that breaking commandments all over the place? Nah."

"Keep an open mind," I said.

"But that's your whole pitiful list—with or without Branch and Raynell Harden—and with nothing at all whatsoever in any form to support the tiniest smidgen of any of it?"

"We haven't been working on it very long," Jerome said.

"You don't like any of them, we'll find somebody else," I offered.

"Y'all left out Louella Purcell," Hen said. "Maybe she did it to make a point about the shoddy sound system, or to embarrass Evan, who doesn't take his job seriously enough."

"He's making fun of us, Jerome," I said.

Hen slapped his hands together decisively. "We're the official po-lice. We need us some evidence. Jerome, I want you to start collecting fingerprints."

"Yes, sir?" Jerome said.

"We'll need to get prints from everybody involved in this case."

"What good will that do? Just about anybody could justify their prints being in the church."

"For elimination, Trudy. Jerome, you go get sample prints from Evan and Miz Saddler, and Howard and Crys Cleary, the Hardens, anybody you can think of."

"Busywork?" I protested.

"It might look like that, but he'll be out where the members of the community can see us serving and protecting, and it will make a couple of important points."

"Which are?"

"First, that the Ogeechee Police Department is on the job. Second, that we believe a serious crime was committed. Might shake something loose, especially when I tell Reverend Harden to let his people know we're trying to eliminate fingerprints that might point us in the wrong direction and we'd be obliged if he'd urge anybody who might have touched that rail, sill, ledge, whatever they call it, to come in and be printed. Some of those Baptists probably haven't ever been fingerprinted. Might broaden their view of life."

"You're not just punishing us, are you?" I asked.

Hen ignored the question. "Trudy, you talk to Josh Easterling's folks. See if they know of anybody with a grudge. Maybe whoever did it isn't somebody we already know about. We need to get us something solid to work with on this case. Now, much as I've been enjoying this healthy exercise of imagination and creative thinking, I've got to get over to the courthouse."

"Yes, sir," I said smartly, smarting. The men got to go out and do things. I had to talk to the grieving family.

CHAPTER 7

Working on a murder case was the most important thing we had going, but it wasn't the only thing. We respond to calls, no matter what else is happening, so when a citizen named Carolyn Reese called to complain that her neighbor's dogs were running around and causing a disturbance, and not for the first time, Jerome cheerfully abandoned the fingerprinting assignment and took the call.

Jerome is our specialist in dealing with women, especially high-strung, flaky, hysterical, or flat-out bizarre women, and I don't even think he minds. Sometimes he gets cookies out of it; almost always he gets hero worship. He doesn't brag about it, but I'm sure he has a fan club. Besides his engaging, unflappable personality, he has dark curls as long as Hen's regulations will allow, a slow grin, and, usually, a gold stud in his ear. Exotic. Dangerous. My taste runs more to stocky, bespectacled newspapermen, but I don't have to stretch much to see Jerome's appeal to women.

While Jerome was out dealing with Carolyn Reese's complaint, I buckled down to my assignment—talking to Josh Easterling's parents. I spent a few minutes formulating a sketchy script for this painful and unusual call, then got the contact information from Louella Purcell at the First Baptist Church, who said she'd been just about to call me because everybody wanted to know when the police tape was coming down so they could get back to business.

I told her I'd have to get back to her on the tape question and put in a call to Charles and Elizabeth Easterling in Brunswick.

"Easterlings'," said a soft female voice.

"Mrs. Easterling?"

"Yes."

"I'm Trudy Roundtree with the Ogeechee Police Department. I'm sorry about your loss."

"Thank you." She hung up.

I dialed again, kicking myself, script notwithstanding, for getting off to such a clumsy start.

"Mrs. Easterling?"

"Yes."

"This is Trudy Roundtree again. I'm sorry to bother you, but I need to talk to you about your son's death."

"Just a minute."

I didn't hear a click, so I assumed we were still connected. A moment later, a man's voice came on.

"Who is this?"

I introduced myself again.

"Is this some kind of a sick joke?"

"No, sir, it is not."

A sigh I could hear all the way from Brunswick. "We're having a really hard time here, Officer. Can this wait, whatever it is?"

"I understand this is a bad time for you, and I'm sorry to intrude, but—Mr. Easterling, there's no gentle way to put this—we have some questions about the way Josh died, and I'd like to talk to you and Mrs. Easterling."

"What do you mean, questions? I thought everybody in the church knew how he died."

"Yes, sir, that's true as far as it goes. How but not why."

"What does that mean?"

"He did die in the baptistry, and he was electrocuted. There's no way to soften that, and, although it may add to your pain, I need to tell you we have evidence that makes it look like somebody tampered with the microphone that killed him."

"Huh." It was a sound like a man might make if he'd been punched in the stomach.

I gave him a moment to get his breath back. "We don't want to take anything for granted. If somebody did it on purpose to kill him, if somebody set out to kill him, we want to find and punish that person."

"I don't understand."

How many ways could I say this? "It is hard to understand, but Josh's death was not entirely an accident."

"I can't believe what I'm hearing."

"Yes, sir, I understand that, but. . . ."

"Who'd want to hurt our sweet Josh?" Mrs. Easterling was back on the line. I mentally faced them both.

"I don't know, ma'am. We're trying to find that out. That's what I need to talk to y'all about. Did Josh have any enemies that you know of?"

I'll spare you the sputtering that followed my question. The upshot was that everybody loved Josh. The biggest confrontation he'd ever had with anybody at all, as far as his parents knew, was when he was four years old and had a problem with a playmate over whose turn was next on the slide, but they'd gotten over that, and Wesley Pritchard, that playmate, was nearly as broken up over Josh's death as Charles and Elizabeth were. Josh had had no violent love affairs. He had a fiancée, who was inconsolable. In every way Charles Joshua Easterling was a sterling fellow, a prince.

I doubted he could be as faultless as his parents made him sound. I called the school. After fighting my way through levels of administration to somebody who actually knew Josh Easterling, and then through a fog of genuine grief and unwillingness to speak ill of anybody (much less the dead and defenseless), I found much the same story. He had been a nice young man, studious, well-liked, Christ-like. My call was transferred to the records department, where I was told he was even a good student.

Still looking for a reason for someone to hurt him, I ran him through the various law enforcement databases and found nothing worse than a parking ticket, which he had paid. I had to conclude the guy was who he was purported to be. Not even a witness protection program could have concocted such a seamless, exemplary life.

I was fantasizing an elaborate murder conspiracy by fellow students who couldn't stand being compared with such a paragon when Jerome returned.

"How'd it go?" I asked.

"Regular two-ring circus," Jerome said.

"Two?"

"Two women for the price of one. Miz Reese, the complainer, and Miz Rhoda Peyton, the complainee. Neighbors, out on the edge of town, about where it turns into farms. Lots of space between the houses. Don't like each other much."

"That accounts for the complaint."

"Uh-huh. Not the first time Miz Reese called about those dogs."

"Does that mean you had a nice day?"

He smiled at me.

"Of course you did," I said, smiling back. "You sailed right in there and sweet-talked both of those women, didn't you?"

"Both of 'em nice enough on their own. The trick is not to get 'em together." He smiled again.

"You bring out the best in women," I said.

"Aw, shucks." If he was trying to convey modesty, he failed.

"So?"

"I assured Miz Reese I'd let Miz Peyton know she needed to do something about those dogs. I won't repeat in the presence of a lady what she actually called those dogs."

"How gentlemanly of you," I observed.

"So I went to see Miz Peyton, who acted like she thought I was a mind reader of some kind because she'd just about decided to call the police, and here I was."

"She going to complain about Miz Reese?"

"Better'n that. First off, Miz Peyton didn't need me to give her the message about the dogs. She's heard it before. Ain't the least bit sorry about her dogs. She'll be happy to pay whatever fine there is for the dogs, if there is a fine, because she could be paying it to some security company and it wouldn't be doing her nearly as much good, and besides she likes dogs. They don't ever cross the road. They don't bark at cars, just people. Reason she was about to call us was to complain about prowlers. If Miz Reese ain't worried about prowlers, it just shows she don't have much sense."

"I see. What about the prowlers?"

"She said she's been seeing people comin' and goin' in the cotton field across the road for a good while now—thanks to her dogs, people can't sneak up on her—but she didn't think much about it till she heard there'd been a raid on a meth lab somewhere around here and it started worrying her. Thought she ought to let us know about it in case there's something going on over there that's against the law."

"She doesn't have a clue what a meth lab is or what it would look like, does she?"

"Not a clue, but she knows it's bad. She reads a lot, and she's been reading about how those places contaminate the air around them, and she doesn't want her air contaminated."

"You think there's really been anybody, or is she just spooked and lonesome?"

"Her dogs ain't been lyin' to her. Somebody's been around over there where she said, all right. I took a look. Didn't find anything but some cotton plants, some pines where the cotton patch runs out, and some trash. Somebody's been over there, all right, but not for any reason I could see."

"Did it look like a game trail or a footpath?"

"Didn't look like it to me. Doesn't really go anywhere. Looks more like somebody just stomped around in the same place. Couldn't tell what to make of it. Can't see kids hangin' out over there. Miz Peyton says when people are over there they kind of go right to the same spot and mill around. Maybe prowlers isn't what you'd call 'em, but they're up to something and it's got her worried."

"Love letters in the hollow tree, something like that?" I confess to having read a lot of Nancy Drew and romantic fiction when I was younger, before I got into real police work and stopped believing in fairy tales.

He shrugged. "She says they walk around over there, like they're looking for something. That's what made her start worrying about it being a drug drop. Even if it isn't meth contaminating the air, she's afraid we'll be having a shootout over there and she might get hit with a stray bullet. Said it would serve Carolyn Reese right if she got shot."

"What do you think?"

"Don't know what to think. Wish I thought she was making it up, but she's not."

"Sounds kind of exposed for people who're up to no good," I said. "And really out of the way for people to go to drop their trash. You don't think that's it, do you? People dumping their trash?"

"She'd've noticed if that was it. She's a sharp-eyed old woman. Says they mostly drive up pretty close to the spot and then get out and wander around."

"It's just not fair," I whined. "You had something interesting to do, and I had to stay here and make a miserable, depressing phone call."

"It was pretty bad out there," he said. "Out and about in the sticky heat, poking around where the prowlers go, messing up my fresh-ironed uniform with tree bark and briars and spider webs and sweat. Lord, sweatin' like a mule!" He grinned. "But that nice lady, Miz Peyton, she was keepin' an eye on me and saw how I was sufferin', and she took pity on me."

"I don't want to hear it."

"Uh-huh. When I finished looking around and came back to talk to her, we sat up there on the porch and had some cookies and a couple of glasses of tea and talked a while. Nice and shady on her porch. Good view of the place she was talking about, across the road."

"I get it. Surveillance," I said, not trying to keep the bitterness out of my voice. "Did any of those shady characters show up while you were drinking your tea?"

"Uh-uh. She says they don't come at regular times. She can't ever tell when they'll come. Sometimes there's more than one of them." He paused for effect. "When I started to leave, she brought out this bag of cookies for me to bring back with me. Told me how much she respected the police in their fight against crime."

"You're a credit to the force and a regular public relations champ," I said, "but I'm still going to tell Hen you were eating cookies with a woman instead of taking fingerprints like he told you to."

"Fingerprints'll wait," he said. "Whatever this is, it's more interesting than fingerprints. After I reminded Miz Peyton about how she ought not let her dogs be a public nuisance, I told her to call us the next time one of her prowlers shows up and we'll get right over there and find out what's going on."

"I give her about a week before she bakes up another batch of cookies and calls, asking for you by name, wanting you to come back and have another look."

"You're just jealous," he said.

Darned right. Why don't I get that kind of assignment, sitting on a porch drinking tea and eating cookies, instilling confidence and trust in our police force? What I get is to intrude on a family's grief. It didn't help my mood to know that when I talked to the Easterlings, I'd been about as subtle as a boar rooting around for acorns.

"You said she gave you a bag of cookies," I said. "Did you already eat all of them, or can I have one?"

His mournful look was my answer.

I sighed. "Well, I've already talked to the Easterlings. I don't think they know anything that will help us. You want me to help you with your fingerprints till something more interesting turns up?"

CHAPTER 8

Howard Cleary lived at the end of an unpaved street on the south side of town, in a house with a tangle of woodsy undergrowth behind it. The house was small, mostly yellow brick, almost hidden from the street by dense bushes. Once I turned into the driveway, I saw that the yard was plain but well kept. There was no color, no flowers. I gave Howard points for keeping ahead of the inevitable mess of needles, cones, and brittle branches from the tall pine in the middle of the yard.

I rang the doorbell and got no response, but the presence of his truck made me think he was nearby. I am a trained investigator, after all.

I found Howard in his workshop, a small sturdy building behind his house. The sign over the door, apparently hand-painted, read, "Tinkerer's Dam."

I could see him through the doorway, left open, I guessed, in the hope of catching any air that might be stirring.

Howard's probably a little shy of six feet tall, but his erect posture and barrel chest make him seem like a very big man. His close-cropped gray-blond hair might be styled like that because it's easy to maintain, or it might be evidence that he's smart enough to know it's a better way of concealing hair loss than a comb-over would be. He was wearing a short-sleeved coverall with countless stains and smears on it, clearly his work clothes.

"Tinkerer's Dam?" I asked, announcing my presence. Like

the rest of Howard's property, the workshop was neat, the product of a man with a businesslike, orderly, no-nonsense mind, not the mess I'd have expected from reading his columns and listening to Phil talk about him. Tools hung from pegboards. Work surfaces, except the one where he was working, going through a pile of Vidalia onions and tossing the rejects into a nearby basket, were clear. The air had a nice onion-y smell that would soon turn unpleasant if he didn't get the over-the-hill specimens out of there.

Howard looked up and wiped his face and neck with a rag that had been lying on the counter. "Tinkerer's Dam. Means it's mine—I'm the tinkerer—but it doesn't amount to much," he said.

"It's clever, but I always thought the word was 'damn,' " I said.

"Maybe it is, but I never could see why a cuss word from a tinker would be any worse than anybody else's, so I go with the version that says a tinker's dam is a little thing that keeps the solder from running off when a tinker is mending a pot. Either way, it's something that doesn't amount to much." He seemed to consider. "Maybe I ought to add that 'n' and see who gets ticked off. How come people can talk like that, cuss with every other breath, but get their hackles up when they see it in print?"

"It's probably different people," I suggested. "The ones with bad mouths and the ones with hackles. You could have gone with 'Jack of All Trades,' " I said, waving at the array of equipment and tools. It looked like he was set up to do woodworking, metalworking, auto repair, yard work, appliance repair, and, for all I could tell, out-patient surgery and dentistry.

"Would have if my name had been Jack," he said. "You got something needs fixin'?"

"Probably," I said. "I don't expect to live to see the day there's nothing around my house that needs fixing."

"You live in that old Roundtree house close to the courthouse, don't you?"

"That's right. Sometimes I wish I had a neat little new place with new plumbing and wiring and insulation and . . . well, new everything. I try to keep after it, but it has a head start on me. I've got a good yard man, but there's a lot of other stuff." I knew I was babbling, and deep down, I probably knew why. I'd had the floors refinished back in the spring and the bathrooms modernized. I'd done such a good job of not getting impatient with all that needed to be done that I was practically at a standstill, partly because the estimates I'd got on the cost of fixing the kitchen, the next most needy part of the house, made me gasp. And there was the issue with Phil.

Howard laughed. "New houses break, too. At least with what you've got, you expect it. Let me give you my card. Not that you don't know where to find me. I don't like to get too much of a workload behind me, like to work at my own speed, but if you're not in too much of a hurry, I can help you out with just about anything you might need in an old house like that—roofing, painting, plumbing, wiring, yard work, building."

He pulled open a drawer and took out a business card. I took the card, mentally flinching. Roofing? I had no idea the last time anybody had looked at the roof.

"Where'd you learn to do all that?"

"No point in looking around my walls for diplomas or certificates of proficiency," he said. "How come people always think school's the only place you learn anything?"

That wasn't fair. I hadn't been looking for certificates. Apparently he hadn't meant the comment personally. It was probably no more than his habitual mental groove finding words. He went on.

"I grew up on a farm, which accounts for a lot of it. Went in the Army, which accounts for a lot more of it, and gives me a pension so I don't have to work any harder than I want to. And I'm naturally an inquisitive kind of person, so I read a lot. And I'm good with my hands, so if I don't already know how to do something, I read up on it and tinker with it until I do."

"Tinkerer," I said, waving in the direction of the sign. The Army. That accounted for the good posture and haircut.

"Right. Well, it doesn't sound like you came to enlist my tinkering skills. What you got on your mind today?"

"A couple of things," I answered. I explained about the need for elimination prints.

"You won't find mine," he said. "I got better ways to spend my time than at church."

"But you were spending time there on Sunday," I pointed out.

"Didn't even touch a hymnal," he said. "You're not going to find my fingerprints in that place."

"Still."

"Waste of taxpayer money having public servants spend time on that. How come you aren't putting your effort into something useful? You said a couple of things?"

"I wanted to see how Crys is doing. She seemed pretty shook up on Sunday."

"That doesn't surprise you, does it? Even for a strong girl, and Crys isn't strong, that woulda been the kind of shock that would shake you up."

"She's not strong? What's the matter with her?"

"Bad blood, partly."

"You're going to have to explain that."

"Her mother was weak. Worst day of my life was when my boy Mitch married that woman. How come young'uns won't listen? Mitch took after his mother that way. She didn't have much judgment when it came to people, either. Couldn't tell him a thing. He married her and let her walk all over him. I always thought it was her idea to rob that place, and it cost Mitch his life. You know about that?"

I nodded.

"How come you make one mistake and spend the rest of your life regretting it?"

Not clear what mistake, or whose, he was referring to, I merely nodded again.

"She got him into all kinds of trouble and then she got him killed. Had to have been her idea. Probably needed drug money. Mitch couldn't support her in the style to which she was addicted. How come women think some man's got to give them everything they want? So he got killed and she got five years over at the women's prison. Call that justice?"

"She must have had a clean record up till then," I said. "That's just about as little time as she could have gotten."

"Played on the fact she wasn't the one with the gun and she had a little girl."

"Sometimes that works," I admitted.

"Yeah. Well. Maybe sometimes it ought to work, but this time they should have looked past that. Tells you all about the kind of woman she was, she thought it was funny to name her baby Crystal Cleary."

He sucked a tooth to give me time to get the joke. I nodded to assure him I got it.

"The way her so-called mind worked, it probably tickled her to think she was getting two jokes for one."

"I just get one, crystal clear."

"Uh-huh. Well, knowing Sandra, she might just as well have been naming her baby after her favorite thing—crystal meth."

"That's just about the worst thing you can do to yourself, and totally irresponsible to do it around kids," I said. "Did Crys have to go through detox?"

Howard snorted. "That woman never cared about anything

but what she wanted, what she thought was a good idea. Never cared about Crys."

His unresponsive response made me wonder if the Crystal Meth Cleary joke was entirely Howard's idea, not Sandra's at all.

"Did Sandra's bad habits affect Crys physically?" I persisted. Thinking of fetal alcohol syndrome and babies born addicted to crack, I wondered if exposure to the toxic by-products of meth could account for the flatness in Crys's behavior that I'd attributed to shock at the church on Sunday.

"Don't know what she'da been like otherwise, but being born to that woman and comin' up in that household couldn'ta been good for her. Yeah, she's nervy."

I took "nervy" to mean Crys had been affected.

"Is there some kind of medication to help her?" I asked.

"Takes something to help her calm down and focus," he answered.

"What's she like when she's not on her meds?" Hyperactive? Violent? A physical and emotional double whammy. Poor kid.

"Like I said. Nervy."

"Lucky for her you were around to step in."

"Only good thing to come out of all that mess was I got Crys safe here with me."

"What happened to her mother?"

I knew enough of the story to keep feeding Howard questions. Maybe if I showed enough interest in his family, he'd be more cooperative.

"OD'd," he said.

"On meth?" I asked.

"Never heard exactly. Maybe booze," he said. He'd finished sorting onions and started wiping the dirt and onionskins off the countertop.

"Was Crys with her when it happened?"

"Crys was here, staying with me, waiting for her mother to get her act together."

"Thank goodness," I said. "How long ago was that?"

"About three years now. Crys was thirteen."

"That's a bad time for a girl, even with nothing else going on," I said. "How'd she take it?"

"Not too bad, to tell the truth. She'd been with me while her mother was in prison—from the time she was eight—so she wasn't all that close to Sandra any more."

And you hadn't done anything to help them stay in touch, I'd bet.

"Rough," I said.

"Rough," he agreed. "Worst thing about it was it made Crys start getting religious, like maybe she couldn't stand this world and needed to be thinking about another one. That's all religion is for a lot of people, a way to make 'em put up with their miserable lives. That, or their religion gives 'em permission to act like the devil because Jesus will forgive 'em. And there are the ones who get it in their heads God told 'em to send their babies on to be with Jesus or shoot the woman who's inhabited by the devil or whatever. I didn't want Crys getting mixed up with people like that. I tried to talk sense into her, but she was too stubborn. Might have got that from her daddy, being stubborn. That church business is just about the only time I can think of when she was dead set on going against me."

Just like Howard to be upset over behavior that would have come as a relief to most adults who had to look out for teenagers. "That made you mad?" I tried to sound merely interested, not like an inquisitor or a psychologist.

"Nobody likes it when somebody goes against them, but I guess just about anything Crys really wants to do is all right with me. Listen, if you don't mind, I do have some work I need to be getting at."

"I'd like to get your fingerprints before I go."

"I told you I wasn't there."

"I'd still like to get them."

"I stand on my civil rights and respectfully decline," he said. "How come government always expects people to lie down and let you steamroll 'em into giving up their liberties without thinking about it?"

"I'm not exactly big government, and I'm not steamrolling. I'm just asking for your cooperation."

As an ex-military man, Howard had to know we could get his fingerprints, even if I didn't happen to have in my possession one of his business cards with his fingerprint on it. He was being obstructionist just for the fun of it. I smiled.

On top of the minor annoyance of his knee-jerk refusal to be cooperative, it struck me that nearly everything he said sounded like the topic sentence for one of his rants. Maybe he was trying it out on me for effect. I found myself liking him less than I had on Sunday, when he'd been so protective of Crys.

When I turned to go, I saw against the wall a well-stocked gun case. I couldn't remember if Howard had ever done a column on the NRA and gun control, but there was no doubt which side he'd have been on. Not quite enough of an arsenal to defend himself in case of a foreign invasion, but plenty so he'd be able to put food on the table in case he had to go into survivalist mode. I spotted a Winchester 30-30, a Remington 12 gauge, a couple of bolt action .22 rifles, and a .55 squirrel gun with a scope, a fairly standard collection around here. Standing out because it wasn't a gun was a beautiful wood-handled knife.

"Wow!" I said. "This must be a collector's item."

"That knife? Sure is. Rosewood handle. Single lock blade. Old boy over in Baxley makes those. Every single one is a work of art. One of a kind. Comes with a presentation case, a serial number, documentation."

I'd obviously hit on something besides his granddaughter and his opinion of the moment that Howard was enthusiastic about. He reached under the countertop and came up with a heavy iron ring with a couple of dozen keys on it. He selected one and opened the case so I could get a closer look at the treasure. I oohed and ahhed with genuine appreciation.

When I got back to the stationhouse, I learned that Raynell Harden had called, asking to speak to the Chief of Police himself, to ask about getting the police tape out of the way before Wednesday activities, since if they weren't going to be able to have prayer meeting and choir practice, they'd need to get the phone tree going to let people know. She also wanted to make sure we weren't suspecting her husband of anything since it should be obvious that he was the intended victim.

Hen must have had an irritating day at court and an equally irritating conversation with Mrs. Harden. His face lit up with a devilish grin. "Doncha think the best thing for us to do, instead of relying on those Baptists to be good citizens, is to go over there about prayer meeting time and do mass fingerprinting?"

"Uh-huh," I said cautiously.

"There's been that push to have parents get fingerprint cards for their children. Don't want to dwell too much on the circumstances that might make it useful, but we can say it's for safety. Let them fill in the gaps."

"We could set up one station for people who think they might have touched any of the relevant surfaces," I said. "And another for children. We are eliminating children from suspicion, aren't we?"

"Yes, ma'am."

"I'm trying to remember who I know that helps kids make pictures out of their fingerprints," I said. "Sort of an art project. We could make extra prints for that."

"Don't want to make it too much of a circus," Hen said.

"We'll get all the other churches jealous and have to do it for everybody. But we could kill a couple of turkeys with one load of shot. We get to let people know we're working on our murder case, and maybe even learn something useful about that or something else, while we are visibly performing a community service." He paused. "Make that three turkeys. Getting even with the Hardens for trying to push me around is a bonus."

"All very admirable," I said. "Hen, did you know Mitch and Sandra Cleary, Crys's parents?"

"Knew who they were. Why?"

"Just got interested in Crys's story, that's all. Feeling as sorry for her as for Josh Easterling's family. But I think Howard's story about what happened to Crys's mother is different from what Raynell Harden told me. I wondered if you know what happened to her."

Hen laughed. "You can't decide which is most likely true— church gossip or the version you got from the man who wrote a column blaming childhood vaccinations against measles for declining scores on school tests?"

"You can't catch me that way. I know better than to rely on anybody's word instead of objective evidence for anything that matters. Not that it matters, but neither one of them makes her sound like a saint."

I told him what Howard had said about his own wife's judgment when it came to people. It apparently hadn't occurred to Howard that saying his wife had no judgment when it came to people didn't say much for her choice of him.

Hen grinned. "Howard may be a little smarter than most people, but most people aren't prepared to admit something like that, and he'd be better off not letting his opinion show so much. Makes it too easy not to warm up to him. The trouble with being generally cantankerous is that being automatically annoying doesn't always work for you. People may get into the habit of not taking you seriously. His thinly disguised opinion that he's smarter than everybody else and his sharp edges keep most people from being comfortable around him. So the sharp edges get even sharper, without anybody to rub them off on. It's a vicious circle."

"I couldn't have put it better myself," I said, thinking of my conversation with Howard.

"Well, now, Officer Roundtree, we've got better things to do than sit around dissing one of our prominent citizens. You get to work setting things up with the church."

"Yes, Your Honor."

Actually, spending some time at the Baptist church might be fun. At least it would be sociable, better than sitting at my desk trying to get Josh Easterling's parents to tell me why somebody might have wanted to kill their darling son. Better than sparring with Howard Cleary.

CHAPTER 9

Hen had decided to make a big deal out of the fingerprint gathering, and the result was that it had the feel of a carnival side show. I had no way of knowing if attendance at the Baptist church's Wednesday night activities was enhanced by the added attraction of a police presence or not, but the place was humming.

It had probably called for the full force of Hen's iceberg blue eyes and good old boy charm to persuade Rev. Harden to instruct Louella Purcell to include information about our fingerprint collecting when the telephone tree got activated to let people know prayer meeting, choir practice, and other meetings would take place as scheduled but not in the sanctuary.

"I left it up to the preacher if he was simple enough, or thought his congregation was simple enough, to try to pass it off as a routine public relations move on our part at this particular time, a security measure for families with children, to help identify them under circumstances we don't want to think about too much, and totally unconnected with Josh Easterling's death," Hen said.

"They've probably figured it out, whether the preacher put any spin on it or not," I said.

"Doesn't really matter," Hen said.

Hen had demonstrated his integrity and proved why he's such an asset to the town by coming along on the mission and bringing in another officer to help. If we were going to do it—

and we were—we'd do it right.

We were set up at a long table in the hallway outside the fellowship hall, a high traffic area but not absolutely in the middle of the church's business as usual.

We had a sort of assembly line. I was the first stop, probably because I'm the only one on the force with decipherable handwriting. My job was to fill out the cards with appropriate identifying information. Then I'd pass the subject on to Mike Ortega, a new hire from Valdosta. Hen figured this project would be a good way for Mike to meet the public and vice versa, and he seemed happy with his assignment, taking care of the messy part, inking the fingers and rolling them on the cards, saying little, smiling a lot. The third step in the fingerprinting process featured a trash barrel instead of a police officer. Hen, with an administrator's eye to the budget, had us bring along baby wipes for the clean-up process instead of the official and pricier orange-scented towelettes.

Mike had nodded his understanding when Hen said, "WD-40 and a paper towel would do the job just as well, but we don't want to push these good church folks too far."

"Got it, *Jefe*," Mike said, a reminder that "Mike," in his case, was short for "Miguel." "Call me Mike," he'd said when he first showed up. "I'm trying to assimilate." Right. His skin isn't as deep a brown as Jerome's, but it's dark enough to give his smile potent contrast. In addition to white teeth and a dimple, he usually lets his smile develop slowly instead of unleashing it all at once, a trick that enhances its effect. "Irritate 'em just enough to make 'em careless, and maybe we'll learn something," Mike said now.

"See there, Trudy," Hen said to me. "I told you from the get-go, this boy's got real potential."

"You just think *hay-fay* sounds better than some of the other things people call you," I said. "I think it's Spanish for mule food." It was weak and I knew it. Even I speak enough Spanish to know *jefe* means "chief."

I turned to Mike. "Don't let *El Jefe* fool you. He enjoys being irritating."

But Hen is subtle, and in addition to all his other good reasons for the fingerprinting, letting the Baptists get a good look at handsome Mike's friendly smile wouldn't be likely to hurt anything and might distract some of them from our other purposes. Hen, innately sociable, was in good form. "Step right up, ladies and gentlemen, boys and girls, cats and dogs. Unless you've already had a brush with the law and we have your fingerprints, I invite you to step right up and do some business with officers Roundtree and Ortega."

Most people, even those who looked puzzled, stepped up. If anybody balked, Hen had another line. "We're looking for prints of innocent people tonight, want to cross them off our lists of suspects. Now if you have committed a nefarious deed of some kind and prefer for us not to know about you, then don't give us your prints. It might not work out for you."

He always laughed when he said it, and I didn't notice anybody getting shifty-eyed and shuffling to the back of the line, not even the non-members, people who were there simply because they knew it was a place where they could get a good meal at a low price on Wednesday nights.

We had a fairly steady stream of customers, with some ebbing and flowing as early birds and latecomers went to and from choir practice, prayer meeting, and whatever other business they had. During a lull, we were approached by a herd of teenagers, likely some of Josh Easterling's flock, at loose ends without their shepherd.

Their spokesman was a tall, good-looking boy with an athletic build. He gestured to the fingerprint paraphernalia. "This have anything to do with Josh?"

"In a way, it does." I repeated my version of Hen's speech for the zillionth time. "We're investigating his death. This will help us to be able to eliminate people who didn't have anything to do with it so we won't waste our time trying to talk to everybody in town. We're asking people to help us by volunteering their prints."

I thought that sounded reasonable. It offered enough information but not too much.

"The Mission Friends are fixin' to come," the boy said. "They're preschoolers. You suspect one of them?"

"Tryin' not to do any stereotyping," Hen said with a straight face. "We'll print everybody. Makes everybody feel safer. You're Kyle Simpson? Paul and Ann's boy?"

"Yes, sir. You writing that down?" he asked me.

"Want to have the right name on the fingerprint cards," I said with a smile.

"I don't get why you're investigating. Wasn't it an accident? Josh, I mean?"

"Well, son, even if it was an accident, we have to find out what we can about what caused it," Hen said.

"Even if? Does that mean you don't think it was?" The kid might be an athlete, but not one of the stereotypical ones who doesn't have enough brains to read the letter on his athletic jacket.

I turned most of my attention to the process of taking prints, letting Hen handle the public relations and public information angle.

"If it wasn't an accident—if somebody wanted to kill him— who do you think it could have been?" Hen asked it in a relaxed, conversational way, but suddenly Kyle wasn't as confident as he had been. He glanced at his friends.

One of the girls—Amanda Goodman, from the card I'd just filled out for her—stopped wiping her fingertips and reached for Kyle's hand. Her question proved she was sharp, too. "So y'all think somebody murdered Josh and it was somebody here at the church?"

"Ooh!" This was another girl, who turned her face against the other boy's chest.

Brooke Stillwagon and Chance Tucker.

Amanda persisted. "Y'all think he was murdered?"

She darted a glance at Brooke, who kept quiet this time, possibly because a third girl had a grip on her forearm. I mentally applauded. I've never appreciated drama queens.

"We have to eliminate that possibility," I said. "That's why we call these—" I gestured at the paraphernalia in front of me— "elimination prints."

"Meaning?"

Hen weighed back in. "Meaning that most of the fingerprints at the scene are irrelevant. If we turn up some that can't reasonably be explained, then they're more interesting to us."

Heather Jackson, the girl with the grip, released Brooke and stepped up with her hands held out. "I guess I'm next."

"Thank you, Heather. We appreciate your cooperation," I said automatically.

"If you think somebody killed him, you need to know some people didn't like him." This came from Chance, speaking over Brooke's head. He was weedier looking than Kyle, maybe basketball instead of football, but it's hard to tell. In a small school system, students get to explore more options than they might in a school where there's more competition.

Brooke jerked her head back to look up at him. "Chance!"

"I'm just saying," he said.

"Who, for instance?" I asked.

"Brooke, for one," Chance said.

Brooke's mouth fell into a pout, and she hid her face against him again. I wondered how long it would take him to get tired of that. Even if I was being drawn into a teenage power struggle, I couldn't resist asking, "Why didn't you like him, Brooke?"

No answer from Brooke.

"He embarrassed her, back when he first came," Chance said, possibly dooming his future with Brooke. "He made a joke about her name, like it was spelled b-r-o-o-k, and she didn't like it."

I didn't much like what I'd seen of her, so I asked, proving why Hen's better at getting along with people than I am, "Something about a babbling brook?"

Heather smiled. I could get to like that girl. Brooke drew up to her full stature, a couple of inches short of mine, and fixed me with what I supposed was her version of a wilting stare.

"That's not funny, and I'm not the only one who didn't like his jokes."

"Do you think somebody who didn't like his jokes mighta been playing a joke on him?" Hen asked.

"I didn't say that." No. She'd naturally be better at hinting and suggesting than at actually making a statement.

"What are you saying?" I asked.

"Just that sometimes his jokes weren't funny."

"But maybe you're on to something," Kyle said to me. "Lots of us thought he was funny. Fun. And he could take a joke, too, not like some people. So maybe somebody thought it would be funny to give him a shock, embarrass him in church."

"Oooh!" Brooke again, of course.

"Whose sense of humor would run that way?"

"Evan's got a weird sense of humor, and he's the one in charge of the mike."

"But he wouldn't have done it if he thought it would hurt anybody," Heather said. "Evan's the kind of person who adopts puppies and feeds crippled birds. He wouldn't want to hurt anybody."

91

"That's right," Brooke said, and for a minute I thought she was going to make me change my opinion of her by saying something nice about somebody. "That's why he hangs around with Crys all the time, like she's a bird with a broken wing. I mean, honestly, she's lame, all right." I briefly wondered if Brooke was bright enough to realize she'd almost made a pun, but decided she was more likely just using slang.

"How would you treat a bird with a broken wing, Brooke? Break the other wing?" Heather asked.

"Now, now, ladies," Amanda said. "Let's behave ourselves here in the church before God and law enforcement and everybody."

"She'd take up for Evan no matter what," Brooke said.

"Wouldn't you take up for me?" Chance asked, pulling her to him, stifling her against him.

"Could I help you with that, the fingerprinting?" Kyle asked. "I'm thinking of going into law enforcement."

"Pull up a chair and let me introduce you to Officer Miguel 'Call-Me-Mike' Ortega," Hen said.

Mike initiated Kyle into the mysteries of fingerprinting just in time for the onslaught of preschoolers, the Mission Friends.

Reverend Harden appeared. "Kyle, Brooke, everybody, we're ready for y'all now back here in my office," he said.

"I'll be right there, sir," Kyle said as the other teens drifted toward the door. "Grief counseling," he said when they were gone. "Mandatory. Or else. Guess I'd better go."

"Guess you'd better. Come back later if you can, and we'll put you to work," Hen said.

"*Hasta la vista*," Call-Me-Mike said. He has his own ideas about the best way to assimilate.

As the teens left, our focus shifted to the preschoolers, sorting out children, teachers, and their parents. The children were variously serious, giggly, squirmy, noisy, messy, interested, engaged, and cooperative. To expedite things, I asked the parents to fill out cards. They'd keep the cards, and they'd be able to read their own handwriting. With parents helping, even without Kyle's help, we dealt with this group quickly.

When the preschoolers cleared out, we were finished, except for a few stragglers. As we were packing up to leave, Heather reappeared, making me wonder if she'd been intentionally keeping an eye on things from a safe distance. "You shouldn't pay any attention to Brooke," she said.

"You mean Miss Clinging Vine isn't what she appears to be?"

Heather looked uncomfortable. "Oh, she's all that. I don't mean to be catty, but I don't get Brooke. Most of us try to be nice to her, to Crys I mean, but Brooke seems to take it as a personal insult, like we can't be friends with her and Crys both."

"Any idea why?"

She shook her head. "No. It's not like Crys is competition for Brooke, or anything like that. Maybe Brooke doesn't like Crys because Crys likes . . . liked . . . Josh and Brooke didn't like him. I don't know."

"Does Brooke think Crys is after Chance?"

"No. Not a chance." She smiled. "He gets tired of it, but we make that joke a lot. Anyway, what I mean is he's not interested in anybody but Brooke. And if he were, it wouldn't be Crys. I mean, really, he's the kind of guy who likes girls like Brooke." She made a gesture of impatience. "I don't know how to say what I mean. Do you know what I mean?"

"Maybe I do. All he can see is Brooke. He's not interested in anybody else. Does Brooke know that?"

"Who knows what she knows?"

"Answer this, Heather. If Brooke was jealous of Crys, could she have tried to spoil her baptism by messing with that microphone?"

Heather laughed. "You're kidding, right? She wouldn't be

smart enough to think of it. Definitely not smart enough to do it."

"I get the feeling you're not especially fond of Brooke."

"We don't hang out much."

"What about Crys? Do you like her?"

"Most of the time. Sometimes she acts kind of crazy and weird, but she's kind of sad, too, and, uh-huh, yeah, we're friends."

"She's sad? Like she's depressed? Or do you mean she's pitiful?"

She thought about it. "Like both, sometimes. I know she's on some kind of meds, Zoloft or something. Maybe having to be on them makes her sad. Maybe the meds make her depressed. I've heard they can do that. I don't get how it's a good idea to take meds because you're depressed if the meds can make you suicidal. Oh, I don't know."

It struck me that for somebody who said "I don't know" a lot, Heather had good insights.

"Is Evan interested in Crys?" I asked.

"No." She looked confused. "I mean, not like a girlfriend." She gave me a small, confidential smile. "I think he's interested in me."

I gave her a smile in return. "Lucky you," I said. "He seems like a nice boy."

Her smiled broadened. "He is. And smart. And not all full of himself and all over you like . . . well, like some guys." She blushed. "Anyway, I just wanted to say, about Brooke, you know."

"Yes. Thank you."

Our stream of customers had dried up. Hen and Mike had been putting our equipment away while I talked to Heather.

"Another thrilling day in the life of a police officer," Hen said, breathing deeply and, apparently, trying to make his elbows meet behind his back. "You'll take care of this stuff, and I'll see you tomorrow," he added as he got to his feet. "I'll just go have a word with the preacher." He turned toward the fellowship hall.

I wasn't interested in another word with anybody. I turned the other way, toward the sanctuary, wanting to unwind and maybe even get a sense of the possibilities in the case without the distractions of light and sound and people.

It was quiet, except for occasional muted voices and clatter filtering from the fellowship hall, dark except for the light that leaked in from the hallway and the multi-colored beams that filtered through the stained glass windows from the streetlights outside. I sat in the middle of the front pew, looking up at the opening into the baptistry centered behind the choir loft and podium, and tried to visualize the scene on that fatal Sunday morning.

I saw families in their Sunday finery, a shade dressier than everyday clothes; fathers and mothers greeting friends, modeling good manners, good behavior—don't run and yell in God's house. I saw teens, the very ones I'd just been talking with, and others like them, jostling, teasing, but trying to rein in their high spirits and be reverent. I saw small children, uncontainable, dashing across the dais—perhaps knocking the microphone out of position. I saw the choir filing in. Could someone in the back row nudge that microphone? Would they? Why?

"You waiting for divine inspiration?" Branch Harden's voice startled me. He was speaking from the doorway that led to the hall, just outside the police tape.

"Not a bad idea," I said.

"I don't think so, either." He paused. "You want me to leave you alone? I could go on. The doors'll lock behind you."

"I give you permission to cross the tape," I said.

He came and sat beside me. "This is a terrible thing."

"Yes, it is."

"People are saying y'all think one of our members murdered Josh."

For some reason I couldn't explain, we both spoke quietly, almost in whispers.

"It's possible the people are right," I admitted. "What did Hen say about it?"

"He said the same thing, but I can't believe it."

We sat quietly for a breath or two. I can't speak for the pastor, but I wouldn't have minded some divine inspiration.

"Raynell's worried," he said.

"About one of your members running amok?" I asked.

A smothered snort assured me he understood my attempt at humor. "That's not how she puts it. She seems to be convinced somebody meant to hurt me instead of Josh. It's making me nervous."

I stifled the impulse to tell him to turn it over to God. "That's possible, I guess. Since we don't yet know what did happen, we can't rule out anything."

"I see." He leaned back in the pew and sighed.

"Who sits in the back row of the choir?" I asked.

"Why do you want to . . . Oh, no."

"I can ask somebody else."

"Well, it's not always the same people."

"Always the men?"

"Usually the basses and tenors, but it depends on who's there. Sometimes the women."

"You know perfectly well I'm not talking about sometimes. I'm talking about last Sunday."

He sighed. "I know. Let me see, now. We had a full choir. We don't have a baptism every Sunday, and besides that, people have taken an interest in Crys, because of her background, you know."

"I know. So?"

"Well, you know, it's hard to say."

"Because?"

Even in the near dark, his relief was evident. His voice took on a lilt that told me he'd found a way out of his dilemma. "Because I don't pay that much attention, to tell the truth. I usually have my back to the choir."

"But not on Sunday. On this Sunday you were sitting out here in the pews to watch Josh Easterling perform the baptism, weren't you?"

"Well, now you mention it, yes, I was, but it happened so early in the service we hadn't settled down yet."

"So you're not going to tell me?"

"You wouldn't want me to guess, would you, and put somebody on the spot?"

"It would give me an idea who I ought to talk to."

"I can't."

We sat in silence for a while, then, from the hallway, heard Raynell Harden's voice. "Branch? Where are you? I'm ready to go."

"I guess I'll go walk my wife home," he said.

"You go on," I said. With him gone, again I summoned up a busy Sunday morning. Choir leader straightening out chairs in the choir loft. Maybe a deacon looking over the ledge to check the depth of the water. The preacher, the organist, the preacher's wife, anybody at all, could have gone up there and messed with the microphone, under some inexplicably wicked or mildly mischievous impulse, and nobody would have noticed. I wouldn't bother talking to the basses and tenors. It could have been anybody.

There were too many questions besides who could have messed with the microphone itself and who could have changed the adjustment so that the victim would reach out for it. The method seemed hit-or-miss for deliberate murder. Was it just chance that resulted in Josh Easterling's death on that day? Was the killer prepared to be satisfied if Josh got a nasty shock, or prepared to try again if this effort failed?

The haphazardness of the plan made me wonder if one of the young people had done it, after all. No, that wasn't fair. It isn't only young people who indulge in magical thinking, letting themselves believe that whatever they want is what will somehow, against all odds, and without any effort, come about. It's the kind of thinking that lets people believe that buying a lottery ticket will solve all their problems, that it's luck more than effort that makes the difference.

I let myself out, making sure the church door locked behind me.

CHAPTER 10

The commotion I found at the stationhouse when I checked in on Thursday morning undid all the benefits of the quiet reflection of the evening before at the Baptist church, even fortified as I was by a cuddle with a couch full of cats and a breakfast of instant grits and pre-made sausage biscuits from the freezer.

I walked in on Henry Huckabee yelling at Howard Cleary, putting his options very clearly, it seemed to me. "I want you to sit yourself down on that chair right there and put a clamp on your tongue if you don't want me to call Jerome in here and have him sit on you!"

A clamp on Howard's tongue? I'd have bet Hen wasn't the first person to want to try that. Having Jerome sit on him was an attractive alternative, though.

Howard drew breath and opened his mouth.

"Sit down and shut up, Howard," Hen bellowed. "I'm the only one gets to raise hell around this place. I got rules against anybody else doin' it. You got that?"

When Howard did sit down and shut his mouth, Hen turned to the other man, whom I'd not noticed until then because he'd already been sitting down with his mouth shut.

"Okay, Jim," Hen said with diminished volume. "Let's hear your side."

I recognized Jim Jackson—the father of Heather Jackson, the friend of Crys Cleary I'd talked to at the church the night before—in a high state of agitation. He was wearing house shoes with his slacks and a mis-buttoned green and pink striped cotton shirt. Compared to him, Howard might have looked reasonable and controlled if you didn't notice the incandescent pink scalp gleaming through his short haircut.

Jackson nodded decisively and began speaking, alternately darting wrathful glances at Howard and self-righteous glances at Hen.

"He came over to my house all riled up, said he wanted to talk to Heather. Said he was worried about Crys, that she wasn't home and he didn't know where she was and he wanted Heather to tell him where she was. Well, I could see he was upset. Nothing wrong with that. I would be, too, if I couldn't find my daughter. Well, Crys isn't his daughter, but you know what I mean. Heather told him she didn't know where Crys was, and that's when he crossed over the line. Said he wouldn't take that for an answer. Blamed if he didn't push his way right on into the house, said he wanted to look around and see for himself."

Howard Cleary opened his mouth.

"Shut up, Howard," Hen said. "Go ahead, Jim."

Jim Jackson pulled at his shirttail, gave up on trying to even it out, and continued with his story. "I've never been a big fan of Howard Cleary, anyway. Thinks he knows more than anybody else about everything on God's green earth, and I sure as sugar cane didn't see any reason to let him get away with comin' in actin' like that, so I told Mary Ann to call y'all. I wanted that lunatic arrested. Still do. Who does he think he is? He can't do that, can he? This is the United States of America, for Pete's sake. Nobody's supposed to be able to get away with that. A man's home is his castle, isn't that right? Can't you lock him up for violating the Homeland Security Act or the Patriot Act or something?"

"Homeland Security doesn't mean your house, Jim," Hen said. In spite of the way he'd been yelling at Howard—or maybe because of it—I got the impression Hen was enjoying himself. He glanced at Howard, still seated but obviously simmering, and spoke to Mr. Jackson. "He says he's a worried grandfather, Jim. Can you cut him a little slack?"

"Worried grandfather, I understand that. That's all well and good, but it don't give him a right to come in like that, like storm troopers, scaring my wife and daughter."

"No, it doesn't," Hen agreed. "Now, Howard, it's your turn. You got anything to say for yourself?"

"He got most of it right. What he left out is that Heather was lying. She knows where Crys is. I was just trying to get her to tell me."

"She says she doesn't know, and I believe her," said Heather's loyal father.

"She's lying. Maybe you're lying, too," Howard said.

Jim Jackson, about half the size of Howard Cleary, nevertheless came close to committing bodily assault upon Howard in the presence of the Chief of Police and an auxiliary officer, me, or trying to. I was disappointed when Hen restrained him. Actually, this was turning out to feel even more therapeutic than lying on a couch under a pile of cats. I felt a warm glow.

"Here's what I think," Hen said. "I think we need to take our time about this. Now, there's more than one way we can do that. One way is for Jim to keep on making a fuss till we see how long a list of things we can charge Howard with. That would take up a lot of time and energy I'd rather be putting someplace else, like maybe looking for pedophiles or drug pushers or jaywalkers, and I got to tell you I'm against it. Another way is for Howard to keep on making such a nuisance out of himself that I lose my patience and lock him up for that till he settles down."

Neither Jim nor Howard seemed impressed with the options so far.

"The third way is both of you to go home and consider your sins"—he glanced at Howard—"and your civic duty"—he glanced at Jim Jackson. "And see if we can't find some way to balance things out and let this episode die a natural death. That's the easy way and the way I'd recommend. It's just one man's opinion, but there it is. Any questions?"

There were no questions.

"Okay, then, Jim, you go on home or to work or wherever you need to go. We'll reason with Howard a while longer."

Jim Jackson harrumphed, but he did leave, shooting Howard a triumphant glance on his way out—a glance that said, "Ha ha! Teacher's keeping you longer than he kept me!"

Hen sat back and took a deep breath.

"So, Howard, you calmed down enough to talk some sense?"

Howard didn't look calm, but he began to sound more reasonable than he had while Jim Jackson was still around to keep the situation on the boil. "Okay, maybe I went off half cocked, but I've got to look after Crys. She isn't the strongest, steadiest girl you ever saw. She's a pretty sixteen-year-old girl, and there're a lot of people out there who prey on people like her. I'm not going home till I find her."

"You don't have to go home. What you have to do is not go back to Jim Jackson's. You got that?" Hen asked.

"Yes, I've got that," Howard said.

"I am not entirely without some sympathy for your situation, Howard," Hen said. "I've got a daughter, and I wouldn't be the least bit happy if I didn't know where to find her, so let's try to calm down and use our heads. You thinkin' somebody took her? She was kidnapped? Left of her own free will? What?"

"I don't know what to think," Howard admitted.

"Then let's start with the least worrisome scenario. If she just left, where would she go?"

"Not around in circles, like you're trying to lead me!"

Howard's veneer of calm shattered again and anger took over. "The only place I could think of was Heather Jackson's. But I already looked there."

"I don't believe she's at Heather's, Howard. Besides that. Where else can you think of? If she ran away, where else would she go?"

"No idea."

"She got any other family, besides you?"

"Some of her mother's people. We don't keep in touch with them."

"But there is somebody. Did you check with them?"

"No. No point in it."

"Give us a couple of names, and we'll check."

"And give them the satisfaction of thinking she wasn't happy with me?"

"You want to find her or protect your ego?"

"She wouldn't go there."

"Howard, I swear if you don't give us some names, I'm gonna get Jerome and Call-Me-Mike in here, and all three of us will sit on you. I'll excuse Officer Roundtree because she's a lady and she weighs well under two hundred pounds."

Much as I'd have hated to be left out of such a satisfying, macho exercise, I tried to cooperate by looking small, ladylike, and harmless.

"Anyway, how would she get there?" Howard said.

"Trudy, where's Jerome?"

"Okay. Okay." Howard spit out a couple of names of some of Crys's mother's people he said he thought lived somewhere near Baxley.

"Good." Hen leaned back in his chair, and the color in his face faded from ripe tomato to the much more wholesome pinky beige of fresh peach ice cream. "Now. Next scenario. She got a boyfriend?"

"No. Not that I know of, anyway, not since Dixon Tatum. But I might not know. From what I hear, teenage girls might not tell their granddaddies about their love life. Another reason I wanted to talk to Heather Jackson."

"You pretty much blew your chances of talking to Heather, Howard. I don't want to hear Heather Jackson's name one more time in this conversation," Hen said. "Now, tell me, has Crys ever run away before?"

"Before? We don't know for sure she ran away this time. Maybe she was in an accident." Howard almost seemed happy to have thought of another possibility, even this one, as though it meant he was gaining points over Hen. "Maybe she's hurt somewhere."

"She got a car?"

"No."

"If she was going away somewhere in a car, whose car would it be?"

"She'd probably ask one of those church kids for a ride."

"All roads lead back to that nameless girl whose father just left," I said.

Hen frowned at me.

Howard nodded and launched another accusation. "And you aren't doing anything to help."

"That's where you are wrong, Howard. We are working hard to make a reasonable plan. We'll swing into action as soon as you give us something to work with. We coulda got started looking for her sooner, for instance, if we'd known she was gone. Trudy, remind this citizen of our motto."

"To serve and protect," I said promptly. Hen loves to remind me of that when I complain about some of the things people expect us to tend to—like the neighbor watering his yard too much and making the complainant's driveway muddy, like kids next door playing the wrong kind of music too loud.

"See there, Howard. We do more than chase criminals. We are here to serve. It didn't occur to you to let us know she was missing?"

"If I'd reported it, what would you have done?"

"I can tell you that one thing we would not have done is threaten to take the Jackson house apart board by board until I was sure they weren't hiding Crys."

"I never said that."

"Jim Jackson says you did. It's right here in his sworn statement."

"Oh, so Jim Jackson says it, and that makes it true." Howard's glower was impressive.

"You're denying it?"

Howard chose not to answer directly this time.

"I don't know why they got so bent out of shape. I didn't have a gun or anything. Just wanted to talk to . . . to the girl."

"Lucky for you, you didn't have a gun," Hen told him.

"Why, so you could waste your time on another bogus charge?"

"Howard, I ought to lock you up for criminal stubbornness."

"You'd lock up a man who's just trying to take care of his family?" Howard was leaning forward now, aggressive, challenging.

"Depends on how he's going about it," Hen answered. "You know you can't go around scaring people to death just because you're worried. I can't even tell what you've got going on in your head instead of thought processes. You trying to see how far you can push me?"

"I'll do what I have to do to find my granddaughter. You do what you've got to do."

Hen sighed. "She take anything with her? Clothes? Toys? Cell phone?"

"I wouldn't know about clothes. I didn't notice anything

missing. Tried calling her cell phone. She didn't answer."

"Okay. You leave it to us now, Howard. You go home and bat out your column on police brutality or partiality or inefficiency or whatever warms the cockles of your so-called heart, and we'll see what we can do. I'll be along over to your house in a few minutes so I can look around and see if my official police eyes see anything you missed."

"Don't you need a search warrant?"

"Good God, Howard! Were you born contrary? That's to protect you from unreasonable search and seizure, not when we're supposed to be on same side, which I thought we were in this case. A search warrant is for people who might not want to cooperate. But you do want to cooperate, don't you? The way I understood it, you are inviting me to come look around for something that might help us find her. Isn't that right?"

Howard would surely have phrased it differently, but he admitted that Hen was basically right.

Hen shooed him off then, after doing an encore of the threat that involved Jerome and Call-Me-Mike if he should have the impulse to bother the Jacksons again, and peace descended upon the stationhouse.

"You know, Trudy," Hen said, once Howard was gone, "by my own actual mathematical calculation, eighty-four percent of our incident reports last weekend were domestic violence. I got plumb weary of seeing the words 'simple battery.' "

"Hen, you aren't saying you think Howard Cleary hurt Crys and then went through all this song-and-dance with the Jacksons!"

"No, not necessarily. I been in this business longer than you have, Trudy, so I can tell you that sometimes what starts out as discipline or a love tap or horseplay gets out of hand, and then people don't know what to do about it. Sometimes they try to pretend it didn't happen at all. Sometimes they'll make up evidence that'll point somewhere else, and just wind up confusin' things so much nobody gets called to account for whatever bad things really did happen. The good Lord knows I ain't proud of having such a low opinion of the human race, but there ain't much surprises me anymore."

"But—"

"So," he continued, as though I hadn't tried to interrupt, "no matter how obnoxious and blustery and offensive and accusatory Howard gets, we got to keep in mind he's a man trying to raise a teenage girl without much help and he mighta made some mistakes."

"I can't tell if you're on his side or not," I said.

"I'm on the side of truth and justice," Hen said.

"I thought that was Superman," I said.

"Him, too," he said.

"But if you think Howard was protesting too much, putting up a smoke screen, why'd you let him go? Why'd you warn him you'd be coming to look for evidence?"

"If he's the villain, he's already done whatever he can do about incriminating evidence," Hen answered. "A few more minutes won't make a difference, except maybe make him a little nervous. But we will not jump to conclusions. We will look for this girl, and we will be vigilant in our search. You will start by getting in touch with those relatives. We'll figure out where to go from there if that doesn't turn her up."

"Right. I'm on it." As I reached for the phone, I made a mental note to warn Phil that Hen had been suggesting column ideas to Howard.

CHAPTER 11

I checked with the leads Howard Cleary had given us of Crys's mother's relatives in Baxley and didn't get the impression that Teddy Westlake was faking when he had trouble placing the name. I believed him when he said he hadn't seen or heard from his cousin Sandra's daughter in years. He wasn't sure how many years. At least Crys's name rang a bell for Teddy's sister Gloria, but she said she had her hands full with her own family, what with the kids and grandkids and her husband's dialysis and all, and she wished Howard Cleary good luck with Crys.

Hen was back by the time I finished my calls.

"Well?" I asked.

"Some progress," Hen said. "I think we can rule out an abduction or an accident."

"Based on?"

"When we looked at Crys's room, he knew right off that her backpack is missing, and her favorite stuffed animal."

"Isn't she a little old for that?"

"From what I've heard, teenaged human females don't know from one minute to the next if they're little girls or women. Lucky for me I've got a wife to take charge when Delcie gets there. Don't know how Howard handles it."

"Maybe he's not handling it very well."

"Maybe not. Anyway, I got him to describe the backpack and the grimy white stuffed unicorn. He thinks she took her toothbrush and her diary. Gotta tell you, I'm relieved to think we've got a runaway."

"I know what you mean. It's the best choice of the possibilities we thought of."

"Uh-huh. Unless Howard was just wanting to cause a ruckus, all he had to do was look around and he could have seen she left on her own, and not in a big hurry, either."

"Well, Hen, he's not a trained investigator. How did he express his gratitude when you explained this to him?"

The laugh that was his answer was loud and infectious. When we calmed down, he asked, "You find out if she's with her mama's folks?"

"Haven't found any of them that admit it. I don't think so."

"Well, you keep after it. I'll check in later."

Right. That made me the primary investigator in the case of the runaway teen. What should I do next? It seemed to me that the most promising line of inquiry was Heather Jackson. Yeah, I know that's what Howard had thought—and look where that led—but it seemed like a different proposition when I thought of it for myself. Notwithstanding denials as reported by Heather's father, I, like Howard Cleary, felt it was a good bet she knew where Crys was. If not that, I'd still have bet she knew more than she had admitted. Even if not that, she was still the best place to start.

I drove to the Jackson home, halfway expecting to find Jim and Mary Ann nailing plywood over the windows to protect themselves from Hurricane Howard.

Instead, I found Heather and her mother calmly shelling peas in a room at the back of the house. It was what we call a Florida room, with windows on three sides, and it was shaded by a couple of big magnolia trees, making it a pleasant place to sit and shell peas. Heather and Mary Ann's calm belied Jim's report of how badly Howard had scared his wife and daughter. Clearly, Jim Jackson's reaction to Howard Cleary had been stronger than theirs. Either that, or they had better powers of recuperation. Maybe it's just easier all around if you don't think you're the one in charge of protecting the herd. Family. Castle. And, of course, testosterone didn't enter into it here.

"Y'all arrest Howard Cleary?" Mary Ann Jackson asked after she'd verified that I would sit down but didn't need a bowl full of peas to work on since I didn't think I'd be there long enough to be much help.

"Hen's considering it. We'll have to see. I came by to make sure y'all are okay."

"We're fine," Mary Ann said. "Howard doesn't scare me. Jim doesn't have much imagination, but I know how he—how we—would feel if we didn't know where Heather was. I feel sorry for Howard, myself. Of course, he didn't have any business bustin' in here like he did, but I do understand it. We were just talking about that." She glanced at her daughter. Heather didn't look up.

"Have you found Crys?" Mary Ann asked.

"Not yet. Tell me about what happened here," I invited.

Their version of events, punctuated by the gentle rustle of empty pea pods hitting the paper grocery garbage bag and the dull thunk of peas hitting other peas in the bowls, corroborated the story of their husband and father. When Mary Ann asked if I'd like a glass of tea, I said yes. As soon as she disappeared into the kitchen, I did what I'd really come to do, lowering my voice.

"Heather, I know you told Mr. Cleary you don't know where Crys is, but something makes me think you do know."

She looked up at me, startled, and tossed an empty pod wide of the gaping trash bag. I waited. She outwaited me, focusing her attention on the compelling bowl full of peas, desperately in need of shelling, in her lap.

"I think you and Crys are friends," I said. "I think you know what's up, or think you do. Believe me, if you know, you ought to tell me. Her grandfather is worried." I wished I had a bowl full of peas so I could throw one at her.

"Yeah. I know." A hint of a smile. "He made that pretty clear."

"Couldn't you at least tell him she's okay, hasn't been kidnapped or in a bad accident somewhere, if you know that's true?"

"No." She picked up another pea and studied it.

"Why not?"

She shelled that pea with excruciating care and picked up another.

"Heather?"

"Because then he'd be after me to make me tell, and Mama and Daddy would know I lied." Finally she looked at me. "Why can't everybody just leave her alone? She's just wants to be alone. She's okay."

"How do you know she's okay?"

"Why wouldn't she be? She wasn't acting nutso or anything. She just said she needed to find some place to go where she could be by herself."

"Did she say why?"

"She needed to think about something."

"Do you know what?"

"It has something to do with Josh."

"Everybody's upset about Josh," I told her. "She'd be better off if she was with friends, with family, with people who can help her deal with it—like the church group. Didn't you say there was a special counseling session on Wednesday night?"

"Yeah, there was, but . . . well, adults are always so sure they know what we're feeling and what's bothering us, and, well, they're not always right."

"Okay." I couldn't argue with that. "So Crys went off to deal with it by herself. How'd she go?"

"What do you mean?"

"She doesn't have a car. Somebody must have taken her."

"Evan. Crys asked him to take her. He has a car. That's why he wasn't at church last night. That's how I know she's all right."

"I think I'd better talk to Evan," I said. "But right now the thing to do is get Crys back home."

"Why? Crys isn't exactly like the rest of us with this, you know. We're all sorry about it and everything, but Crys was, like, more involved. I mean she was right there, close to him when it happened." Heather looked uncomfortable. "She told me she knows why he died, why he had to die, and that's what she has to think about."

"What?" I was glad I had neither a bowl of peas nor a glass of tea to spill.

"That's what she said," Heather said.

"And you, her friend, just let her go?"

She nodded.

"Listen to me, Heather. If that's the truth, if Crys does know something about that, it could put her in danger."

"Why?"

"Don't you understand yet? Josh Easterling was murdered. If Crys does know something about how it happened, about who made that happen, she needs to tell the police. Whoever's responsible, Evan or somebody else, might hurt her to keep her from telling."

Finally, it seemed that I had Heather's attention. She looked at me instead of the bowl of peas. But she still didn't speak.

"Heather, everybody seems to agree that Crys is kind of flaky. Maybe she wanted to go off by herself so she could. . . . Well, she's very upset, in a fragile state of mind, and I don't think she's all that stable in the best of times. Maybe something has pushed her over the edge, where she could do something crazy like hurting herself or hurting somebody else. We've got to find her," I prodded.

As I tried to think of some other approach that might pry information out of Heather, I watched the blur of a hummingbird dive bomb unerringly toward the red plastic feeder outside the window. He hovered, drank, darted off, sped in again and again. Then there were two hummingbirds, but the first one didn't want to share. His own desire for nectar was outweighed by his determination that the other one couldn't have any. He ran him off, squeaking in hummingbird wrath, before he took another drink.

The Jacksons were lucky to have their Florida room on a shady side of the house where they could sit and observe the realities of nature: selfishness, meanness, aggression, even in the beautiful, delicate hummingbird, whose brain was probably smaller than the peas Heather was dropping into her bowl. Did that tiny-brained bull hummingbird think he deserved the nectar or that he had somehow earned it? He hadn't figured out that it was a gift. I guess the lesson is that every living thing is as mean as it thinks it can get away with being. Sometimes I think Hen was right when he protested against hiring me by claiming—jokingly, I'd always hoped—that the job would coarsen me.

I was turning back to Heather when Mary Ann Jackson thrust a glass of tea between me and Heather. Her question made clear she'd been there for a while, listening, learning, and not interrupting.

"Honey, do you know where Crys is?"

"Yes, ma'am." Heather picked up a pea pod and looked at it instead of her mother.

"So you lied to Mr. Cleary and to your daddy and to me?"

"Yes, ma'am."

"I know you wouldn't have done it without what you thought was a real good reason, and loyalty to a friend is a good thing, but I think it's time for you to tell the truth."

A tear started in Heather's eye.

"Crys'll be mad."

"That is not the most important thing going on right now," Mary Ann said.

"Don't tell Daddy I lied."

"We'll handle that when the time comes," her mother said. "Loyalty is a wonderful trait, Heather, but sometimes that's not the most important thing to consider. There may be more going on with Crys than she's told us. We need to help Officer Roundtree find her. Does Crys have a phone?"

Heather brightened. "Yes. She said she could call if she needed anything, so we didn't need to worry about her."

"Let's call her, then."

"She won't answer."

"Heather!" Her mother managed to make the one word carry worry, chagrin, impatience, confusion, concern, and love.

"Let's give it a try," I said. "What's her number?"

No answer. I hoped that meant nothing worse than that Crys was being obstinate. I let it ring and ring and ring, trying to believe that she could, would, call out if she needed to.

Heather broke.

"She's at the orchard," Heather said, crying now.

"Take me to her," I said, trying to make it sound like both a request and an order.

"Good idea," Mary Ann said, taking possession of Heather's bowl of peas.

"I don't think Evan should get in trouble," Heather said. "He was just trying to help."

"That's the least of your worries, young lady," her mother said. "You go take Officer Roundtree to Crys. When you get back, we'll figure out how to deal with your father. And your father and I will figure out how to deal with you."

CHAPTER 12

"Head toward Glennville," Heather said when we were in the car. "I'll tell you where to turn."

We rode in silence for a mile or two.

"Talk to me about Crys," I invited.

"Like what do you mean?"

"I'd like to get an idea of what kind of a person she is."

"I don't know."

"But you're her friend."

"Yeah, but she's hard to know. Sometimes she acts kind of strange. Sometimes she scares me."

"Scares you how? Threatens you? What?"

"Oh, no. Not that. It's just that you can't always tell what she's going to do. That's what we meant when we said she's a little crazy, not really crazy, not crazy like you're thinking, just unpredictable. Turn here," she said suddenly.

I kicked up some dust and gravel as I swerved into a too-fast right turn, onto a dirt road. On the left was a peach orchard, the compact trees heavy and gorgeous with luminous fruit. Not far down the road, the peach trees gave way to pecans.

There aren't many things more beautiful in my opinion than a pecan orchard. Maybe it's as simple as the difference between a short tree and a tall one, but for me a pecan orchard is restful, cool, calm. The tall, leafy trees, spaced in ranks and files wide enough to allow passage of a tractor and a wagon-trailer for gathering the crop, have a well-ordered, welcoming, cooling ap-

115

pearance you just don't get from a cotton patch or a field of corn, or a peach orchard. In contrast, peaches are showy, hot, busy, energetic, dedicated to production. This pecan orchard was well kept, too—no fallen branches or debris to interrupt the restful line of sight.

I drove slowly along the rough road, not only to keep the dust down and avoid shaking our fillings loose as we bumped over the washboard surface, but also to enjoy the ride.

Neither of us spoke until Heather said, "Slow down. We have to turn again." I was enjoying the drive so much I was almost sorry to think we were nearly at the end, even if it meant finding Crys.

This turn took us into the orchard itself, and we eased along between the trees toward a stand of scrub oak along one edge of the orchard. Behind the oaks, out of sight from the road we'd turned off, was a trailer. If Crys was here, it was no wonder Howard hadn't been able to find her, even if he'd actually gone looking instead of storming the Jackson castle.

There were no signs of life.

"Are you sure she's here?" I asked.

"Crys?" Heather called.

A welcome breeze stirred the leaves of the pecan trees. It looks cool under the pecan trees, but it isn't, necessarily, and the heat of the day permeated even the shade. A squirrel chattered from an unseen branch, loud in the orchard, which was far enough from the highway that not even traffic noises intruded. It was so quiet that Crys would surely have heard us.

Heather tried again, raising her voice. "Crys? It's Heather. Don't be mad."

"Whose property is this?" I asked.

"It's ours. Nobody uses the trailer, so we thought it would be a good place for Crys to hide out."

"Hide out from . . . ?"

Instead of answering me, she called again. "Crys, you need to come talk."

"Doesn't seem like she's here," I said. "Did you bring me on a wild-Crys chase?" I swatted at some gnats that had been attracted by my heat and sweat.

"She's got to be around here somewhere," Heather said. "She wanted to come. Anyway, it's too far for her to walk to anywhere else."

The steady silence was beginning to give me the heebie-jeebies. An ill-fitting screen door with gaping holes in the screen was slightly ajar. It grated as it moved in the breeze. The sound itself evoked abandonment, desolation. The door inside the screen door was open. Only the gentle sounds of nature—a buzz, a hum, a bird call—could be heard. I steeled myself to ask, "Was Crys depressed?"

Heather looked shocked. "You think she. . . . Oh! Crys!" Louder, more urgently.

"What?" Crys stood at the corner of the trailer, one hand seeming to support her against the trailer's side. She was wearing shorts and a T-shirt that had been cut off to bare her stomach. She looked dazed.

Heather ran to her. "Are you okay? We thought. . . . We were worried."

"You weren't supposed to tell anybody, Heather."

"I put thumbscrews on her," I said. "We needed to know you're okay."

"I'm okay. I was asleep." Crys peeled herself away from the trailer and turned, disappearing around the corner without inviting us to follow. We followed her to a tattered plaid blanket spread on the coarse, scanty grass.

Crys dropped to the blanket, where she began working loose a thread from the edge. A grimy stuffed unicorn was sharing the blanket with her.

"Don't blame Heather, Crys. She was under a lot of pressure. Howard kicked up a big fuss when you disappeared."

Crys looked up.

"You didn't think he'd notice?"

She shrugged.

"Or didn't think he'd care?"

She tugged on the thread, smoothing the blanket where it gathered up around the thread, giving the impression she was trying to pretend I wasn't there.

Heather sat beside her. "Your grandpa came over looking for you, and I said I didn't know where you were, and he and my daddy got in a big fight about it."

"But you told her." Crys didn't even bother looking at me, "her."

"Come on, Crys," I said. "Now that we've found you, let's get you back home."

She lay down on her stomach and rested her head on her crossed arms, not exactly showing enthusiastic support for my invitation. The waistband of her shorts pulled away enough to reveal a small red heart-shaped tattoo. I could make out letters inside the heart: DT.

"If I wanted to be at home I wouldn't be here," she said.

"Don't you at least want to go somewhere where it's cooler?" I asked, pulling my sticky shirt away from my body.

"It's hotter in the trailer," she said without moving. "No cross ventilation."

"I didn't mean the trailer," I said. "How long you thinking of staying out here?"

"I don't know."

"Are you comfortable?"

"Not especially."

"Why'd you want to come out here?"

It took a long time for the answer to come, and then it came only after Heather, stroking her friend's hair, somehow shook it loose.

"I need to do some thinking," Crys said.

"And you can't do that somewhere more comfortable?"

"I need to be by myself." The words were muffled. Was she crying?

"What do you need to think about?" I asked, fanning my face with my hand, hoping to chase off gnats and generate a breeze. The effort made me sweat even more.

"My life."

My patience, never one of my most outstanding attributes, was at an end, eroded by the heat. "You'll have to think about your life somewhere else. You can't stay here."

"Sure I can. I'm not trespassing. Heather said I could."

"That's not good enough."

"Why not?"

"It isn't safe."

"You think the squirrels might gang up on me?" She shied a cracked pecan from some earlier crop at a squirrel that had been minding its own business. It scurried up a tree and stopped out of sight.

Several mechanically tinny musical notes, a tune I didn't recognize, intruded. Crys pulled back a corner of the blanket, looked at the phone, and covered it up again.

"Why leave it on if you aren't going to answer it?" I asked.

"Just like to know who's calling," she answered. "Sort of a lifeline, keeping in touch without actually touching."

"Heather said you know something about Josh Easterling's death. If you do, you need to tell me."

"No. I don't know anything about that. Why did you say that, Heather?"

"You said you did, Crys. You told me you did." Heather was affronted.

"And you said you wouldn't tell anybody where I was!"

Crys wasn't putting much energy into her arguments, but she wasn't showing any signs of getting ready to go, either.

"Come on, Crys. I'll take you back home."

"I'm not ready."

"And when do you think you'll be ready?"

"I don't know. I've got to think." She threw another old pecan at a skinny liver-colored dog that had sidled up to see what was going on. He sidled off, taking his time about it.

"We can't wait for you to be ready," I said. "You'll have to do your thinking somewhere else. I can't leave you here."

"Sure you can. You get back in your car, put the key in the ignition, you know."

"Okay. I've had enough. If you don't get in the car by yourself, I'll put you in—and if you don't think I can do it, you've got another think coming."

"I don't think you can do it."

"You want to find out? It's up to you."

"You put a finger on me, Gramp will sue."

"Maybe not. Your grandfather wants you back. Do him a favor. We may have to lock him up to keep him from getting in trouble looking for you."

"Come on, Crys," Heather said. "You don't want to be out here by yourself."

I don't know whether it was my threats, Heather's logic, or Crys's realization that she could do her thinking in far greater comfort somewhere else, but she stood up.

"Let me get my stuff from the trailer."

Her stuff turned out to be a backpack and the plaid blanket. She threw some snack food into the backpack, picked up the blanket and the unicorn, and was ready to go.

I took the girls home, Heather first. She seemed reluctant to go inside. I remembered her mother's promise that they'd have a talk about her lying.

Crys didn't say a word as I drove on to her house. She looked at me without expression as she got out of the car, slinging her backpack over her shoulder.

Howard was out the door before Crys was well out of the car. Neither of them spoke, but as I drove away, I saw Howard put his arm around Crys's shoulder and hug her to him. Her arm snaked around his waist, and she leaned against him. Now, what in creation made that girl think she'd be better off all by herself in a derelict trailer in a pecan orchard?

I took that thought with me as I declared myself off duty and went home.

I'd just stepped out of a long tepid shower—hot was out of the question and cold would have been an intolerable shock to my system—and was enjoying the feel of the thick rough towel on my skin, when the phone rang.

"You up for a little culture this evening?" Phil asked. Apparently he'd gotten over being upset with me.

"The Ogeechee Symphony on tonight?" I asked.

He laughed. "I was thinking a movie."

"What movie?"

"Does it matter?"

"No. Surprise me. *Dr. Zhivago* would be nice or *Snow Falling on Cedars.* Something cool. Something with snow. Not *Lawrence of Arabia.* And I don't want anything involving teenagers or methamphetamines."

"I'm taking notes," he said. "I don't know if I'll be able to find anything that meets all your requirements."

"I know you'll do the best you can."

"Your DVD player or mine?"

"Mine. You don't have cats at your place."

"Some people would think of that as a plus."

I'm never sure how many cats are living under my house and

in the nearby woods at any one time. I keep the tame population to about three, currently Muffin (a lovely brown-black mix that makes me think of Aunt Lulu's pecan pie muffins), Puddin' (a creamy yellow with darker sections that suggest bananas in vanilla pudding), and Dumplin' (a pale creamy white). Phil tries to make a big deal out of the fact that they're named after food. It means nothing.

"Some people think Miracle Whip is better than mayonnaise." It's an old, pointless, insoluble argument. Why did I ever get mixed up with a man who has no cats and no mayonnaise at his house?

"You find a good movie; I'll find something to eat," I said.

I ran a comb through my hair, which is all I ever do for it besides keep it clean, slapped on a little makeup, slid into some clothes, and went to see what I could find in the refrigerator. That's always a challenge, but Phil isn't fussy. He always acts happy with whatever I come up with. Maybe that's one of the reasons I'm mixed up with him. Maybe I'd better be careful of how much I take him for granted.

CHAPTER 13

When I checked in at work on Friday morning, I found Hen and Jerome conferring. Jerome was holding a camera in one hand and something that looked like a slightly oversized overweight postage stamp in the other.

"What's that?" I asked.

"A present from one of his women," Hen said.

"You've already been womanizing this early in the morning?" I asked.

"Just the one," Jerome said.

"Oh?" But my hope of learning something, at last, about Jerome's private life was misplaced.

"Miz Peyton's not completely out of touch with modern times," Jerome said.

Oh. *That* woman.

"She said she'd caught her prowlers and she wanted me to come see."

"That doesn't fit with the way I was imagining her," I said. "What did she use? A varmint trap? Karate?"

"She's a pretty feisty old woman," Jerome said, "but she's got enough sense not to tangle with unknown intruders. It turns out she caught 'em with this little ol' digital camera. It's her grandson's. She says she got him to show her how to use it and she kept an eye out till her prowlers showed up again and here we are. Let's see what we've got."

He hooked the camera up to a computer, and the next thing

I knew we were looking at the scene Jerome had described to me when he first went out to see Mrs. Peyton: a road, a cotton patch. Where the cotton ended, a stand of pines took over. The pines made a nice backdrop for the pictures, four in all. Two showed the same man and woman near the trash pile that had grown up between the cotton patch and the pine trees. They didn't look especially dangerous to me, and they didn't look at all furtive, as if they were worried about being seen.

The thing that struck me about the photos was that the man and woman were not paying attention to each other but were looking in different directions, apparently engaged in some activity that didn't include the other. In one, he was looking up into the branches of a nearby pine, and she seemed to be stirring the trash with a stick. In the other, she was poking the tree with the stick, and he was studying it from the opposite side. They weren't having a picnic. They weren't hiking. They weren't cuddling. It was a classic comic candid shot, the two of them together but in separate worlds. Why had they even bothered going out together?

Interesting as that was, the other two photos, obviously in the same setting, were even more so. They were both of a young man. He looked somehow sneakier than the couple, like he *was* up to something. In one, he seemed to be looking over his shoulder as if to see if anybody was watching him. In the other, he was sitting on the ground, holding something in his lap, again looking away from what he was doing.

"Recognize anybody?" Jerome asked.

"Oh, yeah." Not the couple, but even at the safe distance from which Mrs. Peyton had taken the picture, Evan Saddler was clearly recognizable.

"There must be more to that boy than we figured," Hen said. "First he abets Crys Cleary in whatever she was doing, now this. Looks like we'd better have another talk with him. I'll give it a try this time. Y'all been having all the fun."

Hen had just left the building when a call came in from Mary Ann Jackson.

"Howard Cleary's gone crazy again, and you better get right over here. Howard and Jim picked up right where they left off yesterday. It looks like they're going to kill each other—unless I get to one of them first."

Jerome and I lit out, siren screaming, lights bubbling.

Actually, the scene at the Jackson house when we got there was calmer and quieter than I'd expected. There was not even a single homicide. Instead, there was a tableau worthy of any stage production, absolutely fraught with frozen emotion. I wished I had Mrs. Peyton's camera.

Howard Cleary and all three Jacksons were on the front porch, Mary Ann and Heather standing between the two men, Mary Ann facing her husband, Heather nearest the front door, facing Howard. Jim's face showed outrage, Mary Ann's determination, Heather's contrition, Howard's . . . well stupefaction is as close as my vocabulary will let me come. Our arrival broke the spell. They all turned to us, and I was glad to see much of the drama drain from the scene as they took in the presence of Jerome Sharpe.

"What can we do for you folks?" Jerome rumbled. He should have designated a spokesperson. As it was, they all spoke at once.

"Crys has disappeared again!" Howard bellowed.

"I want him arrested!" Jim yelled.

"I don't know where she is," Heather wailed.

"You two stop acting like spoiled children," Mary Ann begged.

"One at a time," I instructed. "Heather?"

Heather didn't look happy about it, but she did answer.

"He says Crys is gone again. I don't know where she is. I promise. I don't know this time. I don't!"

"See there!" Howard yelled. "I told you she was lying!"

"You can't call my daughter a liar right here on my front porch." Jim started for Howard. Howard stepped off the porch into a bed of pink and yellow lantana.

"Get out of my flower bed, Howard!" Mary Ann started for Howard, too.

Jerome stepped in front of Howard, protectively, crushing his own patch of lantana.

"Everybody calm down, now," Jerome said.

Over their sputters, I said, "Heather did lie, Mr. Jackson. You might as well find out from me. She knew where Crys went. She was trying to be loyal to a friend."

"Heather!" Jim turned on his daughter. "You let me. . . ."

"I'm sorry, Daddy!"

"Y'all can work this out on your own time," I said. "Right now we need to be thinking about Crys."

Miraculously, that shut everybody up.

"Okay, Mr. Cleary. Your turn," I said. "What can you tell us?"

He planted his hands on his hips and delivered his report. "Right. Well, Crys was quiet after you brought her home yesterday. Said she was sorry she'd worried me but didn't feel like talking about it right then. She went right to her room, so I tried to leave her alone. Didn't want to come across like a drill sergeant. So I gave her some space. I thought we'd talk about whatever the problem was today, but this morning she was gone again." He looked around at us defiantly, as though challenging somebody to criticize his parenting skills.

"And you thought the way to find her was to come over here and attack the Jacksons?" I asked, rhetorically. "I thought Hen did a good job of explaining why that's not a good plan."

He stared at me, still defiant.

"You know better," I told him. "You should have called us."

"Heather knows where she is." He took one hand off his hip

so he could point at her.

"Get out of my flower bed, Howard," Mary Ann Jackson said.

"No, I don't. Not this time," Heather said.

"Don't y'all get started again!" Jerome said. "It's not getting us anywhere."

"Nobody's happy that Crys is gone again, but this time, I think we can all be calmer about it," I said. "We can look for her without getting into a panic about kidnapping or white slavery or an accident or any other awful things that were running through your mind before." I knew it sounded reasonable. I hoped I was right.

"Heather, come over here where we can talk a little bit," I said. She darted apologetic glances at her mother and father, but it seemed she was happy to step aside and talk with me instead of them.

Leaving Jerome to deal with the other three, I led Heather aside. Before I could decide what to say first, she said, "I really don't know where she is."

"Any ideas?" Like Howard Cleary, I thought if anybody would know something, it would be Heather.

She looked sad. "I don't think she trusts me any more."

"Who else would she turn to if not you?"

We both knew the answer to that: Evan Saddler. I reached for my cell phone and punched Hen's number.

"Hen? You still with Evan?"

"Sure am." There was amusement in his tone.

"Howard Cleary and Jerome and I are at the Jacksons. Ask him where Crys Cleary is."

"Oh."

"Yep."

"Hold on." I held on, trying to hold Heather Jackson in a withering gaze.

When Hen returned, the good humor he'd shown earlier in the day was missing. "Says he knows he did wrong helping her yesterday but he doesn't know where she is now."

"Is he telling the truth?" I asked.

"We'll see," Hen said. "Meanwhile, you keep on it from your end."

We brought our business at the Jackson house to a quick conclusion. Jerome counseled with Howard about his behavior and legal vulnerability and invited him to go home and cool off.

"I'll go looking for Crys," Howard said.

"As long as you go away from here," Jerome said. "You don't want to have Mr. Jackson get a restraining order, do you? You got two strikes now, Mr. Cleary."

Howard Cleary raised his hands in surrender and backed toward his car, as if he thought we'd ambush him if he turned his back on us.

"You get any ideas about Crys, or hear from her, you let me know," I said to the Jacksons when Howard was gone. They all assured me they would. That would be about as likely as a restraining order keeping Howard away from the Jacksons, but we have to act like we believe. What would life be like without faith?

"Howard Cleary flies off the handle pretty good," Jerome said as we drove. "You think he could have gotten mad enough to hurt her?"

"And then tried to cover it up by attacking Jim Jackson again? Maybe so. I'm sure he's devious enough to think of it, but I really don't believe he'd hurt her. You never know for sure what people will do, though, do you?"

"What now?" Jerome asked when we were back in our cruiser.

"Let's go see if Hen can think of something," I said. "He's the boss."

CHAPTER 14

We got back to the stationhouse in time to become part of a small audience, including Dawn and Miguel, for one of Hen's performances.

"Men, and you, too, Trudy," Hen said, in full *Jefe,* Chief of Police, majestic mode, "By now you may have figured out, like I have, that all three of our big current cases—Josh Easterling's murder, Crys Cleary's serial disappearances, and Mrs. Peyton's prowlers—all come together in one person. Evan Saddler."

That didn't seem to call for comment. Jerome, Miguel, and I waited.

"I'm gonna start this briefing with Evan and geocaching," Hen continued.

"What's that?" I asked.

"I'm glad you asked," Hen said. "It's a high-tech treasure hunt. The way Evan explained it to me, it started with the military using global positioning systems for ships at sea, so they'd know where they were. Then hunters and campers and hikers and people like that started using the little hand-held GPS units to keep themselves from getting lost out in the woods. The next natural step was for the people who'd bought these gizmos to look for ways to use them besides when they were at sea or hunting or camping or hiking or whatever, and somebody came up with this game."

"How's it work?" Jerome asked.

"The way I understand it, somebody hides something and

goes to the Internet to post the global coordinates so other people will know where to go look for it," Hen explained.

"What do they hide?" Miguel asked. "Treasure? Maybe food and water?"

"No, nothing valuable or practical, as far as I can tell. Might even be rules against hiding anything valuable."

"People got nothing better to do with their time?" Jerome asked, reminding me of what Howard Cleary had said about spending time in church.

"Guess not," Hen said.

"Miz Peyton's prowlers were some of the GPS people?" Jerome asked.

"They call the things they hide 'caches,' and they call themselves geocachers," Hen, the authority, said.

"Are they harmless?" Miguel asked.

"As far as I know."

"And Evan Saddler is one of them? A geocacher?" I asked.

"That's right. He's one of the ones who hides things. We had us a talk about it, and how it ain't a good idea to put those things on private property without getting permission, and he told me he had permission for his caches."

"So why was Miz Peyton upset?"

"She wasn't," Jerome said. "It was Carolyn Reese got upset when people came around and upset Miz Peyton's dogs."

"Right," Hen said. "And Miz Peyton didn't know about the cachers because Evan hadn't talked to her."

"But you said he said—"

"The cachers weren't on her property. That land across the road from her place belongs to Joe Mills."

"So in the picture Miz Peyton had of Evan, the thing in his lap is what you called a 'geocache'?"

"Yes, ma'am, Officer Roundtree. Good for you."

"What does it look like up close?"

Hen grinned. "The cache? It's an ammo can."

"No kiddin'?" Jerome asked.

"Would I kid about something as important as a geocache?" Hen asked. "Evan showed it to me, and it was an ammo can full of junk."

"What kind of junk?" I asked.

"Junk junk. Mardi Gras beads. A little flashlight like you can get for a dollar at the QuikStop. A Falcons keychain. A mug with a picture of a Brittany spaniel on it. And a little spiral notebook where it looks like all these suspicious characters sign in. We took the cache with us over to show Miz Peyton, and she was so interested in the whole idea she wanted to know more about it. So we sat down and got some iced tea and cookies out of it."

Jerome looked excessively aggrieved.

"Nice woman," Hen said. "But I'm not gonna muscle in on your territory, Jerome."

Jerome smiled.

"Might even be Evan'll get her interested in geocaching."

"Never can tell what a woman with time on her hands might get up to," Jerome said. "She handled that digital camera all right."

"Right, so we'd just about covered that when you called to tell me Crys had disappeared again."

"Did you get Evan to confess about that?" I asked.

"You could call it a confession," Hen said. "He admitted he drove her out to the pecan orchard where you found her yesterday. Not a big deal since we already know that much. It was after that I ran into trouble. By then I reckon he thought we were good enough friends he could take me into his confidence, and I could not get that boy to stop talking."

I could sympathize. Sometimes the only way to get Hen to quit talking is to let him finish telling his story in his own way.

131

"He wanted to know if I was sure Josh Easterling's death wasn't just an accident. I told him I was sure. So then he wanted to give me his theory about what happened."

"I'll bet that was interesting," I said.

"It was. He's worried, he says, about Crys. He thinks maybe she could have done it, killed Josh Easterling, when she wasn't thinking straight because she didn't really want to be baptized but didn't want to admit it and she thought this would give her a way out. Oh, and he didn't think she would have meant to kill him, just to call a halt to the baptism."

"Creative," I said. "Elaborate. Bizarre. That kid's seriously mixed up."

"You talkin' about Evan or Crys?" Jerome asked.

I shrugged. "Probably both of 'em. Actually, I meant Evan when I said it, for coming up with such an odd-ball theory. It could have been a way of trying to divert attention from himself, but maybe it does fit Crys better. Maybe she's messed up enough—a lot of kids that age are—that she can't admit she's changed her mind about something, especially if she had to fight for it in the first place. Howard told me the baptism was one of the few times Crys ever went against him. Called her stubborn. Said she got it from her daddy, who got it from his mother."

"Well, then, there you are," Hen said. "Standing up to Howard couldn't have been easy for her, but she did it. So if she changed her mind, it might have seemed easier, better, to do just about anything instead of admitting it. Howard would probably never have let her forget it."

"She might have known how to do it, too," Jerome said. "She hangs around with Evan. And she hangs around with Howard, too. No telling what she might have picked up."

"Plenty of theories," Hen said. He sighed. "Young Evan wanted to make sure I knew that if we found his fingerprints all over everything at the church it wouldn't mean anything. I told him we knew he worked there. And then Evan wanted me to understand about his love life, Lord take pity on me," Hen said. "Claims to be Crys's good friend, but not a romantic friend. Said she acts kind of spaced out a lot of the time, like she's not there, and it spooks him. For romance, he likes Heather Jackson."

"Heather said almost the same thing, about Evan and about Crys," I said. "For somebody who's so odd and out of it, Crys seems to have some good friends."

"Yeah. Maybe this younger generation isn't all bad," Hen said.

"She may be messed up, but I think she's getting help," I said. "Heather and Howard both told me Crys takes some kind of meds. To help her calm down and focus, he said."

"Find out exactly what it is," Hen said.

"*Sí, Jefe,*" I said, glancing at Miguel. He smiled.

"As to where Crys is now," Hen continued, "Evan says he hasn't seen her since he left her out at the pecan orchard. Swears he hasn't taken her anywhere else."

"Heather might have made him lie," I said.

"Right," Hen agreed. "And it ain't much help, either way. But we might ought to look at places she could get to on her own. If she walked, somebody might have seen her. People walking around here in the summertime tend to attract attention. Where could she go to hide? Jerome?"

Jerome chewed his lip for inspiration, then offered, "A motel? Nah. They'd know she was there, so it wouldn't be much of a hideout, and she'd have to show them some money or a credit card, which we don't know she had. What about her church, or one of the schools? Somebody who knows her way around and is smart enough to stay out of sight could be pretty comfortable in a church or a school, if she didn't mind breaking in."

"Not bad," Hen said. "See there, Trudy? I keep telling you he's not just another pretty face. What else?"

Miguel raised his hand.

"Miguel?" Hen said.

"Well, *Jefe,* if she's really trying to hide from her grandfather and from us, there would be many places around the town and in the edges of the town where she could go. Fish camps. Farm worker camps. Not nice places, not comfortable places, but maybe good hiding places."

Hen beamed like a proud papa. "Very good, men. You, too, Trudy," Hen said. "Okay. Jerome, you go look around at the church and the schools. Take down the police tape at the church, if they haven't beat you to it. We're not going to get anything else over there. And if they already took it down, give 'em what-for. Mike, you go talk *español* around some of the places that use migrant labor. Let 'em worry about if you're checking on conditions in the camps, if you want to. Heck, have some fun."

"*Sí,*" Miguel said.

The illegal immigrant/guest worker/migrant labor issue is as hot here in Georgia as anywhere else in the country. Some would say even hotter. We have a large Hispanic population. Add to that our farm-based economy and the fact that Georgia has some of the toughest legislation in the country with respect to the hiring of illegal immigrants and you get a precarious tangle of enforcement responsibility. Hen's attitude, thank goodness, is to leave as much as possible to the INS and the Georgia Department of Labor. Failing that, the county sheriff.

"Ain't that racial stereotyping, sending Mike out there?" Jerome asked with a straight face.

"*Sí,*" Miguel said again, still smiling. He's catching on to how we get along. "Send Jerome. He don't know Spanish, but it would be a step toward equal opportunity."

"Or I could do it," I said. "I know a little Spanish. *Nachos. Cerveza.*"

"No, Trudy, I want you to take the motels." Hen was not, apparently, in a playful mood. "I got a picture from Howard, so you can all flash that around. Everybody clear?"

Yep.

Besides the motels, for which I did not have much hope, I had another couple of ideas I'd follow up on my own if she still hadn't turned up, ideas that involved loyal friends: The Saddler house. Maybe Evan had lied to Hen in spite of their flowering friendship. Maybe Evan, with or without his mother's connivance, would have taken her in. And there was Bettye Saddler's office at the hardware store. I remembered a couch and a little bathroom. Crys might even have gone back to the Jackson house, thinking we wouldn't think of looking there again. Lots of possibilities.

CHAPTER 15

Anybody in law enforcement will tell you that successful police work is more often a product of slogging away and being methodical than of brilliant flashes of insight, so, although I held out little hope that Crys would have gone to a motel, that's where I headed, per my instructions.

There are three motels in Ogeechee. I started with the one nearest the stationhouse. It was also the best bet if something questionable was afoot since it was the only one of the three that had ever been of interest to the police.

With his well-justified fear that the OPD was out to get him, Walt Harmon at the Come-On Inn would probably have denied seeing Crys even if she'd been sitting right there in plain sight on the threadbare yellow plaid couch next to the registration desk. He did look at the picture of Crys for a long moment before he shook his head regretfully.

"Nobody like that's been around here," he said. "What's she done?" Walt leaned over the counter in a disgustingly confidential way, as though he thought I might be about to describe her underwear or her measurements or give him contact information on a prospective employee in the sideline that the Come-On Inn was known for.

"Her granddaddy's worried about her, Walt," I said, stepping back. I really didn't need a close-up view of his pores. "Nobody's going to hold it against you if she showed up here looking for a room." Well, Howard might if he ever found out, but I didn't feel like delving into that with Walt, who, since I was turning out to be not very interesting, was clearly eager to get on with what I'd interrupted—swigging a beer and watching a body-building infomercial on television.

Since I had no real reason—no probable cause, in police-speak—to think Crys was there, I took Walt's word that he hadn't seen her and asked him to give me a call if he did see her. He said he would, but he didn't even try to make the promise convincing. The wink he gave me as he slipped my card into his hip pocket didn't help.

Celeste Kim, at Ogeechee's newest and cleanest motel, maybe a quarter of a mile west of Walt's place, was as unlike Walt Harmon as her motel was unlike his.

The Mimosa Motel is a family enterprise, and from everything I had heard, the Kims were as hardworking a family as you'd ever meet. Celeste, a small package of energy and intelligence, is the matriarch. She has a bad hip, which is the reason she does the desk work these days instead of cleaning rooms and taking care of the landscaping like her sons and their wives and children do.

The gurgle and splash of water falling on stones in an electric fountain in the corner underscored our conversation as I explained why I was there.

"Oh, the poor girl. The poor grandfather," she said. "But see." She showed me the registry, a notion that would never have occurred to Walt, if he even kept such a thing. "No girl like that. No girl at all, nobody here right now at all. We had some people last night, but no girls, and they are gone now. They were families, no girl like you are talking about."

Having said and re-said her say, she smoothed her dark hair away from her face and waited for me to take my turn.

I thanked her for her time and left, glancing once more through her sparkling window into the well-kept courtyard with its feathery pastel flowers on the mimosa trees. Too bad I didn't have the time to sit there and relax. Duty called. I moved on.

I was no more hopeful of results at the last place, but thoroughness is a virtue in police work as in other areas of life. I turned south, toward Glennville and the Midway Motor Lodge, which is just about in the middle of the county, whether you're slicing north-south or east-west. The motel's ambience is midway between the extremes of the Come-On Inn and the Mimosa Motel—practically nondescript. It looked clean but not especially attractive, with a graveled parking lot all along the front of the strip of units facing the highway. The tired-looking young woman at the desk in the office—Ellis, her nametag read, in big black letters—Ellis Something? Something Ellis?—was no more or less helpful than Ray and Celeste had been. She'd seen no sign of Crys.

As I sat in my cruiser, having fulfilled the letter of my assignment, I realized I was now free to exhibit some initiative. It wasn't much farther south to the turnoff to the pecan orchard. Maybe Crys would think it was safe to go back there, figuring we wouldn't expect that. There's no point in overlooking the obvious, and besides, I liked the drive. And maybe the drive would help my thought processes.

The drive, pleasant as it was, was all I got out of it. There was no sign anybody had been there since I had hauled Crys away. Even the tire tracks in the dust were mine.

Still cruising, mentally as well as physically, I tried the Saddler house. Nobody home. No sign or sound of a soul. The hardware store was next, even though I realized that Crys wouldn't be able to hide out there during the daytime.

Bettye Saddler was there. Evan was out on an errand. Bettye showed me around, cooperative but not happy about it. I could see no sign that anybody had been camping anywhere on the premises, but I will admit that short of seeing Crys's backpack or that beat-up unicorn on the desk in the cluttered office, I might not have recognized the signs.

I thanked Bettye and left, out of ideas. Maybe Jerome or Call-Me-Mike would turn up something useful. The girl had to be somewhere.

But I did have another idea: the Jackson house. Heather had shown she was willing to stonewall when it came to being a loyal friend. Maybe she'd learned that behavior from her mother. And maybe Jim Jackson's unrestrained wrath at Howard Cleary was not so much righteous as diversionary. Odder things have happened. But if they were hiding Crys, how in the name of anything would I get them to admit it?

I pondered my approach as I drove back to the Jackson house. It took a while before Mrs. Jackson came to the door, time enough for me to notice that the lantana had bounced back somewhat since its bad treatment. The tiny orange-and-pink multiple flower heads were almost standing upright again.

"Oh, hello, Trudy," Mary Ann Jackson said, looking politely interested but making no sign of inviting me in. In spite of our recent interactions—friendly, I had thought—from her manner, she might have suspected me of trying to collect money to help desperate hurricane victims or sell magazine subscriptions so I could win a trip to New York. I didn't take it personally. I took her behavior as an indication that my suspicions were correct. Heather had persuaded at least her mother, and maybe her father—who might easily have been persuaded to do something to annoy Howard Cleary, even if his legal standing was shaky—to let Crys hide out there.

"There's something I need to ask Heather," I said.

"Oh."

Of course she knew it would make me suspicious if she didn't invite me in.

"Come on in, then." She raised her voice. "Heather! Officer

Roundtree's here again!" Then, to me, "I'll just go get her."

She led me into the living room, not the pleasant Florida room at the back of the house, and left me while she went to fetch Heather. I listened for any sounds of doors opening and closing, footsteps that couldn't be accounted for by Mary Ann returning with Heather. I heard none.

"We haven't found Crys," I said when the two of them returned. "But I have an idea where she might be."

Mary Ann smiled and made a gesture in Heather's direction that kept her from answering but wasn't quick enough to keep a look of panic from crossing her face.

"We were sure you'd let us know if you had found her," Mary Ann said. "We'll be worried about her till we know she's all right." I had a feeling she was telling the literal truth. You can usually count on good people for that, if not for the whole truth, especially if they reason that they're keeping some details quiet in the service of a greater good.

I nodded. "You have to realize if Howard Cleary finds out you aren't really helping us find her, you're likely to have more trouble with him than you can handle."

Mary Ann shook her head, expressing . . . doubt? Sorrow? Fake mystification? "I don't know what you mean by that," she said. "Crys is a good girl in trouble. Wouldn't friends try to help her through her bad time?"

"You . . . Mama said you said you have an idea where she is?" Heather asked.

Mary Ann shot Heather a warning look.

"I've looked just about everywhere I can think of," I admitted, abandoning my idea of trying to explain that *meaning* well isn't always the same as *doing* well and sometimes it's hard to tell when your friends are manipulating you for reasons of their own, which may not always be what you think. I pulled out my cell phone. "I have only one idea left."

I punched in some numbers. Heather figured it out faster than her mother did, but there was nothing she could do short of snatching the phone from my hands, and she wasn't quick enough for that. Mary Ann's look of confusion changed to chagrin as we heard, from somewhere else in the house, the tinny tones of the song that was the ring tone for Crys's cell phone.

CHAPTER 16

The only thing my cleverness netted me was Crys Cleary's cell phone. Crys wasn't there, but since neither Heather nor her mother could look me in the eye, I knew my instincts were right. Crys had been there.

I was so frustrated I didn't disconnect the call, wanting Heather and Mary Ann to be as annoyed as I was by the continuing tinny ring tone, but it soon became obvious that I'd crack before either one of them. I punched the disconnect and began to sympathize with Howard Cleary's rage where dealing with the Jacksons is concerned. I was dangerously close to venting my annoyance with a stress-relieving stomp in Mary Ann's lantana when my phone rang.

"No kidding! Well, I'll be . . . Sure. Uh-huh. Uh-huh. I'll be right there."

I hoped my enigmatic comments were tormenting the deceitful duo. Indulging a petty mean impulse, I left without telling them Crys had been found. I met Call-Me-Mike, with Crys locked in the back of his cruiser, on the road between town and the tiny municipal airport.

He met me outside the car.

"What's the scoop?" I asked.

He flashed his smile in Crys's direction, but she was staring out the window and missed the full wattage.

"I asked aroun' like *El Jefe* said, an' a friend of a friend's mother's sister's aunt's cousin's boyfriend tol' me he'd seen a strange girl hanging around out by where some of his family was stayin'. One thing led to another. He spread the word around that I'd be comin' to look for her, and they gave her up. Easy as that."

"That's pretty impressive for somebody who hasn't been in town any longer than you have," I said. "I don't even think the grapevine at the Cut-n-Curl could have beat your time."

He grinned. "They might have had their reasons for not wanting me to go looking around on my own." I told you he was smart.

"Looks like you have things under control. So why did you call me?"

He jerked his chin in Crys's direction. "Begged me not to take her home. Said she wanted to talk to you. I didn't see any harm."

"Okay. *Gracias.* Let Hen know we've found her so Howard can quit worrying. I'll try to find out what's going on before I take her home."

"Come on, Crys." I transferred Crys to the back of my cruiser. She'd already demonstrated a flagrant disregard for my advice and my comfort, and I saw no reason to give her the chance to make me have to run her down on foot in the heat. Maybe being treated like a criminal would get her attention.

I turned sideways in my seat so I could look at Crys. "Officer Ortega said you wanted to talk to me. So talk."

"That was Officer Ortega?"

"That was Officer Ortega. I'm surprised he didn't introduce himself."

"Maybe he did." A slight shrug of her shoulders indicated monumental lack of interest. She might as well have said, "So what?"

"You shouldn't let the *bandito* look fool you. He's on the right side of the law."

"Then why didn't he bust all those illegals?"

There was no way I could explain the futility of busting all those illegals to Miss Runaway, whom, I suspected, was stalling. I didn't even try. "He was looking for you. He found you."

"They ratted me out. Why?"

"They didn't want you there."

"Why not?"

I returned her irritating shrug. "If you don't want to be found, you're going to have to find a place where you can blend in a little better, Crys. You were about as well hidden there as a . . . a pine tree in a cotton patch." Hen's a lot better, and quicker, at these figures of speech than I am, but I thought Crys would get my point. If she did, she didn't let on.

"You need to find another hobby besides running away. This is getting old." Nothing. She'd told Mike she wanted to talk to me, so she must have had something in mind. Surely I could wait her out in the hot car.

I should have realized that comfort wasn't a big consideration for a girl who was willing to take refuge in an unused trailer at a pecan orchard or the notoriously unglamorous, uncomfortable, unappealing accommodations at a migrant camp. She looked tired and wilted, but seemed to be impervious to the heat. More impervious than I was, anyway. This wasn't my day for bluffing. I gave up with a loud sigh, as melodramatic as I could make it, and started the engine and the blessed air conditioning.

"Are you going to take me to jail?" It sounded like she said it with something like hope.

"Jail? No. Why do you ask that?"

"It's the only way to keep me from running away again. You might as well know if you take me back home, I'll leave again. And this time maybe I'll go somewhere you can't find me."

"Trust me, Crys, jail is not the answer."

"Why not? They'll give me a place to sleep and stuff to eat

and I can watch TV all day. Lots of people like being in jail better than being out on the streets and having to look out for themselves."

"That may be true of some people, but they're people without much going for them. You've got a lot going for you. You're headed for trouble, all right, but not for jail. Not yet."

"What, then?"

"How old are you, Crys?"

"Sixteen. Why?"

"Well, it would be different if you were seventeen, but sixteen-year-olds are considered children by the State of Georgia."

"What does that mean? The State of Georgia thinks I need a babysitter or something?"

"In a way, that's right. It means the State of Georgia thinks you're not old enough to make important decisions for yourself and therefore has an interest in protecting you, in making sure you're safe and well cared for. If you run away, we have to look for you."

"Been there. Done that," she said. "Then what?" She actually sounded interested.

"Depends on the circumstances," I told her. "If I have to call in the Department of Family and Children's Services and you get into the juvenile justice system, you might get classified as a delinquent because you keep running away. You could get sent to a detention facility or maybe a group home with a lot of really messed up cases, or maybe placed in foster care."

"Sent somewhere? What do I have to do besides run away? Break windows? Start fires? Shoot somebody?"

I was confused by the enthusiasm she was showing for the dire options I had laid out. "I don't know what you think is wrong with your life right now, but I know there's a lot that's right. You're young. You've got a home and a granddaddy who dotes on you."

"Yeah, I know that."

"So, what's going on? If you're just being a typical obnoxious teenager, that's one thing, but I think you ought to know I'm getting pretty tired of it."

She seemed to be thinking it over, but when she spoke it was obvious her train of thought and mine were not parallel.

"If I say Grampa is abusing me, I could go somewhere else?"

Howard Cleary abusing her? It would be hard to believe. Just how much of a schemer was she? How messed up? And what was she up to?

"Be careful what you say, Crys. As a police officer, I am what is called a mandated reporter. If you allege abuse, I am bound by the law to make a report and there will be an investigation. If you're in some kind of abusive situation, you'd be placed somewhere else. But it will take more than just saying it. For instance, I've seen just about all the skin you've got, and I don't see any blemishes. No bruises. Is there a record of broken bones or hospital visits?"

"No." She looked disappointed.

"So? What are you talking about?"

She didn't answer, but I could tell I had her attention, so I tried, in spite of my previous lack of success, to make her understand. "You want to make accusations, you've got to be willing to take the heat. Don't make allegations that aren't true just because you think it would be a way out of whatever mess you think you're in. It wouldn't work because we would investigate your claims."

"But—"

"We would tentatively believe you, and we would investigate in order to find evidence to support your claim. Nobody takes an accusation of abuse lightly. One case we had what Hen calls a whole herd of little heifers, five or six little girls, who should have been too young to think of this, who decided they didn't

146

like one of their teachers and they cooked up a story to get even because she kept them in detention for misbehaving in class. They might have ruined that woman's life if Chief Huckabee hadn't found the notebook where one of them had written down their story so they could all keep track of what they were telling us."

I paused to give Crys a chance to interrupt, but she didn't. "You've already admitted there are no injuries, no hospital visits. Even if people don't believe the lie, lying would cause no end of trouble for Howard and for you. Sometimes that's as rough as the abuse. If you want me to protect you, Crys, you have to tell me what's going on. Tell me the truth about what's going on," I amended.

I started driving toward town to give her a chance to think that over. I'd thought I'd gotten through to her, so I was disappointed when she said, about time we reached the center of town, "You can't keep me from leaving again, you know."

"Crys, I'm running out of patience. Unless you start talking—and making sense—I am taking you home. Whatever's going on, that's the best place for you."

"What do you know about it?"

"I know enough to tell you this. Whatever's going on, whatever kind of trouble you're in, this is not the way to deal with it."

"I'm not in trouble."

"Then what's this all about?"

"I don't want to go home."

"I'm a trained investigator. I picked up on that." We rode in silence till I reached Stubbs Street, only a few blocks from the Cleary house, and slowed to make my turn. She cracked. Sort of. As least it was a different approach. Tears. I wasn't convinced they were spontaneous, but they were real.

"Please don't take me home. I'll talk to you."

Like she'd just thought of it. Like that wasn't what I'd been telling her to do. Still, it was a breakthrough. "Fine. That's why I'm here." I turned away from the Cleary house. With the pressure deferred—I didn't need to keep after her and she didn't need to worry that I would—we were quiet while I drove. "Talk," I said.

"I don't want Gramp to get hurt."

"I don't understand you. You think running away and driving him berserk with worry is not hurting him?"

"That's not what I mean. I mean really hurt."

While I waited for more, I put on a little pressure by casually turning back toward the Cleary house.

"That's all. I don't want him to get hurt. See?"

"No, I don't see. How do you think Howard might get hurt—and what does that have to do with your running away?"

"You'll think I'm crazy."

Too late, Crys. "Try me."

"Well, I don't know who'd hurt him. God, maybe. I don't know."

"You're leaving me behind again. Slow down. You think maybe God wants to hurt Howard . . . because . . . ?"

"I don't know. Because he loves me, and I love him."

I tried not to show my alarm, my instant horrible concern, as I asked, "Crys, what are you saying?"

"Oh! No. Not what you're thinking, not what that sounds like. It's just . . . see, okay. I just don't know what to do."

She wasn't crying, but she looked so miserable I wished she would cry, let off some of her pent-up emotion. She became more and more agitated, working herself up to trying to make me understand. Finally, "Everybody in my life who's ever loved me. . . . He's the only one left."

"You're not making a lot of sense."

"They're all dead. All but him."

That took my breath away. While I was struggling to get it back, I drove on through town, past the courthouse, past the stationhouse, out into the countryside. Crys went on talking, more relaxed now, leaning forward, closer to me, eager now for me to understand.

"See, my daddy got killed when I was just a little kid. I was eight. I know he and Mom were mixed up in something bad, doing something they shouldn't have, but I don't care. He was my daddy. And Mom had to go to jail. And then, when Mom got out and I was going to go live with her—after she got a job and a place for me—she died. She wasn't doing anything wrong. She wasn't mixed up in anything bad. She was going to work hard so we could be together. She told me so. But she died. And then . . . then . . . I had a boyfriend, the first one I'd ever had that I liked, and he said he loved me . . . and he . . . he died, too."

"Dixon," I said.

She startled. "How'd you know that?"

"The tattoo. DT. I saw it out at the pecan orchard the other day."

"Oh. Yeah. We went to Savannah and got tattoos, just little ones that meant we loved each other. It was practically the last thing we did together, Dixon and me, before he . . . well, I'll never get it taken off, no matter what. It was supposed to be hidden, like a secret between just us." In the rear-view mirror I could see her soft smile as she twisted her arm behind her so she could touch the tattoo. Then a mischievous glint appeared in her troubled eyes, reminding me she was, after all, a sixteen-year-old girl. "And I forgot about it and put on some low-rider jeans and Gramp saw it and I swear he just about went postal. Told me I'd have to get it taken off. Told me I was lucky if I didn't get AIDS from the needle. And I told him if I went to have it taken off, then maybe I'd get AIDS from that needle.

It's the biggest fight we ever had."

From what I've heard about families with teenagers, that sounded reasonably normal. Just to be sure, I asked, "What kind of fight? Did he hurt you?"

She looked surprised. "Just a word fight. Gramp wouldn't hurt me."

Well, excuse me for being confused. "You've had a lot of hard blows, Crys, enough to shake anybody, but you say he wouldn't hurt you, and I simply do not see how running away from home is going to help anything."

She was quiet then, looking out the window, frowning. Finally, she found some words. "See, the thing is, what I'm trying to tell you is, everybody who's ever loved me is dead. It's like being around me is dangerous to your health or something. Like I'm a curse."

"That's rough, but I don't see the connection."

"I'm trying to keep Gramp from dying."

"Crys, everybody dies."

"But not so soon. Daddy. Mama. Dixon. Even Josh. They weren't old. They weren't ready to die."

Now we seemed to be getting somewhere. Strange as that line of thought was, it did make some kind of sense. She was still shaken up over witnessing Josh Easterling's death.

"And you're thinking by staying away from Howard you can keep him from dying? It doesn't work that way."

"How do you know? You may know about the Department of Family and whatever, but you don't know everything. Maybe it does work that way."

"Crys, people die. Those deaths didn't have anything to do with you. My mother and father died when I was young, too. Younger than you are. They were gone in a flash, in a car accident. My grandmother took me in." I was seeing more parallels the more I thought about it. "I got married. My husband was killed in a hunting accident. Just a few years ago, my grandmother died. You could say I'm alone, just like you are, but you still have your granddaddy, like I had my grandmother. He will die one of these days, but I don't think it's going to make him live longer if you run off—and I'm pretty sure it won't make his life happier. Come on. Think about it. You aren't stupid. You're at an important point in your life, with a lot ahead of you, and you don't want to make a big mistake—a mistake like your mother and daddy did—that'll mess up things down the road. We've been over this. Down the one road, you're headed toward social services, some kind of foster care or juvenile detention because you're incorrigible. Down the other road, you have somebody who loves you and wants to take care of you. Seems like a no-brainer to me."

"But I can't. I can't. He'll die. I know he will."

I'd carelessly circled around, and we were nearing the Cleary house again.

"No. Please." Crys started beating on the car door.

"Okay. I've got an idea. We'll go sit on the front porch at my house and drink some tea."

"And you won't make me go home?"

"Not right this minute."

"Okay."

It was a transparent stalling maneuver, but since it suited us both for the moment, I was willing to settle for it. As usual, I parked at the back of the house, and we came inside through what used to be the back porch before it was closed in to make a TV room. I introduced Crys to the indoor cats and poured us each a glass of iced tea and led the way through the house to the front porch. It was shady, sultry. I sat on the swing and pointed her toward a cane rocker.

"It's cooler inside," she said.

"I like it out here. Sit down. I'm ready to listen to you if

151

you'll try to make sense, but I want to start out by saying you are not a curse. What you are is a distraction. Think about this, Crys. Josh Easterling did not just die. Somebody messed with the microphone that gave him the shock that killed him. And the more time we spend running around trying to keep track of you, the less time we have to spend trying to find out who did that."

"What about this," she said, stroking Dumplin' thoughtfully. "If you don't want to keep having to waste time looking for me, you could let me stay here."

I paused, tea glass halfway to my mouth, which was hanging open. "Here?" I finally managed to ask. "Oh, I get it. You don't like me and you think I don't like you, so you think this would be a safe place? And since we don't care about each other, I'm not in danger—and even if I am, you don't care?"

She winced and looked confused, but nodded. "Sort of. I won't be any trouble. I could sleep on the couch back by the kitchen. I can clean house, do your cooking. I do that for Gramp. I'd do anything you say."

"You are serious."

She nodded.

Serious and desperate, I realized. It wasn't an idea I'd have thought of, and I wasn't crazy about it, but there was something to be said for it, at least as a temporary measure, just until we could figure out something better. Unorthodox? Somewhat. Stupid? Probably? Still. "Okay."

"Okay?" Her evident surprise showed how little she'd expected me to agree.

"Okay, maybe. I'll have to talk to Hen about it, let him know where you are. Maybe you can stay here, for tonight, anyway, till we can figure out something else."

"No! Don't tell him. Don't tell anybody!"

"I have to tell Hen. I'm not about to let the whole police

department get crosswise with the law because you think you're a curse. And Hen will tell Howard you're okay. You don't want him to keep worrying about you, do you?"

"Okay, yeah. But you won't tell him where I am, will you? He'd come get me."

"Definitely not." I didn't want him coming to my house and stomping on my lantana and my cats and whatever else was in his way. "But just in case I haven't already made this as clear as I can, here's the deal: You run away again before we get this all straightened out, and you are in big trouble, with me and with the Chief of Police, as well as the State of Georgia."

"Yeah." She smiled. "Kiddie jail or the loony bin or a foster home. It's clear as crystal."

"I mean it, Crys. We're spending a lot of time looking for you that we ought to be spending investigating a murder."

"I get it. I get it."

"I hope so. Okay. You can stay. I'll find you some sheets, and you can make up your bed while I go tell my boss what we're doing."

She put down the cat and followed me into the hall, where I rummaged in a cabinet for some sheets, then followed me into the spare bedroom. I left her there and called Hen.

"Wondered when I'd be hearing from you," Hen said.

"If I'm interrupting your supper I can call later."

"Just finished my third bowl of crab stew."

Lucky me. Maybe he'd be in a good mood.

"You take Crys Cleary home?" he asked.

"Depends on whose home you mean."

A low growl rumbled through the phone. I figured I'd better talk fast. I talked fast. "My home."

"And your excellent reason would be?" At least he'd stopped rumbling and was making actual words.

"She doesn't want to go home, and I think I ought to find

out why. I'll let her stay here tonight and see where we are
tomorrow."

"Let me get the crab juice out of my ears. I thought I heard
you say. . . ."

"I did say. And I've thought about it. I know it's not necessarily a great idea, but I think it'll be okay."

"Glad to hear you are actually thinking."

"I'm not offering to adopt her, I just don't think we ought to
get DFACS into it yet. I just think if she can spend the night
here, it might be good for her."

And more of the same. By the time I'd convinced him it
wasn't a stupid idea, I was worn out and giddily grateful that he
said he'd talk to Howard Cleary.

"You call him, he'll be on your back porch before you can get
the door locked. Besides, it's my job. Besides, I might enjoy it."

"Thanks, Hen."

"You're welcome, Trudy."

It takes a lot out of a person to follow up hours of trying to
reason with a disturbed teenager with having to defend a shaky
interpretation of the intricacies of the law and social work. I was
barely able to stay on my feet.

I looked in on Crys, who was sleeping peacefully, Dumplin's
gray-and-gold tail lying across her neck like a velvet ribbon, and
that dirty unicorn tucked under her arm. Luckily, I am well
supplied with cats. I found Muffin behind the couch and took
him to bed with me. I don't think he even woke up.

My encounter with Crys had started a couple of different,
vaguely formed trains of thought, one concerning Phil Pittman
and the other concerning Josh Easterling. I needed time to
think and see where those trains of thought would take me, but
I was having trouble thinking clearly. I wondered if the trains
would collide somewhere down the track. Heck, even some of
the cats who'd loved me—or were wily enough to make me

think they did—had come and gone. Before I had made any progress in figuring things out, I joined Crys, Muffin, and Dumplin' in dreamland, where the trains collided in a nightmare that had Phil Pittman running off to hide from me in a migrant camp and Josh Easterling driving around in a police cruiser trying to find him until a gigantic Howard Cleary, wearing hunter camouflage, came stomping all over the landscape waving a cat in one hand, a squirrel gun in another hand, and Crys in a third hand.

CHAPTER 17

"You look like something one of your cats wouldn't even drag in," Hen said in greeting when I reported in the next morning. He always looks the same: solid, competent, and ready to tackle whatever the criminal element throws at him. Maybe if I had people fawning over me all the time, catering to my every whim, I'd look better.

I slumped into a chair across from him. "That's how I feel, too."

"This Crys thing not working out?"

"I didn't sleep well. Actually, I'm thinking of adopting Crys. By the time I got out of bed, she'd straightened up some of my clutter and had bacon frying. She'd have had my eggs ready, but she didn't know how I like them. Made me nervous, but I know she meant well."

"Good experience for you, seeing what it's like to be around somebody else in the morning, see if you can get along with living with somebody else."

"What are you getting at? I'm perfectly fine."

"Getting at?" The look of innocence on Hen's face was as out of place as sugar in cornbread.

When I had something to say about Phil and me, and the likelihood of us waking up in the same place in the morning, I'd say it to Phil, not Hen. I changed the subject to something I wanted to talk about. "You talked to Howard?"

Hen beamed at me and put his boots up on his desk, leaning

back in his chair in a conversational pose. "Yes, ma'am, I did. The way he's been acting lately, it was a pure pleasure to be able to sit on him."

"He begged to be sat upon?" Maybe my day was getting better.

"Oh, yes, indeedy. You know what a good mood I was in when I started with him, full of crab stew and all. Told him he could quit worrying about Crys, we had her in a safe place. Even stayed in good humor enough to laugh when he started in on how if I didn't bring her right home he'd call the sheriff or the state patrol or the FBI or somebody to come down on me and my entire corrupt department."

"You did? Stayed in good humor?"

"Teri's crab stew is hard to beat, Trudy. You know that. I explained to him Crys was upset and making all kinds of wild claims and we had concerns for her safety and if he had any sense he'd want us to make sure she was safe. 'From me?' he wanted to know. 'And vice versa,' I told him, which slowed him down a little. I put it a little plainer. 'Howard,' I said, 'if she starts making wild-eyed accusations to the po-lice and the Department of Family and Children's Services and gets hysterical at the idea of going home, where you are, it will be better all the way around if she stays somewhere else till we find out what's going on. She could say anything at all, no matter how far-fetched, and we'd have to check it out.' While he was thinking that over, sputtering and threatening me the whole time, I raised my voice a couple of decibels and explained that if he didn't behave himself he might not be home to welcome her when we do get things straightened out because I'd take a great deal of pleasure in incarcerating his sorry loud-mouthed self. Up till lately, I've always thought of him as a harmless, mostly entertaining, crackpot. Now I'm not so sure."

"Well," I said. "I'm sure glad you agreed to talk to him and were in such a good mood."

"Bought us a little time, is all," Hen reminded me. "Now you tell me why I did that."

I did my best to tell him why I thought Crys needed not to be at home. "I'm not sure I can make sense, but here goes. She doesn't really want to make horrible accusations about Howard. They'd be lies if she did. I'm sure of it. It's just that she's wrought up."

"Okay. Wrought up. What's that got to do with her running off?"

"Stripped of all the hysterics and dramatics, it comes down to Crys's not wanting to go home because she's afraid something will happen to Howard if she does."

Hen frowned, but a jerk of his head invited me to clarify that statement.

"She's got the idea that the people who love her all die."

"Uh-huh. You tell her that don't make her special?"

"I did. I tried to. But I started thinking about it. She's sixteen years old, and she's had a lot of losses. You and I have talked about that a little, feeling sorry for her, but we haven't really thought about it. At least I haven't. Hadn't. Until I was listening to Crys. But think about it now, Hen."

"Think about what? That she's had a lot of losses? Yeah, she's young to be an orphan."

"Not just her mother and father. There was her boyfriend, too. And now Josh Easterling."

"She's putting them all in the same category?"

"Yes. People who loved her."

"And she's got it figured that she's some kind of bad luck charm? That's some kind of a stretch."

"Yes, maybe it is, but that's how she sees it. What's bothering me is the niggling idea that maybe, in some odd way, she's right."

"I think we're getting close to some kind of voodoo here, Trudy, not policin'."

"I know that's what it sounds like. You're probably right, but policin' isn't getting us anywhere on the Easterling case, and maybe I'm stretching for a way to come at it from another direction. It doesn't look like we're going to nail anybody for that. We know it's murder, but we're not going to be able to prove who cross-wired that microphone. We know it didn't get cross-wired all by itself or by accident. Somebody did it, but it was a smart somebody. Or maybe a lucky somebody. Or a twisted somebody."

"Or a smart, lucky, twisted somebody," Hen said. "The way the universe is put together, forensic science can't pick up evidence that isn't there. Lordy, life just ain't fair. Here we got us a real live murder mystery, and we don't know what to do with it. Maybe I'd better see if I can find money in the budget for a public information officer and get started on a goodwill tour to take everybody's mind off it."

"You mean something more aggressive than the public service fingerprinting at the Baptist church the other night?"

He nodded. "That was good as far as it went, but it might not be enough to distract the citizenry from the fact that we aren't solving our murder case."

"We could back off and say it was an accident, after all," I suggested.

"Much as I hate to admit I'm wrong about something, I'd do that even if I had to gag on it, if I believed it was true," Hen said.

"No," I said, "I'm with you there. I don't believe it was an accident, either. What about suicide?"

He didn't even dignify that suggestion by acknowledging it.

"Unless you're ready to eat humble pie and go with that press agent angle," I said. "I do have one idea."

He brightened. "I'd just as soon eat biscuit puddin' made out of horse biscuits as eat humble pie. What you got?"

"Sandra Cleary. Dixon Tatum. If those deaths are all connected—not, not because Crys is a jinx, but connected somehow, and not accidents—we might be able to find the connection. And if we do that, we might be able to find evidence that was overlooked in one of those cases, evidence that would lead us to somebody who has killed more than once. And even if we don't find anything, looking into those other deaths would make us feel more like we were doing police work."

He looked happier than he had since telling me about his encounter with Howard Cleary as he corrected me. "It'll *be* doing police work, Officer Roundtree. And it'll put off having to hire a public relations firm and trying to explain the sorry state of our investigation to the mayor. Let's see what we can find out."

"Something else just occurred to me," I said, emboldened by the fact that he wasn't laughing at me.

"What's that?"

"Crys is not really a stable person. Her friends use words like 'crazy,' and 'wild,' and 'scary' when they talk about her—her *friends.* But she's not completely goofy. Maybe she's not reliable about taking her meds, and that messes her up. I don't know, but I do know my cats like her. Heck, *I* like her. She neatened up my house. She told me she cleans and cooks for Howard. But still, maybe in some way she is in the middle of all this. Maybe she's more directly responsible. Maybe in some confused way she thinks she needs to prove to the universe that she's not worthy of being loved. Her losses go back to her daddy. She couldn't have had anything to do with that. She was too young at the time, and it's pretty clear what happened to him. But maybe that's what unhinged her, if she's unhinged. I know it's a stretch, but it's not so clear cut what happened to Sandra, her mother."

"Couldn'ta had anything to do with that, either," Hen said, frowning. "She'da been what . . . ten? Eleven? You saying she's some kind of bad seed, killed her mother for . . . what? Getting her daddy killed? Abandoning her by going off to jail?"

"She wasn't a little girl, Hen. It was just a couple of years ago. She must have been thirteen or fourteen, and you know girls that age are a tangle of hormones and irresponsibility and impulsiveness at best. All of them, not just the ones who are certifiably unstable. If you don't know it yet, you'll know it before you're ready, when Delcie gets there."

He shuddered and waved Sandra away. "Crys, now, she'd have had to be pretty far out of touch to electrocute that preacher when she was pretty near in the water with him," he countered.

"Purt' near but not plumb, Hen." I can talk like that if I want to. "She was almost in the water, true, but only almost. If she knew what was going to happen, all she had to do was be sure to stay out."

I'd said all I had to say. Hen sat in silence for a bit, if you don't count the clomp of his boots on the floor or the squeak of his chair as he swiveled this way and that, leaned backwards and forwards. Finally, "Okay, let's stretch our imaginations and say fragile, almost-crazy Crys Cleary is our perp."

"Okay."

"Then what are you doing keeping her at your house? We've got to get her away from you. Or vice versa."

"Well, I hadn't got that far in explaining my theory, but if she's a bad seed, I'm safe."

"Why's that?"

"We talked about it, sort of, believe it or not. I'm not in the same category as the people who love her, so I'm safe. I think."

"We'll find somewhere else for her, anyway. If she's really crazy, no telling what'll make sense to her."

"Yes. You're right. If she's connected with the killings, maybe Howard is next. Maybe she's running away from him to keep us from suspecting her."

He shot me a look that made me realize I was sounding crazy, scary, unhinged. Desperate for a theory. I took a deep calming breath.

He scratched a note on a pad on his desk. "I'll see about Crys. . . . We'll put off getting DFACS involved as long as we can. She gonna be at your house when we go for her?"

"I threatened to shackle her to a ball and chain if she ran away."

He snorted. "Might not have made the impression you had in mind. We'll see. And in the meantime, we'll look into these other deaths. Maybe we'll find something. There's a chance that there'll be something to find because whatever happened was so obvious nobody thought about looking below the surface. I'll talk to some people about what happened to the boy. Some kind of hunting accident, I think. Wasn't right here in Ogeechee, so I'll have to find out who was on that case. And you can start with Sandra Cleary."

"I'm glad you're taking this theory seriously, Hen."

"I wouldn't say that's what I'm doing, exactly, and I wouldn't dignify it by calling it a theory, but you make a good case for us not having any other way to turn. Anyhow, you can do it, but wait till I've greased some wheels."

"What?"

"Happened in Macon, didn't it? I ran into an investigator from Macon when I was getting some more schoolin' in case management and inter-agency cooperation up in Hotlanta last time. Got his card here somewhere. Gimme a while to find it. Then I'll give him a call, see what he can do to help us out."

I was so pleased Hen hadn't given me a horse laugh that I almost cheerfully found desk work to occupy me while I waited for him to grease some wheels in Macon. I thought about calling Crys, but didn't want to interrupt her, just in case she was cleaning my house.

CHAPTER 18

Since not even the people who know and love me best would put patience high on the list of my virtues, I was relieved when I didn't have to spend too much time puttering around on desk work unrelated to what I wanted to be doing before Hen called me back.

"Two things," he said. "First, I've got another place for Crys to go. Howard may be a nuisance, but he's not stupid. Won't take him long to check your place. You let her know Mike's coming to pick her up."

"Check," I said.

"And I've got it set up for you to meet with Lt. Patrick Barnett over in Macon and find out what he can tell you about Sandra Cleary's death. Said he'd fax the file over here, but you need to go look around for yourself, anyway. And you gotta be tactful here, Trudy. Don't want to give anybody the idea we think they didn't do a good job on this case the first time around."

Just like him to lecture me on manners, the grown man who is perfectly capable of wiping out the banana pudding bowl with his forefinger if his mama isn't watching. "Of course not," I said.

"We gotta act like we believe if they did miss something, it coulda happened to just about anybody."

"But not to us, eh, *Jefe?*" I've been trying to remember to add *jefe* to my list of titles for Hen. He seems to like it better

164

than some of the others: Exalted High Omnipotence, Your Eminence, Worshipful Lordship, and even Your Majesty, for examples. There's no accounting for tastes. Or maybe he just likes Miguel better than he likes me.

"No, Officer Roundtree," he said, using his favorite title for me when he's getting tired of my wit, "it couldn't have happened to us. We are much too good at what we do to let the obviously accidental death of a poor pitiful ex-jailbird with a drinking problem go uninvestigated, even if it did happen while we were dealing with a series of bomb threats, the disappearance of a bank president, and a car-theft ring."

"All that really goes on in Macon?" I asked.

"Maybe not regularly, but that's the general picture I got from Barnett of what law enforcement in Macon had on its plate about the time Sandra Cleary went on to her eternal reward, whatever it was. The fact that the bomb threats turned out to be teenagers with no idea how to make a bomb, the poor snake-bit bank president had driven his car off the road into the underbrush during a frog-stranglin' rain storm and stayed there for a couple of days before anybody found him, and the car-theft ring turned out to be a sideline of a local used car dealer, in no way undermines the stress the po-lice were under. Sandra Cleary looked like a drunk who got careless about what she was mixing with her alcohol, and they didn't have a lot of interest in looking any further and making the investigation harder than it had to be."

"Yes, sir."

"So, soon as you've talked to Crys, you can quit moping around here and get over to Macon and see if you can stir up anything."

"Yes, sir," I said. I was out of there like a scalded cat. Macon sits where Interstate Highways 75 and 16 converge, a little more than halfway to Atlanta from Ogeechee. The Highway 16 part is a pleasant rural drive compared to the Highway 75 part, especially if you can ignore the drivers who are ignoring the speed limit, confident that the law won't get after them until they hit ninety. I can ignore them. I, of course, while eager to reach my destination and begin exploring the possibilities in my frankly flimsy theory, did not flout the law, but used the hour or so to clarify my thoughts about life and death, love and marriage, crime and punishment. The usual.

Patrick Barnett must have been having a slow day. He had apparently gone into action as soon as he was through talking to Hen. He had a copy of Sandra Cleary's file waiting for me on his desk. "Let me introduce you to one of the guys who worked that," he said and led me to another desk.

Officer Thom Sawyer looked up from his desk to speak to Barnett and me. (Yeah, Thom Sawyer, and if he thought spelling it that way would save him grief, him with his straw-colored thatch and enough freckles for two or three people, he'd surely been disappointed through the years, which may have affected his attitude, of which he also had enough for two or three people.)

"Yeah, I remember that," he said, scratching under his armpit. "Landlady called it in. Skinny faded-blonde loser decided to take the easy way out of her miserable life. Booze and pills. No reason to take a second look." (Like you idiots are doing, his attitude said.) Clearly Hen's charm hadn't worked on Sawyer—or maybe it was Barnett's interpretation of Hen's request that was at fault.

I've been known to muster some significant attitude once in a while, myself, so I asked, "No signs of forced entry? No signs of anybody ransacking the place?"

"You got a hearing problem? I just said there was no reason to ask any questions, and a broken door, smashed furniture, blood, woulda raised some questions."

I smiled. "Suicide note?"

"No suicide note doesn't prove a thing, just means she was careless."

"What kind of alcohol? What kind of pills?" I was still smiling.

Thom Sawyer was not smiling. He wasn't even looking at me any more. "It'll be in the file. Anything else I can help you with?"

"We're looking for evidence that might link Sandra Cleary's death to a series of deaths."

"A serial killer in . . . where did you say you're from? Ogee-chee?" Now he smiled, a prizewinner, if you're into condescending smiles.

I resisted the childish temptation to overstate the crime situation in Ogeechee in order to win his respect. Instead, I said formally, "Not all the deaths occurred in Ogeechee, or I wouldn't be here taking up your valuable time. We don't know where the investigation will take us."

He demonstrated how valuable his time was by wiping his nose with the back of his hand and beginning to rummage in a desk drawer.

"Thanks, Thom," Barnett said and led the way back to his own desk. "Serial killer?" Barnett asked when we'd moved out of earshot of Sawyer. "You make that up?"

"Not entirely," I said. "We don't know. . . ."

". . . where the investigation will take you. Gotcha." He handed me my copy of the file. "Now you know all we know. What little there is, is in there. Cut, dried, and packaged. Knock yourself out."

"Thanks for your help," I said. I turned to the file, which, it turned out, wasn't actually much more helpful than Thom Sawyer had been. The usual post-mortem examination of the body had showed a lethal combination of alcohol and tranquilizers, as Sawyer had told me, ingested within an hour or so of Sandra's death, which had occurred not long before midnight on the evening she died, three years ago. The file did not, of course, explain how or why that combination of ingredients got inside Sandra Cleary. If there was more to Sandra Cleary's final moments than the cut, dried, and packaged data in the file, it was up to me to find it out. I was hopeful. One positive aspect of my meeting with Sawyer was that it was easy to believe the Macon investigators might have missed something. Nothing short of finding a slavering vampire with his fangs stuck in her throat would have gotten Sawyer's attention.

According to the file, Marlene Booth, the manager of an apartment building called Robins' Roost, had called the police when she found Sandra's body. I drove out there to see if I could find Marlene Booth or anybody else who might still be around that remembered Sandra and the circumstances of her death.

Since it was a little south of town, the name Robins' Roost might have been intended to lure Air Force personnel from nearby Warner Robins. Even if that wasn't the idea, the name was poetic, reasonably clever, and, it turned out, miles too cute for the actuality.

The wooden sign, which needed to be re-painted, stood at right angles to the highway in an expanse of asphalt that was succumbing here and there to weeds with an astonishing desire to live. Some patchy grass around the base of the sign and a large crape myrtle in need of some pruning were the extent of the landscaping. The weedy asphalt widened to make a parking area in front of the building, a two-story faded yellow stucco rectangle. I guessed there'd be four units—two up, two down—with an entry hall and staircase dividing them.

So this was where Sandra Cleary was roosting while she tried to get herself together. It was depressing to think how low she must have been if this was on the way up (if you believed Raynell, Mrs. Reverend Branch Harden) or giving up (if you believed Thom Sawyer). Still, life force being what it is, this unlikely place must have provided enough soil for her tentative new roots.

The card in the slot on the door of the ground-floor left apartment said Booth. Maybe I was in luck. I saw no doorbell, so I used my knuckles, rapping long and loud to overcome the noise from inside, a television set.

The volume on the television dropped. "Who is it?" The voice was cheerful, alto, and seemed to be coming from some distance into the apartment.

"Officer Trudy Roundtree from the Ogeechee Police Department. I'm looking for Marlene Booth."

"What's it about?" I pictured the woman, trigger finger poised over the remote, ready to raise the volume on her TV show and shut me out if she didn't like my answer.

"Could I come in and talk to you, please?"

"What's it about?"

"Do you remember Sandra Cleary?"

"Just a minute."

It took just about a minute before the door opened to reveal a heavy woman putting a lot of her weight on an aluminum walker.

"I'm Marlene. Come on in," she said, backing away to give me room to edge past. She closed and locked the door behind me. "The place is a mess, but I don't get around too good these days. Just push that stuff off the couch and have a seat."

I did as I was told, moving what looked like a month's supply of newspapers onto another pile of papers on the floor as my hostess positioned herself in front of a recliner and adjusted herself on the hydraulic seat, which began to lower her into sitting position.

"Waiting for a hip replacement," she said. "Can't be too soon for me. Tired of living like an old lady. I'd offer you something, but it's not worth the effort."

I was glad of that. There was a smell in the place that didn't inspire confidence in what might come out of the kitchen.

"Sandra Cleary, you said. Haven't thought about her for a while. She can't be in trouble with the police again, so what's this about. Ogeechee, you said."

I smiled, trying to ignore the mess, the smell, and the noise from the TV. "We've got a case over in Ogeechee that might be connected with the way she died. I was hoping you'd remember her and could fill in some blanks for me."

"Oh, I remember her, all right. I'd remember her even if she hadn't died right upstairs in 2-A. I was the one found her, you probably know, since you're here, and I got to tell you it just about broke my heart. She used to stop by for a minute on her way home from work, and when she didn't stop that day, I got a little worried. She never did go anywhere except to work, and I thought maybe she was depressed about her daughter's birthday. I called up there and didn't get an answer, so I went up to see about her, thought maybe I could cheer her up. That's before my hip got so bad I quit doin' stairs. And I went in to see if she was all right, and she wasn't. That's how I found her, there on her couch, dead as anything."

"You liked her, then?"

"I did. She'd had some bad breaks. Now, I know some people would say she asked for a lot of that trouble herself, but it looked to me like she'd learned something from her hard knocks and was turning things around. She had a daughter, you know, and she was tryin' real hard to save some money so she could have her daughter with her. I could sympathize. I have a daughter, too, and I know my life wouldn't be worth living if I didn't have her."

"There's some question about how Sandra died," I said.

"Mixed up drugs and alcohol is what I heard. You sayin' that's not right?"

"According to the police report I have, that much is right. The question is whether she did it on purpose or not."

"Whose question was that? And what difference does it make to anybody now?"

"Just an unanswered question," I said.

"Well, you'll never make me believe she did it on purpose, if that's what you're getting at. She just wasn't like that."

I wish I had a dollar for every time I'd heard that sentiment from somebody who'd been surprised at what a friend or acquaintance had undeniably done.

"So you believe it was an accident."

"Had to be."

"If she didn't mean to kill herself, that raises questions about how it could have been an accident. Was she a heavy drinker?"

"That poor woman's in her grave and still can't get any peace!"

A key rattled in the door lock accompanied by scurrying noises and a voice with an edge to it. "Mama, I need you to watch the kids while I go to the store."

The woman who opened the door was obviously Marlene's daughter. Same rich voice, same soft bulk. She brought with her three children. Two of them seemed bent on impeding her progress by holding on to the hem of her shorts as they played peekaboo around her legs. She held the third, still in diapers. If Marlene Booth was their babysitter, a concept that seemed shaky to me, it helped explain the mess and the smell in the apartment.

As soon as the door closed behind the group, peekaboo suddenly changed to let's pinch each other. High-pitched shrieks, delight or pain or terror, joined the rest of the rich atmosphere.

Marlene raised her voice. "This is my daughter I was telling you about. Deena, this police officer wants to talk about Sandra Cleary."

Deena took the boy by the arm and pulled him around to the front. "Ray, you stop that right now and go get some ice cream sandwiches for you and your sisters."

The shrieking older children ran toward the kitchen, separated from the larger room by a half-wall and counter.

"Mama, can they have some ice cream sandwiches?" Deena asked belatedly.

Marlene waved a dismissive hand. Deena opened a couple of the newspapers from my neat pile, spread them on the floor, and plopped the baby on top.

"I miss Sandra," Deena said, raising her voice to a new level, to reach over the noise of the TV and the scraping sound of the children dragging a chair in front of the refrigerator. "We talked about our kids a lot. I just had Ray then, and since her girl was older, she knew a lot more about babies than I did."

"She was just asking me if Sandra drank a lot," Marlene said.

Between the TV noise, the children, the smell, and all the clutter, I was fast losing interest in Sandra Cleary's possible problems. It was such a long shot, anyway, that I was surely wasting my time, and it would be a blot on the reputation of law enforcement everywhere if I had to run screaming and gasping from the room instead of leaving with dignity while I still could. I was about to bid them a fond adieu, but Deena's answer got my attention.

"I told you then, Mama, I never saw her drink." Deena perched on the arm of the sofa. "She told me she'd found out she had what she called an addictive personality defect, meaning when she found something she liked, she didn't know when to stop with it. It could be drugs or alcohol—"

"Or sex?" her mother interrupted. "You got an addictive

172

personality defect, too?"

The interruption didn't faze Deena. Maybe she thought it was Marlene's idea of a compliment. Maybe it was Marlene's idea of a compliment. Deena turned to me.

"Mama thinks I've got too many kids, not that she don't love 'em all three to pieces. I liked their daddies for the sex, but that don't mean I want any of 'em around all the time. No reason to marry any of 'em. They'd think they had the right to get in my business, try to tell me how to raise my kids. Then they get mad when you're tired of 'em and you have all that divorce crap, which costs money I'd rather spend on something else. Nah. I can do just fine without that. Me and Mama and the kids, we get along just fine without some worthless man."

She stopped for breath before going on. "Anyway, Sandra said she didn't want to get started on anything that would bring her down. Sure surprised me when they said how she died. Sorta like Marilyn Monroe, wasn't it? I always thought something bad must have happened to throw her into a tailspin, if she was drinkin' and druggin' again."

"You talkin' about Marilyn now or Sandra?" Marlene asked.

"Did you have any ideas what that bad thing might have been to put her in a tailspin?" I asked, hoping to head off a trip down a rabbit trail.

Deena stepped over the baby so she could go into the kitchen to scream at Ray, who was eating an ice cream sandwich and holding another high in one hand while his sister cried.

"You give Renay that right now if you know what's good for you!" Deena said.

"If something put her in a tailspin, like you said, I don't know what it coulda been," Marlene said. "She had a couple of jobs where she could walk to work, just down at the shopping center, and they liked her. She didn't make much but enough for her to get by on and save a little, and she wasn't a spendthrift like some people. Didn't seem to care if she had a boyfriend or not, not like some, so it wasn't that."

"Maybe it wasn't anything big," Deena said. "Maybe it was all just wearing her down. Waiting to be with her kid again, feeling bad about how she'd messed up and had to miss seeing her grow up."

"Yeah," Marlene said. "She did get down once in a while about all the time she'd missed with her baby while she was in jail. She was away for five years, you know, five years. Missed all that time from eight to . . . what . . . thirteen?"

Deena was breaking off bits of an ice cream sandwich and feeding it to the baby, whose wails and flailing arms suggested he or she didn't appreciate the gift. Neither Marlene nor Deena seemed to mind that the baby was spreading the ice cream and cookie mixture all over its clothes, its face, and the newspapers.

"Did y'all tell the police this?" I asked. "That she wasn't suicidal and didn't drink?"

The women looked at each other. A shampoo commercial told us how easily we could all be sexy as all get-out.

"I don't remember anybody askin'," Marlene said. "I'da sure told 'em if they did."

"All I know is I had a two-year-old and was pregnant again by another no-good fly-by-night smooth talker, so I didn't have much time to think about anything else," Deena said.

Much as I'd hate to cut Thom Sawyer any slack, I was beginning to understand why he might have accepted the obvious answer to why and how Sandra Cleary died. These two wouldn't have been any help in an investigation. And since Sandra, in Hen's words, might have been a poor pitiful ex-jailbird with a drinking problem, that would have done nothing to make Thom Sawyer look any deeper. But I needed either to look deeper or put myself in his class. I tried looking deeper.

"If y'all don't think she would have killed herself deliberately, and if you don't think she would have been drinking and done it accidentally, what do you think? What does that leave?"

Apparently, "don't think" was more operative for these two than "do think."

"I don't know," Deena said. "What are you saying? You mean you think somebody did it to her? Made her drink herself to death?"

"There were pills, too," Marlene reminded her, barely beating me to it.

"Never knew she was on any pills," Deena said. "Maybe she had a date and he gave her pills, some kind of date rape drug. That would kinda make sense. I don't think she'da spent the money on liquor, but somebody mighta talked her into having a drink, and you know how it is with them addictive personalities. She kept on drinking, didn't know when to stop."

"If she had a date, wouldn't she have mentioned it to one of you?"

"Of course, she would," Marlene said. "I just don't know what to think. That doesn't sound right, but I've seen people do things I never would have expected. You can't ever know what people will do, can you?" Marlene shook her head. "Deena, show her that picture you took of us."

Deena was in the kitchen pouring oyster crackers into plastic bowls. "I don't give my kids hard snacks like some women do," she explained to me when she saw I was watching. "I heard of a kid choking on a carrot stick, so I give 'em things that'll dissolve real easy." Having staked her claim on responsible mothering, she responded to her mother. "Where's that picture, Mama? I don't see it."

"There, behind the TV."

While the children threw spit-soaked oyster crackers at each other with more enthusiasm than accuracy, I looked at the framed photograph Deena took from a shelf behind the television set and handed to me. It showed a woman who could have been an older, tireder version of Crys Cleary sitting with a younger, dressed-up version of Marlene Booth on a low couch. On Marlene's lap sat a child whose face was partly hidden behind a red balloon.

"That was when she had a party for Ray's birthday," Deena said. "That's Ray, there on Mama's lap. Look here, Ray. That's you."

Ray leaned over me to get a good look at the picture, planting his small gummy hand on my slacks. He shrugged, not much interested in whoever that was with a balloon in front of his face. Still leaning on me, he resumed trying to spit crackers at his sister. I summoned all my professional training to keep from flinching when she returned fire.

"She said she wanted to have the party for Ray because it was gonna be Crys's birthday, too, and she couldn't get over there to see her," Marlene said, "so she was goin' to pretend it was for both of 'em."

"You can see there on the coffee table in front of us," Marlene said, waving her fingers in the direction of the picture. "She always had a picture of her daughter, said she was keeping her eyes on the prize."

"That was so sweet," Deena said. "She kept a sort of a shrine. She said it was like the Catholics or Buddhists do, with things to remind her of her husband—he was killed before she went to jail, you know—and her daughter. Nothing else mattered in the world as far as she was concerned."

"Look, you can see the present she had for Crys." Deena pointed, but I was having trouble concentrating on anything besides Ray and Renay and the baby, who was now crawling off the newspapers, gummy hands and all, and was heading in my direction.

Deena continued, oblivious. "You can't see it very well, just part of its head, poking out from behind Crys's picture. Sandra was afraid Crys was too old to like stuffed animals, but I told her it was the thought that counted, and if Crys didn't appreciate it, it was just too bad. Anyway, I slept with a teddy bear till I got pregnant, didn't I, Mama?"

"Wasn't a teddy bear got you Ray," Marlene said. "Come to think of it, though, Ray's daddy was a hairy son of a gun." She laughed.

Deena ignored her mother. "Sandra said she'd just keep it till she could give it to her, and the very next day she was dead. You think maybe she was depressed over bein' around us all together and her not even getting to see Crys on her birthday?"

"It's possible," I said, standing and edging away from the children.

"Had a time keeping Ray away from that knife," Deena said.

"That knife there, next to the picture of Crys on the coffee table." Marlene pointed again. I tore my eyes away from the children and darted a glance at the picture. "The knife was for her husband that got killed. I felt so sorry for them poor kids. Thought they were going to have a good life together with their little girl, and look what happened. She didn't have much of anything, and most of that was pitiful, but she held on to these things. Made it all that more of a big deal when she wanted to spend a little money on the party. I didn't take it wrong that she wanted to get out of here."

"Well, I did," Deena said. "It's good enough for me and my kids, and that precious girl of hers would have had Ray and Renay to play with."

"Babysit for you, you mean," Marlene said. Back to me: "She was just trying to put it together, finding out where Crys would go to school and how she'd get there. She'd already talked with social services to find out what she needed to do, and she was workin' on it."

"This is a nice souvenir," I said, nodding toward the picture, trying to keep them from going off on another of their routine arguments, as I dodged Ray again.

"Talk about souvenirs, Mama, you still have Sandra's stuff? Maybe if Officer Roundtree is doing some CSI cold case thing, she'd want to look at Sandra's stuff."

"What stuff?" I asked.

"The stuff she left," Deena said. "You can't take it with you, you know."

"There wasn't much," Marlene said. "I rent the apartments furnished, even the kitchen stuff, to make it easier for the airmen, you know, so it's not like Sandra had to bring in a lot of her own stuff."

"Do you still have it?" I asked.

"What did you do with it?" Deena prodded.

"What little there was I put in boxes, waiting for somebody to want it, but nobody did, and I forgot about it. If it's not one thing, it's another, like they say, and when Deena had trouble delivering Renay, and then Renay was sick for such a long time, and then my hip started giving me trouble, and then . . . well, it was always something."

Deena interrupted, speaking to me. "Sounds like Sandra's stuff's out there in the storage, if you want to look at it."

"I sure do want to look at it. I don't know what I'd be looking for, but you never can tell what will be useful. I'll give you a receipt for it and take it with me back to Ogeechee. When we're sure we don't need it for evidence, I'll see that it gets to her daughter."

"Like she'd care. Never came to see her mother."

"Come on, Deena. The girl couldn't drive yet, couldn't come on her own. She couldn't get over here to see her mother any more than Sandra could get over to Ogeechee to see her. It's not like that granddaddy—Sandra's husband's daddy—the only other relative we ever heard of, and we heard plenty about him, let me tell you, was makin' it easy for Sandra."

"Howard Cleary? Do you know him?" I asked.

"No. Just goin' by what Sandra said. If he or the girl ever came over here, I missed it—and I think Sandra would have talked about it, don't you, Deena?"

Deena shrugged. "Never heard of him being here."

"Would you have known him if you did see him?" I asked.

"Not unless Sandra introduced us," Marlene said. "She sure didn't keep any pictures of him around."

For a moment their boisterous laughter drowned out the children and the television.

Then Deena frowned. "Seriously, you know, that man did nothing but try to make trouble for her. Threatened to get her declared an unfit mother."

"What about other visitors? Did she have friends?"

"Just us, far as I know," Deena said.

"Some woman came to see her a time or two, right after Sandra came," Marlene said. "I didn't see her or anything, and I sure don't know her name now, if I ever did. I didn't get the idea she was much of a friend, either."

"Somebody from DFACS?" I suggested. "Somebody connected with the police or the court?"

"Maybe," Marlene said. "Might have had something to do with Crys. Come to think about it, she might have been from Ogeechee. But that was a long time before Sandra died. Like I said, not long after she moved in."

She looked to Deena, who had nothing to add. I had no more questions.

"If you'll find Sandra's things for me, I'll get out of your hair," I said.

It took a while for Marlene to find the key to the storage unit and describe Sandra's boxes to Deena and tell her exactly where in the storage unit they would be found. It took another while for Deena to find them and bring them back inside so Marlene could take a look to be sure she was giving me the right boxes and the right number of boxes, but finally I had Sandra's boxes in the back of my car. Four boxes. That was all.

It's not often that I'm glad to be outside in the hot, humid Georgia summer air, but this was one of those times. Even the noise of traffic as I left town was a welcome change from the whining children and the television underscoring the conversation. The air, hot and humid as it was, blasting off the highway, smelling of hot tar, felt cleaner than it had inside Robins' Roost.

CHAPTER 19

The hundred-mile drive back to Ogeechee gave me hardly enough time for all the thinking I had to do. I had put it off while I dealt with Crys Cleary and again when I went to Macon to see what I could find out about how Sandra Cleary had died, but now I was ready to have a talk with Phil. Maybe not so coincidentally, the talk would be colored by those earlier encounters.

I swung by the stationhouse to leave Sandra Cleary's boxes and let Hen know I was back. Hen told me Call-Me-Mike had successfully put Crys in our own backwards, homemade version of a witness protection program.

"Said he hated to interrupt and haul her off while she was cleaning your house, though," Hen said.

"I'll have to talk with him about his priorities. I don't know why he had to be in a hurry. I hope she got to the pantry."

"What's all this stuff? You started doin' a little housecleaning on your own and think we've got room for your extra junk down here?"

"These four boxes are the fruit of my trip to Macon. They seem to be all that's left to remind anybody of Sandra Cleary. I'm beat, ready to call it a day, so I thought I'd wait till tomorrow to go through them. If there is anything that will help us, it's been waiting for more than two years. You want to go through them with me tomorrow?"

"I'll trust you to notice if there's anything useful. I'm taking it you didn't find a smokin' gun in Macon."

"My hopes weren't that high, after all this time. If there ever was a smoking gun, the smoke cleared years ago."

I stopped at the *Beacon* office on my way home and found chaos. Still, I asked Phil, "Can you come over tonight?"

"Looks like I'll be here kind of late," he answered. "We've got computer problems like I've never seen. One of the hard drives has started mangling files."

Ah, yes. The curse of progress. Was it Ogden Nash who said progress was all right, but it went on for too long?

"Eek," I said sympathetically. "You want me to bring you some supper?"

"No. Don't do that. I'm sending everybody else home because I'll be fuming and fussing and generally unpleasant company. And I've got to wait for a guru to get here and see what he can do for us."

"I'll fix you something later."

"Trudy, between worrying about how much damage there is and trying to reconstruct the lost material, I'm not in a mood anybody wants to put up with. Wouldn't want to put that kind of a strain on our relationship." He flashed a half-hearted grin, but the furrow in his brow came back almost immediately. Clearly, I didn't need to hang around, but darn it, I was ready to spend some quality time with him. I tried to set aside the idea that he was getting back at me for my wishy-washy ways where he's concerned, which would have served me right, but that possibility made me even more determined to see him later and to prove I could be nice.

"I'll go on home, then, but I think it's my turn to muster some patience and understanding. Why don't you come over when the crisis is past?" I've always had trouble letting go, once I get an idea into my head.

"No telling what time it will be." He was still not paying

enough attention to me.

"Ah, what is time to two people in love?" At least that got his attention. He gave me a puzzled frown. "Seriously, Phil," I added, so he'd know I'd been sort of kidding, which puzzled him even more, "Do come by. I'll be there. I've got nowhere else to go, nobody else to see. I've had sort of a stressful day, too. Just come on when you can, and we'll unwind together."

He gave me a big smile. "When you put it that way, how can I resist. It's a deal. But, I warned you. No telling what time it'll be."

"Fine. I'm warned." I gave him my most seductive smile and left.

With the sights, sounds, and smells of Marlene Booth's apartment still in my mind, when I got home I went to work setting a totally different kind of scene for my talk with Phil. I wanted peace, order, gentle fragrance. Surely I could manage that, especially since I found my place unusually tidy. Maybe Crys had been using up nervous energy, but I didn't mind being the beneficiary. The cats had tried to restore things to their idea of normal, but the mess they'd made with the odds-and-ends basket next to the television set was easily cleaned up.

Nice as the inside of the house looked, I still decided on the front porch for my rendezvous with Phil, however late it should be. I found that looking forward to seeing him was helping me recover from my day. I was in a happy homemaker mood that doesn't hit me very often.

I brought out a small table from the living room and covered it with a lacy cloth I'd found in a drawer in the dining room buffet. When Grandma died, she left the house and what was in it to me. Years later, I'm still discovering things, like gifts from a loved one that had been stuck in some dead-letter office but finally made their way to the intended recipient.

I'd also found a red rose blooming in the shade behind the

garage and floated it in a crystal bowl. A hurricane lantern with a fat candle—unscented, so as not to compete with the rose—gave a warm glow. A bottle of cream sherry. Two liqueur glasses Grandma must have bought because they were beautiful, not because she drank. Liquor, liqueur, hooch, spirits, moonshine, and medicinal wine were equally abhorrent to her. What in the world is my younger generation coming to?

As I toasted pecans in butter with just a dash of hot sauce, I mused over my reactions to Deena. There was no question she had something to do with my mood. I almost envied her easygoing attitude toward men.

I considered trying to figure out a way to provide music for Phil, but backed off. No point in freaking him out completely. The tidy house would alarm him enough. Besides, the muted creak of the chairs and the floor boards of the porch, the occasional rustle of a bird or lizard in the bushes next to the porch, the highway traffic so far away it was a hum, those sounds would surely be music enough to a man who'd spent most of his day listening to the greedy insatiable whir of computers eating data and the increasingly strident voices of people who had provided the fodder.

No doubt most people prefer their own sights, sounds, and smells, but I can't help thinking almost anybody would prefer mine to those in the Macon apartment. Setting my scene, and then surveying it with satisfaction, had been so relaxing that I was asleep when Phil arrived, curled up on the swing with Dumplin' on my chest, both of us, no doubt, purring with satisfaction. It was the cat's leap off the swing, setting it into motion, that woke me. By the time I heard Phil making his way through the house from the back, I was sitting up, had smoothed my hair, and was ready to interact in the quiet, dimly lit, sultry evening.

"Out here," I called. Although I'd been enjoying listening to him coming closer and closer, calling my name, I didn't want him to start worrying about me.

"Sorry I'm so late," he said. "You did say 'whenever.' "

"I put the time to good use," I said. "Sit here." I pointed him toward one of the rocking chairs beside my elegant candle-, rose-, and sherry-laden table.

"You didn't clean house, did you? For me?" He seemed alarmed.

"No, don't worry. That's a long story, part of my long day."

"But you are up to something?"

"Don't worry about it," I said.

"Oh, I wasn't worried. Not at all." He leaned back, glass in hand, and put his feet up on the banister, his knees bending and stretching as he rocked back and forth.

"Don't you fall asleep, now, and drop that antique glass," I said.

"You fell asleep." I couldn't tell if his eyes were open. I know I heard a sigh.

"I was safely lying down, and I wasn't holding anything."

"I could do that."

So I made room for him on the swing.

I set the swing in gentle motion. And we had our talk. By which I mean that I talked. I told him about Crys and her fear that people who loved her would die, about my concern that I had the same fear and that it was making me afraid to admit to loving and being loved. I told him about Deena and her children and her attitude toward men and marriage.

I told him that, after all, I thought maybe we should get married.

"You're not saying this to cheer me up because you know I've had a bad day, are you? This is pretty extreme, but okay. I just want to know."

I ignored the interruption. "I just want you to know that I

don't think I can make a lot of changes all of a sudden. I've seen too many things that can go wrong. And I'm not as young as I used to be."

"Who is?"

"And, anyway—"

"Trudy, you're starting to hyperventilate. Don't stress out over this. Let's just get one thing settled at a time."

"Okay." I gave the swing another push and took a deep breath.

"In with the good air. Out with the bad air," Phil said.

"Right."

"We'll just deal with the details as they come up. We don't have to have a plan for the rest of our lives right this minute."

"Right." In with the good air. Out with the bad.

"Relaxed?" he asked.

"Relaxing," I said.

"So, then, you want to look at a wedding in early autumn, when it might be cool enough to have it outside?"

"Sure," I said, and immediately felt myself beginning to hyperventilate again. It's so definite, so final. Wedding. Family. What a wimp. Still, that's who I am.

"I don't know about children," I said. "I like them okay, but Delcie might be enough." I dote on Hen's daughter.

"Parenthood is over-rated," Phil said. "I'll bet I could get Howard to do a column on it. Sounds like his kind of topic, don't you think? Something along the lines of how it's better to have your grandchildren first?"

"Too frivolous for him, I think," I said, oozing contentment.

We were quiet for a while then, both of us relaxed and relaxing as the swing did what swings do.

It wouldn't do for us to fall asleep together on the front porch swing, although the least bit of common sense would tell any gossipmongers who caught the scandalous sight that if we'd been up to anything salacious, we'd have done it inside.

Phil sighed. "We could rock along like we've been doing," he said. "But I'd rather not."

Not the most passionately romantic avowal of everlasting love, but exactly right for Phil and for me.

The mention of Howard had thrown my mind back into the murder case. I began telling Phil about my day, the trip to Macon, the sad way Sandra Cleary's life had ended.

"I'll save you from all that," Phil said.

"My hero," I said. But the image of the photograph of Marlene and Sandra at little Ray's birthday party stuck in my brain. There was something wrong with that picture. Not wrong, exactly, but something that set a little red flag waving. What? Not the kid with the balloon in his face. What? I knew it would come to me eventually.

"We could have my mother's ring re-set for you if you'd like that," Phil said. "Or shop for a new one. It's up to you."

"What?"

"A ring," Phil said. "It's traditional."

"Oh."

"Second thoughts already?"

"What? Oh. No. I just had an idea about the murder."

"Romantic evenings are over-rated," Phil said.

"I'm sorry," I said.

"Don't be sorry. This was a good effort on your part, Trudy. I'm proud of you. It's a start. We can work out the rest of the details later—what we'll name the children, should we accidentally have some; where they'll go to college; whether we'll live here, at my place, or both; will you keep the name 'Roundtree' or become . . . Gertrude Pittman? Has a nice ring, doesn't it? And what will be in bloom in, say, October, if we decide to have the ceremony back there by the garage? And what kind of punch? Please not that stuff with lime sherbet in it. And I'll bet you'll have to get a new dress, won't you? Better start worrying about that. Unless you want to let Teri and your aunt Lulu do it."

"I'll let them do just about all of that, Phil, unless I change my mind because you're making fun of me."

"A helper, Trudy. I'm just trying to be a helper."

"Okay. We don't have to decide on everything right this minute."

"That's right. Take another deep breath."

I did. "Good," I said.

"Good night, Trudy."

"Good night, Phil."

CHAPTER 20

My first order of business at the stationhouse next morning, because I couldn't think of anything more pressing, was to weed through Sandra Cleary's things and hope to find a flower. Luckily, I was in an up-beat frame of mind, feeling that life was good and that Phil and I were heading in the right direction. Otherwise I'd have been depressed as all get-out as I unpacked the boxes and spread the contents on the table in the break room.

One box held clothes, including tired uniforms for Sandra's two fast-food jobs. The few non-uniform clothes—I guessed she didn't go much of anywhere besides work—were clean and in good repair. She'd liked bright-colors, or once-bright colors, which made me like her, since they hinted at an optimistic attitude, but these garments looked forlorn, as though it had been a long time since they were new and they knew their potential had pretty much been used up.

There was a large plastic purse that held a used lipstick, some crumpled tissues, a keychain with a single key on it, and a wallet with ten dollars and an old picture of Crys in it.

One box held what you might call personal decorative items: some framed photographs of Sandra, Crys, and a man I guessed to be Mitchell Cleary, although I saw no resemblance to Howard. Several glass prisms, suncatchers, in different colors, with hanging cords attached. Crystals, of course. I was getting a picture of Sandra Cleary that was more like the picture Marlene

189

and Deena had painted than the one Howard had tried to convey. Objective evidence.

A jewelry box covered in white imitation leather stamped with gold rosebuds held a few strings of multi-colored beads, a couple of bangle bracelets, and a flaking gold-tone necklace with the word "Mother" spelled out in dangling letters. I imagined Mitch and Crys picking it out for Sandra two lifetimes ago.

Marlene Booth had obviously used some judgment when she packed up Sandra's things. There were no perishable items—no food, no half-used bottles of shampoo or aspirin or mouthwash, although Sandra must have had that kind of thing around. Had Marlene thrown it out? Had she kept it for her own use? And where had she drawn the line between what to keep, what to trash, and what to store?

Hen joined me and poured himself a cup of coffee before surveying my sad display.

"Turn up anything?" he asked, not quite repressing a shudder when he tasted the coffee.

"You mean like a suicide note or a prescription for something she shouldn't have been mixing with alcohol? That would have been nice."

"It was a long shot," he said. "You knew that. I don't see anything here that looks like evidence of anything worse than poverty. Still, you got a nice drive over to Macon on city time, so the day wasn't completely wasted."

"Oh, the day was filled with rich new scenic and olfactory experiences, all right, even if it didn't produce what I'd expected."

"Sounds like a story, there. You want to tell me about it?"

I did, but not till I had a little more distance from Thom Sawyer and Marlene and Deena, and especially Ray and Renay, not until I'd polished the story into something that I could laugh at along with everybody else. I was still too close—too annoyed—to think it was funny, although I could see the potential for humor. I'd keep the development with Phil for later, too. "Not now," I said. "You want me to see if Crys wants any of this?"

"Sure. She probably doesn't have much to remind her of her mother. Better wait till we've finished pokin' around and we're sure we don't need any of it. Some of those little knicknacks might appeal to her. Crystals, huh?"

"Right." I began repacking the boxes.

"You giving up on the idea that we'll find something wrong about the way Sandra Cleary died?" Hen asked.

"I hate to give up on this angle, Sandra Cleary's death, since I want to believe these deaths are related somehow. Did your look into how Dixon Tatum died turn up anything that will help?"

"Not much. Ran into his daddy yesterday, though, and I asked him to come in this morning to tell us what he can about what happened. We'll see what good that does us."

"Poor man."

"Yep. You'd know better than most how he feels."

"I never claim to know how anybody else feels, but . . ." I know there are a lot of things that can come zooming around a corner and blindside people, countless unexpected paths to heartbreak, but since my husband died in a hunting accident, thinking about that kind of accident still has the power to make my heart sink.

Hen poured out his coffee and left me. I'd just finished packing up Sandra's things when he reappeared. "Lloyd Tatum's here. Come listen to what he has to say."

Lloyd Tatum was a slim man, tanned with outdoor work so that his skin was the same color as his hair and his eyes, which were behind rimless glasses. He looked to be in his mid-fifties.

He was wearing work clothes, khaki pants and a plaid cotton shirt, and carried an Atlanta Falcons cap which he held by the brim, waggling it in abrupt jerks.

"Thanks for coming by, Lloyd. I appreciate it," Hen said when we were all seated in his cramped, cluttered office.

"I don't recall if you said why you wanted to talk to me," Lloyd said.

"I don't think I did say," Hen said. "And I'm sorry to bring it up, but we're looking into the possibility that the way your son Dixon died might tie into another investigation."

"What investigation?" Lloyd looked from Hen to me in surprise. "I don't get it."

"Lloyd, let me ask you this: You ever have any idea it wasn't an accident?"

I turned away from the pain in Lloyd Tatum's face, my eyes stinging in sympathy. He hung the cap on his knee and removed his glasses so he could rub his eyes. "No." He shook his head to confirm it, then slowly looked up at Hen. "What're you gettin' at, anyway?"

Since it was obvious what he was getting at, Hen didn't answer that. "Tell us about it, Lloyd."

Lloyd shook his head, clearly indicating he didn't understand what Hen was after but would humor the Chief of Police. When he spoke again, his eyes were closed. "We were hunting at my brother Conrad's place up toward Cobbtown, Conrad and his boys, Dixon and me. Howard Cleary was planning to go with us, but something came up, so it was just the five of us. We'd hunted there a hundred times, maybe a thousand, know the ground. Not much of anybody else hunts there since it's private property, and my brother's careful who he lets on. Next to playing football, huntin's what Dixon liked best in this world. You ask about it being an accident. I never doubted that's what it was. I've asked myself over and over how it coulda happened, but that's what an accident is, isn't it? Something that just happens? Dixon knew how to be careful. He knew about guns, been around 'em all his life, and we took all the hunter safety stuff together. Shouldn't have happened. But it did."

"I know you've thought about it a lot," I said. "Can you tell us how you think it happened?"

Lloyd Tatum took a deep breath and put his glasses on. He picked up his cap again and began bouncing it up and down by the brim. "Yeah, I've thought about it a lot. It was hard to piece it together. We've talked it over since, me and Conrad and the boys. What it looked like was Dixon propped his gun against a big log while he climbed over, and it slipped and went off, or maybe he tried to jump over the tree with the gun in his hand and didn't quite make it and it went off. Something like that."

He sat there, looking off into the past, until Hen said, "Tell me about how y'all found him."

Tatum put down the cap and took his glasses off again. "It started gettin' late, and it had been a while since anybody had seen Dixon, so we went lookin' for him. It was Billy found him, his cousin, Conrad's boy. Set up a holler. We called nine-one-one and got help on the way, but we all knew it wasn't going to help."

"He was lying next to the log? And his gun was nearby?" I asked.

"That's right. No tellin' how long he'd been lyin' there. I just hope he died quick, didn't lie there waiting for somebody to come help him." His voice broke. "Lord, I don't think I could stand it if I thought we coulda saved him if we'd gone looking for him sooner. We'd heard a couple of shots from his direction but didn't pay much attention, knew he'd come get us if he needed help with a kill. I'll never get over it to my dying day."

"A couple of shots?" Hen asked. "Close together?"

Lloyd frowned, thinking, then bounced his cap in an I-don't-know gesture. "Close enough together for me to remember it was a couple of shots."

"You take a look at his gun?"

A look of pain crossed Lloyd Tatum's face. "Hated to touch it, but, yeah, I looked at it. Didn't see anything wrong with it. Watched while Fred checked to see if it had been fired, which it had. Took it home and locked it up and haven't touched it since. His mother . . . well, she blames me. Never did like the guns and the huntin'. I don't hunt any more. Just don't enjoy it the way I used to."

The silence stretched out until Hen said, "Thanks, Lloyd. Sorry to put you through this again."

Lloyd Dixon slapped the cap against his thigh. "You're not gonna tell me why you're asking?"

"We'll sure tell if you anything comes of it," Hen said. "Let me walk out with you."

They left and I sat, trying to see if there was anything useful in what Lloyd Tatum had told us. If there was, I'd missed it.

When Hen came back, he brought with him Fred Wiltshire, a sheriff's deputy.

"Stay put, Trudy. You'll want to hear what Fred has to say. Make yourself comfortable, Fred. I'd offer you some coffee, but I don't want to get on your bad side."

Fred took the chair recently vacated by Lloyd Tatum, leaned back and crossed his arms in a posture that seemed to be defensively aggressive, if there is such a thing. He grinned in a way that made me think it was too late for Hen not to get on his bad side. I remembered that he and Hen had gotten cross-ways awhile back over Fred's handling of a domestic violence case that had involved the sheriff's department as well as the city police. Even though he surely had not said it to Fred's face, in a fit of pique Hen had said that Fred was the kind of officer that could give Neanderthals a bad name. But Hen is a good man and a good policeman, and he knows how important it is for people in the same line of work to get along. I was interested to see how he would manage to get along with Fred long enough to find out what he wanted to know.

I could see Hen was trying to be nice. Fred, Neanderthal or not, could see that, too, and he smiled a little Neanderthal smile as he said, "What's this all about? Sounded pretty mysterious." He probably thought he had some kind of edge since Hen was making an effort to be pleasant. "I was aiming for discreet," Hen said. "It just came out mysterious. You're one of the ones who investigated Dixon Tatum's hunting accident."

"Yeah, I was. Wasn't much to investigate. Pretty clear what happened. Happens every year. People get to having a good time, doing something they've done all their lives, and they get careless. Especially somebody like Dixon Tatum. Now, I wouldn't say this in front of his daddy, but the boy went around askin' for trouble. You know that as well as I do. Had a good-sized collection of tickets for speeding and reckless driving, even one DUI. Only thing surprised me about him bein' killed in an accident was that it didn't involve that car of his. Comes of being a football star, if you ask me. Those boys get to thinking they're indestructible in real life like they are on the football field. Probably don't think life's worth livin' after high school, anyway, so they don't worry about it. Worst thing anybody can think of is blowin' out a knee or getting hit on the head, and they don't think about that much. You think his folks would come down on him, try to straighten him out? Think again."

"There wasn't anything about his death that raised any questions in your mind?" Hen asked, nodding in a way that might have suggested he was agreeing with Fred's opinions. "No idea that what you found was what somebody wanted you to find—that it had been staged in any way?"

Tiny as Fred's mind may be, it was big enough to let in the

notion that Hen was questioning his work. He reared back and narrowed his eyes. "What d'you mean?"

"I mean we've got some stuff going on that's making me take another look at some deaths that passed for accidents," Hen said. "Deaths that were meant to pass for accidents. If you think back, can you think of anything at all that wasn't exactly right?"

"If I didn't think so at the time, I'm sure not about to think so now." Fred's eyes pinched into a frown under his Neanderthal brow. "You got a problem with the way we investigated that boy's death?"

Hen looked as surprised as if the very notion had never entered his mind. "No. That's not what I'm sayin', Fred. What I'm sayin' is if it wasn't an accident—and it might have been an accident just like everybody thinks—but if it wasn't, then somebody would have gone to some trouble to make it look like one."

Fred leaned back again, still prickly, still suspicious of Hen, but he'd decided to string along. He shrugged. "Looked like a huntin' accident to me. 'Course, by the time we got there, any evidence of anything else woulda been stomped all to heck by the Tatums and the EMTs." He nodded, satisfied, then added. "Only thing to say it wasn't his own fault and pure-D careless-ness was Lloyd Tatum carryin' on about how he couldn't get over Dixon being so careless, and I already told you how much I'd go by that."

"Lloyd's still not over that," Hen said. "Probably won't ever get over it. I wouldn't ever get over it, if it had been me and mine."

Fred shrugged that off. "Now you raise the question, though, Hen," he said thoughtfully, surprising me. "I did wonder a little at the angle of the shot."

"What do you mean?" I asked

Fred darted a glance in my direction but directed his answer to Hen. "If he'd dropped the gun and it discharged, you'd have thought the bullet would come from low down, angling up, wouldn't you, maybe catch him under the jaw or come up through the ribs, if it happened the way it looked like, with him climbing over the log and the gun goin' off?"

"I would." Hen leaned back now and took a deep breath, his posture suggesting somebody who was pleasantly surprised. He probably was pleasantly surprised that Fred had made an intelligent observation.

"Well," Fred said, "I remember sort of noticin' it looked like there wasn't much of an angle at all. It was almost straight on. We didn't stand the dead boy up and check the angle or nothin', but that was an idea I had, just a little bit of an idea, and with all the hullabaloo I forgot all about it."

"That's interestin'," Hen said.

"That's what I figured," Fred said. "It could happen by accident. No way to prove it didn't, so that's why I never brought it up."

Hen nodded.

"That's why I let it go." Fred nodded. Vindicated, he now became more verbal. "Especially since, far as anybody knew, the only other people out there with guns were the boy's daddy and his uncle and some of his cousins. If one of them did it, it was still an accident, and they sure as hellfire wouldn't help us try to pin it on one of them."

"Don't take this wrong, Fred, but did you have any question the bullet came from the boy's own gun? You check to see if there was an empty casing?"

Fred's glower told us he'd taken that wrong. "Uh-huh, and I zipped my britches up before I left the house that mornin', too."

Hen nodded, responding to the useful information, ignoring the extraneous. "His uncle Conrad still the mayor over there?"

197

"You suggestin' I'd cover it up if Conrad Tatum shot his brother's boy?"

"No, sir, I am not," Hen said. "I'm just askin', tryin' to get the whole picture."

Fred was clearly torn between two grievances—his distrust of Hen and his dislike of Conrad Tatum. He sighed, much put upon. "Yeah, Conrad Tatum thinks he's a big man over here. But that's not all there was to think about. I had to think about what if I made a big stink and then couldn't prove anything. I'd have to move to the North Pole and learn to fish through a hole in the ice and go huntin' on snowshoes. See, Dixon's rifle had been fired, but so had everybody else's. We looked around some, got the general lay of things, but not like it was a crime scene. Even if we'd thought there was something that didn't add up— and I'm not saying we did—looking after the boy was the main thing."

"I'm followin' you," Hen said. "But proof aside, evidence aside, now, I'm askin' what you thought."

"You're asking if I thought somebody did it on purpose?" He waited for Hen's nod. "Heck no. Had to've been an accident. Either Dixon did it or one of his kin did. No reason to investigate somethin' like that when we've got real bad guys out there breakin' the law just because they enjoy it. They were a bunch of family out hunting, and they were all broken up over it. If one of 'em was more careless than he shoulda been—or more malicious, come to that—I don't know how anybody'd ever prove it. We about through here?" He stood.

"Just about," Hen said. "And I appreciate your taking the time to go over this with us. You see the autopsy report?"

Fred didn't bother to sit back down. "He died of a gunshot wound. Bullet went right through him."

"Nothin' about it that got your attention?" Hen asked, definitely pushing Fred's patience.

"Died of a gunshot wound," Fred said.

Hen and I sat quietly for a bit after Fred had grunted, smiled his Neanderthal smile, and departed.

"So, that wasn't much help," I said. "The sheriff's department has officially decided Dixon's death was an accident, just like the Macon police did with Sandra Cleary. They're probably right. Even if they're wrong and it was murder, we're never going to prove it."

"That sums it up," Hen said. "Mighta been able to learn something if they'd found the bullet so we could match it with a rifle, or if they'd made a record of the scene so somebody a little more motivated coulda looked to see if everything added up, but that didn't happen."

"Grandma used to say 'if' is the biggest word in the English language," I said, reaching for platitudes because I was so disappointed. "What next? It looks like we have three maybe-murder cases and no chance of proving any of them."

Hen smiled. "Grandma sure didn't believe in second-guessing and pining over things. She also used to say something about your luck getting better the harder you work."

"I'm not afraid of hard work, but I do like to feel like there's some purpose to it. You have any particular kind of hard work in mind?"

"Not yet."

"Well, while you're waiting to come up with something, let's go back to my conversation with Crys, when she told me about everybody dying."

"Uh-huh, and when you told her God hadn't singled her out for that."

"Right. But there was one thing. What she said was 'people who loved me' not 'people I loved.' I think that's a little backwards, don't you?"

"A little self-centered, maybe," he said. "I don't get what

you're drivin' at."

"I'm not sure, either. But when my parents died, when my husband died, when Grandma died, the way I thought about it was that I'd lost people I loved, not that I'd lost people who loved me."

"Not a whole lot of difference, is there?"

"Certainly not enough to build a murder case around, but we get a different angle on it if we think of the victims as people who loved her."

"How does Josh Easterling fit into that? If anybody suggested they had that kind of relationship, I missed it."

"I know I'm sounding desperate, but, well, let's say there's a serial killer out there bumping off people who love Crys. Maybe that circle of people keeps getting wider as the killer gets more notches in his or her belt and gets more confident of getting away with it—maybe Sandra Cleary was notch one, Dixon Tatum notch two. The killing gets easier and the requirements get looser. With Josh Easterling, the killer has widened the circle to include people who have influence over Crys, not just people who loved her. Easterling did have influence over her. Howard told me he didn't like Crys joining a church—getting baptized—but Easterling talked her into it. Maybe he thought Easterling had an inappropriate degree of influence over her."

"You givin' up on your idea that Crys is the killer?"

"I never liked it much. I like this better."

"It's a stretch, Trudy. We haven't had a smidgen of a hint of any kind of improper behavior on Easterling's part."

"Maybe not by your standards or mine, but if we're talking about a killer we're not talking about a rational human being. Talk about improper, I've started thinking there's something improper about Raynell Harden's attitude. She's been making such a fuss about how she thinks Branch was the target instead of Josh that I've started wondering if she's trying to distract us.

Maybe she was carrying on with Josh and killed him when things went bad."

"You don't think Raynell Harden is just a loyal wife who's been through a traumatic experience?"

"She might be, but you're proving my point, sort of. I mean, I'm just arguing that things can look different to different people, and especially to people who aren't thinking normally in the first place. If the killer was somebody who thought it was okay to kill people in Crys's life, that person might see impropriety where nobody else would."

"Can't argue with you there. Evil is in the eye of the beholder. But I don't see how that fits Raynell Harden, especially if you're trying to find a link to Sandra Cleary's death and Dixon Tatum's. What you're saying is that wherever Crys goes, we're going to have to worry about who she's with, worry that the killer will think whoever it is loves her too much or has too much influence? No, Trudy, I just can't get there."

"What if the killer is Howard?"

"Howard? Ah."

"It would explain a whole lot of things. If it's anybody else, Howard would have been one of the first victims, certainly he'd have come up before Dixon Tatum or Josh Easterling."

"Another possibility is that your theory is complete hogwash, remember," he said.

"I know that. But *if.*"

"Okay, I'll pretend I think you're onto something, Officer Roundtree. Maybe we *have* had our wires crossed this whole time. Let's think about how this looks if Howard's behind it all."

I tried to give him time to think it over, but I couldn't keep quiet. The more I thought about it, the more sense it made to me.

"I think it comes together, Hen. Dixon Tatum had enough

influence over Crys he talked her into getting a tattoo. That infuriated Howard. If Howard's the killer, it fits in with Crys's theory about people close to her dying, but explains why Howard's still alive. And Lloyd said Howard was supposed to go hunting with them, but changed his mind. It could be interesting to know where he was when Dixon was shot. It's been a while, but sometimes people do remember where they were on special occasions. Or remember where other people were. Or weren't."

Hen nodded. "You go see what you can find out. And I've got me another idea. Why don't we see about getting the sheriff's posse out there to look for the bullet?"

"You're kidding."

"What makes you say that?" he asked, beaming, proud of himself.

"I don't even know where to start," I said. "For one thing, people go hunting out there all the time. There must be buckets full of bullets out there. Okay, then, moving along, finding one particular bullet—and proving it was the one particular bullet—would be worse than looking for a needle in a haystack. It would be like looking for a hayseed in a haystack."

"Maybe not. A lot of these old boys are pretty good shots. Mostly their bullets end up in deer. What else?"

"Wouldn't the sheriff's posse have better sense than to want to go crawlin' through the woods in the kind of heat we've been having?"

"Sense don't come into it; you know that as well as I do. When they sign on for the posse, they're signing on to help out the sheriff, and if that's what he wants 'em to do, that's what they'll do. They wouldn'ta signed up if they were the kind of men—yes, they're all men—who want to take things easy. They're the kind of men who like sufferin' a little in a good cause. Makes 'em feel righteous and manly. You're just kickin' up because you didn't think of it. Yeah, Trudy, I'm seein' real possibilities here. First thing, though, I'll go have a talk with Conrad Tatum, tell him what we've got in mind, get him and those boys of his to go out there with me. If I can get them all to agree on how they found things, it might save us, the sheriff's posse, I mean, having to comb through the whole woods."

He stood, the very picture of a man with a purpose, eager to swing into action, even though the action would entail no more than picking up the phone. As I recoiled from the force of his enthusiasm, he issued instructions to me in a sharp, decisive voice. "In the meantime, I want you to go talk to Crys. See what she remembers about the day Dixon died. Maybe she'll know where Howard was."

"Glad to. I'd sure rather do that than go out in the woods looking for a bullet in a haystack. Where will I find her?"

When he told me, I laughed out loud.

CHAPTER 21

"She really got with the secrecy of the thing," Hen said. "I'll call and let her know you're comin'. Gotta give her the password, or she won't admit she's got her."

"And the password is?"

"Geocaching," he said. "It's her favorite new word."

He was reaching for the phone when I left.

Not five minutes later I was knocking at the front door of Mrs. Peyton's house, a well-maintained farmhouse from a time well back in the last century. She came bustling from the back, wiping her hands on a cloth.

"Looks like I'm interrupting something," I said.

"We've been doing some canning," she said. "Beats me why we still call it canning, when we use jars and a freezer instead of cans, but I guess it would sound funny if we called it 'jarring' or 'freezing'."

"Yes, ma'am," I said, trying not to smile too broadly, in case she hadn't meant to be funny.

She flapped her cloth in my direction, maybe to indicate she'd seen my smile and didn't mind.

"We've put up . . . I'm going to say sixteen pints of peaches. Just finishing some peas when Chief Huckabee called."

"Y'all at a good stopping place?" I asked.

"Good as any," she said.

"I'd like to talk to Crys, then," I said.

"Crys who?" she asked, flapping her cloth again, gazing out

the window.

Oh, yes. The password. "Crys Cleary," I said. "Geocaching."

She smiled. "Crys and I are both sort of revved up, got lots of nervous energy from everything that's goin' on. Before we even cleaned up from the cannin' we started diggin' into the pantry, cleaning it out. We've got a big mess, but it'll wait while we take a rest. Come on back."

I followed Mrs. Peyton to the kitchen and what looked like utter confusion. Every surface—table, countertop, floor—was covered: jars (some empty, some glowing with red, green, and gold fruit and vegetable color), pots, pans, dishes, empty bags (both paper and plastic), fully and partially filled bags of grits, rice, flour, beans, and who knows what else: boxes, buckets, bowls, appliances, mysterious kitchen gadgets.

"Figured if I was ever goin' to get this pantry cleaned out, I'd be smart to do it while I have somebody willing to help me with it," Mrs. Peyton said. "That girl doesn't say much, but she's the best help I've ever had."

Crys, grimy, disheveled, smiled.

"Wish I'd thought of it while she was staying with me," I said. It did look like Crys was a willing worker, no sign of the kind of sullen reluctance I might have expected from somebody in her situation.

"What's this?" Crys asked, holding up what looked like a red gingham apron with a big pocket in the front and rickrack around the edges, except that there was no way it could go around a housewife's waist since the top of it was closed and held a coat hanger.

"It's a clothespin holder," Mrs. Peyton said.

"What's it for?" Crys asked.

I wanted to say, "For holding clothespins."

Mrs. Peyton said almost the same thing but in a much less snarky tone than I'd have managed. "You hang it on the clothesline so it's easy to reach the clothespins when you're hanging things out and easy to put them back when you take things down."

"I don't put things on a clothesline," Crys said.

"I don't much any more, either, since I got an electric dryer in the house," Mrs. Peyton said. "Sure beats hauling the clothes outside and waiting for them to get dry and then hauling them back inside. I don't need that old thing any more. Put it in that box for the Goodwill."

"The Goodwill's not good enough for it," I said. "It ought to go to an antiques store."

Mrs. Peyton smiled at that, and Crys stopped her motion to toss it into a box that was already nearly overflowing.

"Could I have it?" Crys asked, "I mean, if you're going to give it away, anyway?"

"Sure, honey. Help yourself," Mrs. Peyton said. "You going to start hanging things on the line to dry?"

Crys shrugged. "I think it's pretty, and it would be a keepsake. I could use it for my dirty laundry, my underwear, something."

"Be my guest," Mrs. Peyton said. "I like you having a keepsake of me."

"Much as I hate to interrupt anybody who's having such a good time doing something productive," I said, "I do need to talk to Crys again."

Crys looked to Mrs. Peyton, who said, "We needed a break about now, anyway. Y'all talk, and I'll see if I can find my way through this mess and make us some iced tea."

Crys led the way to the front room and looked at me. Expectantly? Patiently?

"Looks like this is working out okay," I said, gesturing to include the room, the house, Mrs. Peyton.

"Uh-huh," she said. "Miz Peyton's nice. But I miss Gramp.

How long do I have to stay here?"

"I don't know. All I can tell you is that you'll be better off here until we can find out what's been going on—and before you say it, I do not believe you are under a curse. I think there's another explanation. If we're lucky, things will get back to normal before too long."

"What's normal? I don't think I've ever felt normal."

"Well, at least we ought to be able to fix things so you won't feel like you have to run and hide from everybody who cares about you."

The thought didn't seem to cheer her up. "You acted like you thought I was nuts."

"If I gave you that impression, I'm sorry. Actually, our conversation gave me a lot to think about."

She gave me a small smile. "So you came out here to talk about it some more?"

"In a way, yes. One of the things I started wondering about is if there might be some kind of connection between Josh Easterling's death and Dixon's, and even your mother's. Maybe there's something weird going on that doesn't include your being some kind of a curse, or whatever it is you think is goin' on."

She transferred her gaze to the cotton patch across the road. "I told you: I'm the connection."

"Even if that's right, maybe it's not the kind of connection you think it is," I insisted.

She looked back at me. "You're as crazy as I am."

"I'm not about to argue with you on that point, but maybe neither one of us is crazy."

She smiled. "Oh, I'm crazy, all right, but maybe your idea isn't crazy. But maybe it is. You're the big investigator. How are you goin' to find out?"

"I'll keep plugging at it till I get somewhere. For starters, let's try this: If I'm going to look for a connection, I have to know more than I know now. Tell me what you can remember about how Dixon Tatum died."

She expelled a lung full of air, every particle expressing exasperation that I could be so dense, so callous, so . . . adult. "Dixon? You're seriously thinking it'll cheer me up if you can make me believe the police are going to investigate a hunting accident over a year old?"

"No, Crys. This is not a new counseling technique, and cheering you up is not my main objective right now. You know we are actively investigating the death—the murder—of Josh Easterling, which is definitely not a year-old hunting accident. I want to find out if his death is connected with a couple of other deaths."

"How? He didn't even know Dixon or my mother. You try to act like you care, but you don't even listen to me. I told you the connection. Me. People who cared about me."

"Okay, let's say that much is right. That is the connection. But that's not what killed them. Maybe we're both wrong about the deaths being connected, but the only way to find out is to look into it. What have you got to lose?"

She had to think about it. "Nothing, I guess."

"Okay. Good. Now, I know this will be hard, but I want you to think back to when you heard about Dixon's accident."

"If you're calling it an accident, what are you investigating?"

"Don't be so contrary, Crys. Even accidents have causes. Work with me, okay? What do you remember about that day? What were you doing when you heard about Dixon? Who told you?"

Her hand snaked behind the chair and returned with the ragged unicorn I'd seen before, clutching it like Linus Van Pelt and his favorite blanket. She seemed to be talking to the unicorn when she began talking.

"It was Saturday, October fourteenth, but you know that

since you're investigating. We'd won the football game on Friday night, and everybody was still excited because we hate the Tigers, and I was getting my housework done. Gramp didn't like Dixon very much, like I told you, and I didn't want to give him any reason to keep me from going out. We were going to go out with some other kids from school and just hang out, nothing special, and it was kind of open when he'd pick me up since he was going hunting and didn't know what time he'd be back."

When she came to a stop, I prompted. "Do you know who all went hunting with him?"

"His daddy, I know. His uncle. Maybe a couple of his cousins. Ben and Billy, I think. Not a big bunch. They went hunting together a lot."

"Was it always the same group?"

"More or less, maybe. I don't know. Gramp is friends with Dixon's daddy, and he used to go with 'em sometimes."

"Was Howard with them the day Dixon was shot?"

"No."

"You're sure."

"I'm sure."

"Okay. Was there any particular reason he didn't go?"

"Not that I know of, except I think he didn't like goin' unless it was just with the older guys. Gramp talks a lot about how much he and my daddy liked going hunting together, and I think he still misses Daddy, especially in deer season. Maybe being with just the old guys doesn't make him miss my daddy so much, like he would if he was with younger guys and their daddies. So maybe that's why he didn't go that day, if he knew Dixon and Ben and Billy were going."

"Was he at home all day?"

She gave a short humorless laugh. "Sounds like you're asking about an alibi. Isn't that how the police do it? 'Where were you on. . . .' " Then, possibly influenced by my failure to be amused by her attempt at humor, she gave up trying to be funny. "No, he wasn't at home all day. He's always out doing errands, working for somebody, picking up things to fix or delivering things he's already fixed. Even if he didn't have anything special to do, I know he went somewhere, because he doesn't like to be around when I'm running the vacuum cleaner."

"Could he have been out in his workshop?"

"Yeah, maybe he was. No. Well, maybe part of the time, but he went off somewhere because that's how he heard about Dixon and came back home to tell me. That's all I know."

"Do you remember about what time of day it was when Howard brought you the news?"

"Afternoon. Late afternoon. I had finished my chores. I remember I was in my bedroom trying to decide what to wear later, and Gramp came in and hollered for me and . . . and . . ."

She wiped her eyes with the unicorn's dingy mane.

"Do you remember exactly what he said?"

She gave me an odd look. "Exactly? Probably not. It was something like 'Dixon's had an accident,' and I thought he meant in his car, and I asked if he was hurt, and he said he was hurt pretty bad, and when I asked what hospital they took him to and if he'd take me to see him, that's when he told me he was dead."

"Rough," I said.

"Yeah." She wiped her eyes again.

"Did Howard say how he found out?"

"Why do you want to know that? I guess you can ask him if it makes any difference."

"You never can tell what will make a difference in an investigation," I said. "Or where a valuable piece of information or evidence will turn up. I know this is hard for you, but if we stick to it maybe we won't have to go into it again. Anything else you remember about the day Dixon died?"

"Well, I didn't go out, I remember that. I dressed up anyway, though, and some of the kids from school came over because they knew he was my boyfriend, and we just sat and cried. It's kind of blurry."

I took my time making some notes of what Crys had said. There didn't seem to be anything useful, but it gave us both a moment to back away from painful memories. I flipped the page in my notebook to get her attention and asked, "What do you know about your mother's death?"

She looked startled momentarily, and angry. Apparently, I hadn't given her enough time to come back from recalling Dixon's death.

"You're pokin' all my sore spots, you know that?"

There was no answer to that, so I waited rather than go through my "it might help us see a connection" speech again. She gave me a wispy smile, and I gave her mental points for trying to cope. "I don't *know* anything. Everything I know is hearsay. I wasn't there," she said, so I gave her points for trying to use humor, too.

"Hearsay's good enough for now. This isn't a court of law, and you aren't giving evidence. You're trying—I hope you're trying—to help me in my investigation, even if neither one of us is sure where it's going."

"Sure. Okay. About my mother, what I remember is that she died on my birthday. I've been thinking of changing my birthday."

I nodded my understanding. Yes, even I am sometimes at a loss for words. Imagine having that memory every time your birthday came up. I had to clear a lump out of my throat before I asked, "Anything else?"

"Not really. Gramp said she was drinking. Had been drinking. That was a big thing with him. Actually, he probably said she drank herself to death." She nuzzled the unicorn before adding, "He didn't like my mother."

With that, Howard Cleary fell off the bottom rung of my ladder of esteem. How could he be so cruel? Disliking Sandra Cleary was one thing; poisoning her daughter's memories of her was uncalled for, but I couldn't think of anything to say that wouldn't make me guilty of trying to poison Crys's feelings about Howard. I couldn't even choke out a platitude like, "I'm sure he only wants the best for you."

"Well," I said.

"Yeah," she said. "Well. I don't think Gramp ever really liked anybody but my daddy and me." She hugged herself and added, "You didn't actually think I was going to be any help, did you?"

"Sure, I did. I wouldn't have come to poke all your sore spots just for the fun of it. I'm desperately looking for something that will point this investigation in some direction that will take us somewhere. Right now, I feel like a dog with its leash tied to a post. All I can do is go around in circles. Sorry to put you through it." Actually, what Crys told me had sparked something. Maybe it was just a question and the answer wouldn't help me, but it was something I could check. That was more than I had when I started with her.

I let her go then, back to the kitchen and the peas and calm, friendly Rhoda Peyton. As soon as I got back to the stationhouse, I consulted the Macon police file on Sandra Cleary. As far as I could tell, it confirmed my hunch, but I wanted more.

Hen and Miguel had their heads together over a sheaf of papers, so Hen merely waved me away when I said, trying to tamp down my growing excitement, "I may be on the track of something in the Sandra Cleary, Dixon Tatum, Josh Easterling case. Okay with you if I go back to Macon?"

CHAPTER 22

I used my driving time to Macon to try to untangle my thinking, annoyed that I'd allowed myself to be unprofessional on my earlier visit. I had let the sensory overload in Marlene Booth's apartment distract me from what might turn out to be a key point, might be the thing that turned our investigation around. Oh, well. As Hen had pointed out, it was a nice drive on city time. I kept my speed under control even though I was impatient to see if my half-formed hunch, based on a quick glance at a photo, would break the case.

"Well, look who's here! Come on in." Deena answered the door, dashing my hopes that I'd be able to talk quietly with Marlene. On the other hand, I was pleasantly surprised, once inside, to see no Ray, no Renay, no baby.

"Don't bother looking for the kids," Deena said. "My friend Awana has 'em. She wanted me to keep hers this weekend so she and her man can go off for their anniversary, and I told her I'd trade her, so me and Mama have the whole day without 'em to do whatever we want to, and we're just sittin' here watching television, missin' 'em. Don't hardly know how to act without 'em around."

"You're here about Sandra Cleary again, aren't you?" Marlene asked from her recliner. "You sure did bring up some memories. We've been talkin' about her a lot."

"Yes, I'm here about Sandra again. I've got another couple of questions for y'all."

"We told you everything we know already," Deena said, "but you don't have to rush off. Can I get you a glass of tea?"

I declined the refreshment and got right to the point. "I didn't go into it much when I was here before, but we think Sandra Cleary's death may be connected with some other deaths."

Deena's eyes grew round and big. "You talkin' about a serial killer? Some serial killer got her? Came right in here and killed her?" She looked around in a panic-stricken way, but I'd have sworn the dangerous idea, safely in the past, excited her.

"It's possible," I said, "but I don't think—"

Marlene got into the act, setting her tea glass down on the floor. "Ohhh! You think they're comin' after us next? Is that why you're here? We been asking ourselves why the police were interested, after all this time, hadn't we, Deena? I guess that explains it. You offering us some police protection?"

Even without the children, a visit with these women was like slogging through a swamp.

"No, I don't think there's a serial killer coming after you, and no, I'm not offering police protection. If whoever killed Sandra wanted to do something to you, he's had three years to do it. I think you're safe."

They exchanged glances that seemed to be compounded of relief and disappointment. Maybe life was too calm for them without the children around.

"Do you know who it is?" Marlene asked, but before I could answer, she made her own suggestion. "Maybe it was Ray's daddy, and he got the wrong woman."

"No, it wasn't a case of mistaken—"

"No, Mama. That rascal wasn't much smarter than a chigger, but he'd've been able to tell us apart," Deena said.

"Gave you an itch to scratch like a chigger, too, didn't he?" Marlene asked, underscoring it with a raucous laugh. Deena nodded agreement.

I raised my voice. "No, it wasn't mistaken identity. Whoever killed her knew exactly who she was. That's why you don't have anything to worry about from our serial killer. It takes a lot of emotion for somebody to want to commit murder, so murder victims are almost always killed by somebody they know. It's somebody they feel strongly about for some reason, even if it's a reason that wouldn't make sense to anybody else. Whoever killed Sandra Cleary was after her, not just anybody."

Deena heaved an exaggerated sigh. "Guess I'm safe, then. Nobody feels strong emotion about me but my kids and my mama. Not a one of them no account so-called men I got tangled up with."

"So what you want from us?" Marlene asked.

"I want you to let me take another look at the photo y'all showed me of Ray's birthday party, the day Sandra died."

"That's easy. It's there behind the TV set, right where it was the last time you were here," Marlene said. "Get it, Deena."

Deena fetched it. It only took a glance to confirm what I'd half-thought I remembered. I felt a thrill of triumph. Crys's talk about how much Howard had enjoyed hunting with his son had reminded me of the beautiful handmade knife I'd seen in Howard's workshop. Here, in the picture taken the day Sandra died, I saw that knife, the token of her husband that Sandra had put in her makeshift shrine. The knife that was present at the party the night Sandra died had somehow moved from Macon to Ogeechee and found its way to Howard Cleary's gun case. Howard had been at Robins' Roost, had fed Sandra liquor and pills, and had been unable to resist taking that souvenir of his son. I must have beamed.

"What's got you so excited? What's going on?" Deena asked.

"See here, this knife?" I pointed. "I saw it not long ago. I think Sandra Cleary's killer took it with him."

Marlene made a choking sound and fell back in her chair

with such force that she spilled her tea.

"Mama, I swear, if it isn't the kids makin' a mess, it's you!" Deena moved quickly to the kitchen, returned with a paper towel, and began mopping up her mother. Marlene waved her away.

"What makes you say that?" Marlene asked me.

"Say what?" I'd been distracted again.

"That the killer took the knife."

"It wasn't in the photos the police took of the scene."

"Oh." Marlene's hand fluttered to her heart.

I wasn't sure she'd understood what that meant. "The knife was here for the party but missing when the police took pictures after her death."

"You like that picture so much, we've got more," Deena said. "Want to see them?"

"Yes. More evidence. Yes. More details. More information. Context. Great. And I want to know if there's anything else you can remember—any other details at all—about the party or what it was like when you found Sandra dead?"

Marlene gave a shaky laugh, hand still fluttering. "I'm lucky to remember to put my clothes on when I go to the store. That's been a while."

"But you can remember," I persisted. "Just try. It could make the difference between catching the man who killed Sandra and letting him get away with it."

"Not just Sandra," Deena said. "You said a serial killer. Who else did he kill?"

Caution finally caught up with me. "Maybe nobody. This is just a theory, so far. Let's take one step at a time. Can we go over the party again? Maybe you took some other pictures at the party that would jog your memory?"

"I'll go see if I can find them," Deena said, "but this was the best one. Y'all don't say anything interesting while I'm gone, now."

Deena left to go look for the pictures. Marlene smiled. The fluttering of her hand had slowed.

"Well, we told you everything we thought mattered to you, but I don't think we told you it was a funny party. Funny ha-ha. Sandra had gone to some trouble for it, made some of that cereal and chocolate chip stuff that looks like dog food, and she just laughed when we said she shouldn't be teaching Ray to eat dog food. And we had Kool-Aid. It might not sound like much of a party to some people, but it's what she could do, what she wanted to do, and it meant a lot to us, especially since it turned out to be the last time we saw her. This may sound funny— funny peculiar—but in a way, if somebody did kill her, it makes me feel better than thinking she was so low she did it to herself, like we were letting her down and weren't helping her make a go of things."

I was searching for a response to that when Deena returned from the back with a handful of photographs. I already had what I'd come for, so I was willing to graciously, casually, make conversation.

"Thanks, Deena. Marlene was telling me about the refreshments."

Deena laughed. "Ray really went after that dog food."

"Was it good or just odd?" I asked.

"Yum," Deena said. "Powdered sugar and cereal and . . . what else, Mama?"

"Nuts, wasn't it?" Marlene asked.

"Yeah. Nuts. Marshmallows?" Deena asked.

"I think the marshmallows go in something else," Marlene said. "But maybe—"

Enough of that gracious, casual conversation. I interrupted. "It sounds like something kids would like, all right, but let's get back to Sandra. I'd like to try to narrow down the time frame the killer had to work with. Do you remember what time it was when y'all left, after the party?"

"Up in the afternoon, wasn't it, Deena? Musta been about . . . oh, maybe three o'clock or something like that. Deena was taking Ray to see his daddy later on, goin' for pizza or something. Isn't that right, Deena?"

Deena was nodding. "Uh-huh. I took some of that dog food to Big Ray."

"I bet he didn't think it was funny," Marlene said. "Probably thought it was the real thing and you were insulting him."

I hurried to ask. "And you found Sandra dead the next morning?"

"That's right," Marlene said. "We told you that."

"I'm just trying to make sure I've got it all straight in my head. You said there was no sign of a break-in, no sign anybody else had been there?"

"That's right. The place looked neat, just like she always kept it. Of course, it was easier for her to keep things neat. She didn't have a lot of clutter around like I do."

"That's how she was, liked things neat. She used to joke about it, said she learned that in prison. She probably cleaned everything right up as soon as we were out the door," Deena said. "She was clean. Poor but clean. Not like Mama. Mama's rich and messy."

It was a good bet that these two didn't have simmering grudges. They kept their barbs, if that's even what they were, right out in the open. Marlene, in any case, didn't take offense. She continued as if Deena hadn't interrupted.

"It looked like she'd cleaned up from the party and then maybe sat down and took the pills or whatever she took and stretched out on the couch to wait, like maybe she wanted that shrine of hers to be the last thing she saw. Maybe having a party for somebody else's kid made her sad." Marlene nodded slowly, thoughtfully, unhappily.

I held up the framed party photo and pointed to the items on the table in front of the women and the balloons and Ray. "Help me figure out what else the killer took. That knife isn't the only thing that didn't show up in the boxes you gave me. This picture of Crys was in one of the boxes, but what about the birthday present Sandra had for Crys? What about the liquor, for that matter? The report I have from the Macon police doesn't say anything about them taking anything like that. So what happened to it?"

"Hmm," Marlene said.

"So what?" Deena asked, frowning, darting a glance at her mother.

"Besides wanting to know what else is missing, I'm also trying to figure out why the killer would have taken any of this stuff."

"Maybe it wasn't the killer," Marlene said.

"Who else could it have been, Mama?" Deena asked, looking at her mother in surprise.

Marlene took another drink of her tea. "How would I know. Maybe a burglar."

"What?" Deena frowned.

Marlene took another long drink. "Or I mighta thrown some things away when I cleaned up."

"The vodka, Mama?"

"Well, I might have."

"Did you?" I asked. "How did you decide what to trash, what to pack, and what to keep?"

Marlene looked offended. "I didn't notice anybody helping me clean things out. I did the best I could."

Something was going on, and I couldn't tell what. "I'm sure you did. Was it still there with her? The vodka and the pills."

"Well, yes. Some pill bottles with painkillers and muscle relaxers and sleeping pills. I wondered where she got all that stuff. Never knew her to be sick. Did you, Deena? Anyway, what it looked like was she mixed it all up, the vodka and her Kool-Aid and a bunch of sleeping pills and pain medicines and all. Not a drink I'd want to try, but I guess it didn't matter to her what it tasted like."

"Mama, you're acting shifty," Deena said.

"Oh, well, once it's been opened."

"Mama? Did you keep it?"

"Why not? It's not like it was going to do her any good, was it? I figured since the police didn't take it, there wasn't anything wrong with me keepin' it, in case I ever wanted to have a party."

"Do you still have it?"

"Matter of fact, I do. I don't much like vodka. I don't see any point in liquor that doesn't have any taste, unless you're drinking just to get drunk, and I may have my faults, but that isn't one of them."

"So you kept it, but you didn't drink it?" I asked.

"That's what I said."

It wasn't exactly what she'd said, but I let it pass. "That bottle might be evidence. Maybe some of the drugs were dissolved in the vodka. The bottle might even have the killer's fingerprints on it. Can you get it for me?"

"You want me to get it, Mama?" Deena asked.

"I'll do it."

Marlene struggled out of the chair. Deena helped position the walker, and Marlene made her way to the bedroom.

"She thinks I don't know where she hides her liquor," Deena whispered.

When Marlene returned, she pulled a half-filled vodka bottle from the pouch hanging from her walker. She ostentatiously held it by the neck, protected from her fingerprints by a scrap of toilet tissue.

I took it from her, also handling only the tissue. "Thanks. This might be important," I said. "If you weren't drinking it anyway, there's no great loss." My joke fell flat, and I had the feeling I was wearing out my welcome.

"What else, Mama?" Deena asked, surprising me, but apparently not surprising Marlene, who turned and retreated again. "You're acting like you're up to something."

Marlene turned and disappeared again into the back room.

Deena whispered, "Mama's not greedy but she hates for things to go to waste. No tellin' what else she kept, but the truth is Sandra didn't have all that much that anybody would want."

My heart sank when I saw what Marlene was holding when she returned this time. The knife. The knife I'd been so sure put Howard Cleary at the scene of Sandra's death. My face must have shown my disappointment.

"I didn't see the harm," Marlene said defensively. "It's not like she was stabbed or anything, and Ray was so taken with it, I thought it wouldn't hurt to keep it for him, when he was older."

"Is that all?" Deena asked.

Marlene sank into her chair. If there was any more loot, she wasn't going to admit it. Not now, anyway.

"I'm sorry." Marlene did look contrite. If my face reflected the way I felt, it's a wonder she didn't take pity on me and pat me on the head or offer me some dog food.

"Does it mean there isn't a serial killer and you don't know who killed Sandra?" Deena asked.

I shook my head. "It means I don't have the evidence I thought I did. Maybe I had it figured out all wrong. Maybe she wasn't murdered." I said it, but I didn't believe it. Still, it didn't matter what I believed. One of the big differences between actual police work and the cozy soft-boiled mysteries Aunt Lulu likes to read is that the clues and intuitions that are so helpful to those amateur sleuths aren't enough. Actual law enforcement needs actual evidence that will hold up in an actual court of law.

"Wish we could help," Deena said, "seein's how it was Sandra and it's a serial killer and all."

"I appreciate that," I said. "There's one more way you can help."

I brought a fingerprint kit from my cruiser.

"Uh-oh!" Marlene said when she saw what I intended. "I may have to think about this, now, if I want to get in your system."

"It's just for comparison," I said. "So we won't get excited if we find your prints on the vodka bottle."

Deena snickered, and her mother turned on her. "You leave your prints behind at any crime scenes you ain't told me about, Deena? They get your prints, they'll be able to track you down, especially now that law enforcement"—she nodded in my direction—"knows right where to find you."

Luckily, this exchange was merely another example of their mother-daughter relationship and not an expression of real objections to being printed.

As they were cleaning their fingers, and since I was already annoyed and they were already on edge, I mentioned, graciously and casually. "We'll want to get statements from you both."

"What?" Marlene's fluttering hand, which had calmed down when she confessed about the knife and the vodka, began fluttering again.

"What does that mean?" Deena demanded.

"It means you'll write down, or tell somebody else who will write down, what you know about the last time you saw Sandra and when you took these pictures. You'll be helping the police find a killer."

"That doesn't sound like what Big Ray was doing when he said he was helping the police," Deena said. "We in trouble? Mama in trouble over the knife and the vodka?"

Much as I wanted to get even with the two of them for being so slippery, I admitted Marlene wasn't in trouble.

"Well, then, I guess we could do it," Deena said. "Couldn't we, Mama?"

"For Sandra," I said. "I'll get back to you."

As I was leaving, I passed a frazzled-looking woman with six children in tow, surely Awana, I deduced, since I recognized Ray and Renay and the baby. The other three small children must have been Awana's. Bad as this visit had turned out, at least my timing had been good. I'd missed them. I repressed a nightmarish flash of what it would have been like to try to take fingerprints with the six children and another woman in Marlene's living room. Be grateful for small blessings, Trudy.

I was halfway back to Ogeechee before I thought about the party photos Deena had brought out. I still had them, but in all the to-do about the knife and the vodka, and taking fingerprints, I'd never gotten around to looking at them. I'd mail them back. I didn't think I could face another visit to Robins' Roost. As far as that went, I wasn't really all that excited about facing Henry Huckabee and admitting that my hunch had been wrong.

CHAPTER 23

I was so let down over my failure to be able to accuse Howard Cleary of murder based on his possession of the knife that I still hadn't recovered by the time I got back to Ogeechee. I didn't even wait for Hen to ask me how it went.

I told him about my visit in Macon, elaborating on my high hopes that the knife in the picture I'd seen before was now in Howard Cleary's possession and would show that he'd been in Sandra's apartment. I emphasized the heartrending pathos of the moment when Marlene Booth tottered out of her back room with the knife, dashing my hopes. I showed him the vodka bottle.

He raised an eyebrow, no doubt ready to listen and learn.

"As far as I can tell, this might prove Sandra was sneaking liquor even though her friends think she wasn't. Anyway, this is all I have," I concluded.

"So based on this vodka bottle, which we will test for fingerprints since it is at least something we can hold in our hands, our theory would be that the killer took the vodka to her place and somehow or other got her to drink it."

"Something like that. Along with pills. Zoloft. Crys takes Zoloft. Oxycontin. Anybody can get some of that. Sandra Cleary's friends in Macon say she was off alcohol, but he could have spiked her Kool-Aid with the pills and got her groggy enough that he could force the vodka down her. I wouldn't put it past him to put a funnel down her unconscious throat. Then he could go on his way and let the drugs and alcohol take their course. And proving it is just about as likely as finding a bullet in a haystack."

"Officer Roundtree, we didn't get to choose the hand we hold, but we will play the hand we got dealt."

"Yes, sir," I said. "But this isn't a card game. Are you trying to sound like Abraham Lincoln?"

"Well, I do have a thing or two in common with old Abe—my honesty, my humility." His attempt to look humble was a miserable failure, seriously undermined by his look of self-satisfaction. "And when I don't have a clue what's going on, I like to stall and say something that sounds kinda wise and folksy, whether it makes any sense or not. But I'll say this in plain English: If we don't get something to go on pretty soon, we'll just have to quit on this case and go back to pullin' in the regular old druggies and drunk drivers and tracking down the occasional ragin' geocacher. Now, just relax and let me tell you what I've been doin'."

"Please do," I said.

"Got things set up with the sheriff to get his posse out tomorrow mornin' bright and early," he bragged, "and did some groundwork to get things ready for 'em."

"What did you have to do to get ready?" I asked, too depressed to be more than a straight man.

"Well, first off, I had a meeting with Fred Wiltshire." He raised a finger to illustrate his number one.

"Fred? Why?"

"So he won't mess things up for us when we get the posse out there. You know my opinion of Fred. He's slow and mean and ornery, but he is stubborn, so I figured I'd give him a kind of a head start on the whole thing, get him on our side, and that stubbornness would work for us."

"I didn't get the feeling he was likely to be in your fan club. If he was willing to hang out with you and get a head start, I'll have to give you credit for unsuspected supplies of charm and diplomacy."

"Give credit to his gut. I fed him, but you'da been plumb proud of my charm and diplomacy, too. We smoked the peace pipe in the form of some Brunswick stew at Harry's Bee Bee Que, and I explained to Fred our idea for giving the posse some exercise on this problem we've got. Told him I needed him to help me figure out, *if* somebody had shot the boy on purpose, how it could have been staged so nobody, not even the sharpest mustard in the jar—which he is not, by the way, and I'm pretty sure he knows it and that's what makes him so ornery—would have had any suspicion. We talked about that some, two professionals workin' on a problem, and we agreed that every good ol' boy in the woods would be smart enough to know how to go about stagin' a huntin' accident, startin' with the self-evident fact that if you shoot somebody in the woods during huntin' season, accident or not, nobody's gonna notice the shot, so you'd have a little time to clear out. And on top of that, in this particular case, with Dixon's daddy and uncle and cousins milling around, 'most any evidence that an evildoer left behind would have been messed up beyond all usefulness where we're concerned. We pondered that a while, ol' Fred and me, then we decided—under my skillful leadership—to turn it around and work on it from the other direction. Not what the killer might have done, but what we'd have to have to prove it was murder, *if* it was murder, and to prove it on the killer."

"Sounds pretty highfalutin for Fred. Was he any help or was he just slurping up Brunswick stew and letting you lead him around by his taste buds?"

"No, he wasn't much help," Hen said, "but I didn't expect him to be. He's got about as much imagination as a senile mule. What I was really after was to get enough of the concept into his head so he'd be *some* help. Like I said, he's stubborn."

"And to this end you made the noble sacrifice of havin' to

eat some of Harry's Brunswick stew."

"All in the line of my duty as I saw it." He grinned. "But you don't need to go tellin' Teri what I had for lunch, now. It was a sacrifice, but she might not understand about the nobility and come to the conclusion I don't need any supper."

"My lips are sealed. Don't keep me in suspense. Did all your charm, diplomacy, nobility, and Brunswick stew pay off?"

"Yes, ma'am, if you mean did it get old Fred on our side. 'Course, it didn't hurt that he'd rather be out in the woods any time of the day or any time of the year than just about anywhere else."

"Did y'all actually do anything besides eat? I was gone a good while."

Hen looked hurt. "By the time we'd got through our bucket of Brunswick stew, we decided what we'd need, in the hypothetical event that Dixon Tatum did not shoot himself and we wanted to prove it, would be a rifle bullet that we could be sure was the fatal bullet and we could trace to a particular rifle in the hands of a particular individual. You remember, Fred told us the bullet went clean through the boy, so we didn't have that. Could have been anywhere in the woods. The way my suspicious mind works, it suggests to me the hypothetical killer had to be sure the bullet would be a through-and-through."

"If I'm following that suspicious mind of yours, that would mean that either it was a high-powered rifle that the killer could count on going through, or he knew Dixon well enough to get really close to him for the shot."

"Yes, ma'am. And either option makes the rascal about as cold-blooded as a toad."

"A toad. Yes."

"And another thing, huntin' accidents bein' such a regular thing. Mostly, whoever did the deed 'fesses up right off. So, since nobody started wringing their hands and hollering,

'Lawdy, lawdy, I thought he was a buck,' we got to ask ourselves why not."

"Do we have an answer for ourselves?" I asked, getting interested.

"We answer ourselves that whoever it was couldn't stand the limelight, that if we started looking at accidents around this person we might have questions."

I nodded, liking the drift. Not an ironclad notion. I could see where Dixon Tatum's cousins might not have jumped up to confess, for instance, and anybody who might have been poaching in Conrad's woods might also have been shy about coming forward. Still, it was a thought.

"I got Fred to take me out to the spot where Dixon was shot, and we went over the whole scenario together," Hen said. "He showed me the log it looked like Dixon tripped over, showed me where the boy's rifle was lying when they found him."

He looked at his raised index finger as though he'd never seen it before, then remembered what it was doing sticking up in the air and added another finger, giving me a nod to remind me he was enumerating the things he'd done to prepare for the posse.

He pulled out a notebook and opened it to show me a sketch and some photographs. Rough but understandable, it showed the cardinal compass points, the position of the body, the rifle, and the significant log. "So I had the lay of things in mind when"—he now waved three fingers—"Conrad and his boys got there, and we went over it again. They had to argue about it some, but they finally agreed that this is more or less the scene they found. No big surprise, since it fits with the story we've heard before, and if there was anything obviously wrong—say Dixon was here by the log and his gun was over by the tree— somebody would have smelled skunk before now."

"Did it help?"

"We'll know after the posse's finished and we see what they find. What will be the most help is our imaginative reenactment of Dixon's last moments. Ben Tatum, now, that boy's got a future on the stage. Really got into the whole thing. Stretched himself out and kept on floppin' around till all three of 'em agreed it was how Dixon was laid out. Stood like a statue while we studied angles and trajectories and what the force of the bullet would have done to the boy. All that dramatics sort got on Fred's nerves, but he didn't argue with any of it. I got a picture of Ben lying there. These other shots'll give you an idea of the layout."

I studied the photographs. "Not as well as your lovely drawing," I said. "But, yes, I get the picture."

"We got no guarantees," Hen continued, "but I'm dead sure there's something there for us to find, if we can just find it."

"This confidence is based on . . ."

"Based on what nobody mentioned, not Fred, not the Tatums. No gunshot residue. If Dixon's gun is what killed him, there should have been GSR all over him. Either that or he must have had arms six feet long, which might have been helpful to him if he had ambitions as a football player, but you'd think somebody would have mentioned it if he looked like an orangutan, now wouldn't you?"

"Yes, sir, I would."

"So I'm going with a third possibility," the Chief of Police said, smug with assurance. "He was killed by a different gun."

Somebody or other has said that Fortune, that whimsical goddess, favors the brave. That's probably true. Somebody else, and this is the version I'm more comfortable with, said Fortune favors the prepared. Virtuously determined to be ready to move into high gear when and if any of our long shots came through, I set about cleaning up odds and ends and organizing the meager materials I'd accumulated in what I was determined to call—and equally determined to prove to be—the multiple murders.

First, I fielded what had come to seem like the daily call from Raynell Harden, assuring her once again that we were working to clear the good name of Baptists everywhere and her husband in particular, and we *still* had found no reason for her and her husband to worry that somebody was out to kill him. I didn't admit that we hadn't really been looking in that direction.

With that daily chore attended to, I turned to the Macon police file on Sandra Cleary. The photographs gave up no new secrets. Stripped of the legalese and medicalese, all it told me was what Thom Sawyer had told me: Zoloft, Oxycontin, and Valium mixed with vodka had done her in. There was no mention of any other drugs stronger than generic aspirin in the apartment.

My mind was as prepared as it was going to get. I called it a day and went home, leaving the outcome to Fortune.

CHAPTER 24

True to their word, the sheriff's, Fred Wiltshire's, and the posse's, they were all out just after the sun crept far enough up over the pines to give them light to work from and before it had been up so long it was flexing its muscles and making them all wish they'd volunteered to deliver meals on wheels from an air-conditioned van.

Hen went out with them, and when he showed up, noonish, I all but attacked him. "Did y'all find anything?"

"Not so fast, Officer Roundtree. Let me tell this in my own way."

Did I have a choice? "Certainly, Your Reverence. I apologize. I am ready to listen and learn."

He was so taken with himself that he didn't even bother giving me a look intended to reprimand and squelch me. I know that look. But he took his time settling down, puttering around making a fresh pot of coffee, checking with everybody about what had been happening while he was out, generally stalling because he knew I was dying to know what had happened.

Finally, *finally,* he sat down, put his boots up on desk, leaned back, and smiled. Naturally, he did not start with the important stuff. "Hot and sticky out there. Put the commitment of all those would-be heroes to the test, but they stuck with it. Now, I want you to picture a dozen men walking along within arm's reach of each other, except where they had to dodge a bush or a tree. They'd rounded up a bunch of those hand-held metal detectors they've been using to screen backpacks at the schools and swept them back and forth as they inched along. Those fellers had some real values clarification goin' on, trying to figure out whether they'd rather wear clothes to protect them from the underbrush or wear as little as possible to keep from melting into a puddle."

"I thought you'd narrowed the area for the search with your reenactment," I said.

"We did, but we wouldn't want anybody to accuse us of not being thorough, now would we? Besides, with Fred and the rest of those ol' boys all fired up, no point in shortchanging them on their chance to serve."

"I'm sure they appreciated that," I said, biting my willful tongue to keep it from asking again what, if anything, they had found. "Metal detectors?" I asked instead.

He grinned, no doubt in appreciation for my self-control, and answered. "Turned up some used shotgun shells, a handful of spent rifle cartridges, a keychain, two what we used to call church keys, two quarters, one dime, one nickel, and six pennies, all carefully noted on our map and tagged for identification."

None of that sounded useful to me, but he was obviously pleased with himself. Apparently we were playing a game in which it was up to me to figure out what questions to ask. I pondered. Routine search. Routine results. What was he so happy about? I never would have guessed. While I was still trying to find a good question, he told me.

"Thanks to our painstaking reenactment, we had a pretty good idea where to find what we needed if it was there to be found, and Lord'a'mercy, if we didn't find something."

"What? Where?" My tongue asked before I could control it.

"The trees are so thick out there that, unless the bullet went off into the wild blue yonder or down into the ground, chances were it would hit a tree. And the bullet we were looking for would not have gone off into the wild blue yonder or down into the ground," he continued tediously, deliberately. "You remember Fred sayin' the angle of the shot the boy took was almost straight? In our reenactment we had that cousin of his, Ben, who was about Dixon's size, stand up, and we looked at whereabouts that bullet woulda gone."

"And?" I asked.

"And we found a tree that was weeping pine tar from the insult that had been done to it."

My enthusiasm, no doubt held down by the weight of my waning hopes, was restrained. "You found a bullet hole in a place known to be a hunting ground. Pardon me while I swoon from the surprise of it all."

"Now, now," he said, saddened by my naiveté. "We don't know that what we found was a bullet hole."

"Then why are you so all-fired pleased with yourself?" I asked, exasperated.

"I'm plumb tickled at our creativity," he said. "If there is a bullet in that poor tree's wound, we don't know where exactly it is, and diggin' around for it would most likely mess up whatever it could tell us."

"So you've got nothing, after all?"

He finally took pity on me, forlorn as I was, my hopes dashed. "Not nothing, Officer Roundtree, not nothing at all. We talked over the best thing to do, and Conrad Dixon went and got his chainsaw and we insulted that tree even further by taking a slice right out of it." He glanced at his watch. "By now Jerome has probably amazed and delighted his buddies at the crime lab up in Hotlanta by hauling in that hunk of tree and asking them to get that bullet out and see what they can tell us about the gun it came from."

"Wow! And what if it turns out it was a pine beetle instead of a bullet that insulted the tree?" I wanted to believe, really I did, but this was a stretch. However, I had finally asked a question Hen wanted to answer directly.

"It won't. Before we sent Jerome up north, we took that wounded tree by the hospital and had it x-rayed. There's a bullet in there, all right."

"It's a long shot," I said, automatically skeptical, as I tried to imagine the scene at the hospital when Jerome Sharpe and Henry Huckabee showed up with a wounded tree. Knowing Hen, I wouldn't have been surprised if they had taken it in on a stretcher, but I didn't want to ask.

Hen was so pleased with himself my skepticism didn't faze him. "We never had any sure shots or short shots in this mess, if you remember," he said. "We did a good day's work. We provided those men on the posse a chance to prove they're good citizens. We found a bullet. No, don't interrupt me, I know that bullet might not prove anything. But think about this: In this low-key cozy Southern murder mystery we've got goin' here, the mystery isn't so much 'whodunnit' as 'how can we prove it?' With all those television shows out there that show crime labs nailing their perps based on a single sequin or hair or piece of sand—remember the one where they caught the guy based on a trace of a Vidalia onion on his boots?—even somebody who's pretty savvy in the way of the world might not be abso-tively sure just what we can prove and what we can't. So when word gets around, if it hasn't already, that the high sheriff and his posse, as well as the forces of the Ogeechee Police Department, have been pokin' around in some places connected with those earlier deaths, it might rattle somebody. No matter how cool he is, it might shake up our villain to know we're lookin' at something he thought was a dead issue."

"If there really is a villain and if said villain is paying attention and if said attention-paying villain is shakable," I groused, ignoring what I feared was a feeble joke. "And what good will it do to shake him up? Make him careless when he commits his next murder? And who will *that* victim be? One of Crys's school teachers? Heather Jackson? Mrs. Peyton? Okay. Yeah. You're right. I know you're right. We're making progress. I think. We've got a vodka bottle in the Sandra Cleary death and a cross-section of a pine tree in the Dixon Tatum death. Should we take another look at the case that started this whole chain of investigations?"

"Good thinking, Officer Roundtree. When in doubt, review all your evidence and assumptions. I know it wouldn't exactly be funny, but wouldn't it be something if after all our creative theorizing, it turns out poor Josh Easterling died because somebody really was trying to rid the world of Branch Harden?"

"Raynell Harden would never let us hear the end of it," I said.

CHAPTER 25

I won't try to pretend that the next stage of our investigation, or, more correctly, our non-investigation, into Howard Cleary and his connection (if any) to the deaths of (in chronological order) Sandra Cleary, Dixon Tatum, and Josh Easterling felt very good. It felt like treading water. My vodka bottle had revealed no prints except Marlene Booth's, a little odd, but nothing to build a murder case on. We were waiting to hear from Atlanta about the Tatum bullet.

I couldn't think of another thing to do on the Josh Easterling case, and Raynell Harden was getting on my nerves. She'd moved from worrying about her husband and had started calling to suggest alternative lines of investigation, in spite of assurances from me, Hen, Jerome, Dawn, Miguel, and anybody else who had the misfortune to talk with her, that we had not a smidgen of a hint of anything to do with the pastor. She protested so much that I began to wonder if there was something I was missing. Hen's cheerful assurance that I was unquestionably missing a lot did nothing for my state of mind. In my efforts to make some sense out of Raynell Harden's tedious repetitions of verse after verse of her one song, I began suspecting that she was ineptly, clumsily, trying to direct our attention away from her husband as a suspect. Then my good sense, or, possibly, my innate contrariness, took over, and I began suspecting *her*. Was she cunning enough to think we'd believe that so much smoke must lead to some kind of fire—

trash fire, brush fire? If she was that cunning, would she have overlooked the possibility that with her in my face all the time, I'd start suspecting her of . . . no, surely not a murder that called for an understanding of electrical connections. My imagination wouldn't stretch that far. It did stretch far enough to suggest that she might have had more than a pastor's-wifely interest in the honorable and stellar young minister.

Exasperated and in the hope that my insensitivity might get her out of my hair, I asked not-so-subtle questions along that line: "Did you know Josh Easterling had a fiancée? Would you describe your marriage as a happy one? Do you ever feel that your husband doesn't understand the demands on someone in your position? Did you ever have meetings with Josh Easterling without others present?" She hung up on me with a theatrical harrumph. I should have thought of it sooner. I should have been ashamed of myself, too, but since there was something in her manner that made me wonder if I hadn't hit on something, I patted myself on the back for giving her a beneficial heads-up and for providing just about my only entertainment during our wait.

Just about. Fun as it had been to annoy Raynell Harden, it was nothing more than fun, a good example of an idle mind (mine) being the devil's playground, or something like that. I had no doubt that all three deaths were connected and that we knew who was responsible.

"What do we know about how Mrs. Cleary, Howard's wife, died?" I asked Hen, from the depths of desperation.

It shows how worn down he was over the whole thing that he even bothered to answer. "Go check it out. Look it up, or go ask Mama."

I'd rather talk to Aunt Lulu than dig through old records, so I started there. I found her in her kitchen, surveying a bushel of zipper peas, and I thought briefly of suggesting she get in touch with Mrs. Peyton to see if she could borrow Crys to help with canning the peas, but I remembered that Crys's whereabouts were a secret and, besides, I was on a fact-finding mission.

"Loretta Cleary? Hm. At least she didn't live to see her family coming apart. She died before Mitch and Sandra took up their life of crime, when she had a pretty baby granddaughter and no idea what was ahead."

"What did she die of?"

"Pulled out from the post office, paying more attention to her mail than the traffic, and ran right in front of a logging truck. The driver was more upset than anybody else, but everybody who saw it said there wasn't a thing he could have done about it. Takes a while for those big old trucks to come to a stop. He tried, though, tried so hard he scattered logs all over the highway. I'm surprised you don't remember that."

"It happened while I was living in Atlanta, and I do remember hearing about it. I just didn't remember who it was who got killed. Thanks, Aunt Lulu."

"You got time to help me with the peas?"

"No, ma'am. I'd really like to stay here and sweat over the boiling pots with you, but I have crime to fight."

"You back already?" Hen asked when I returned to the stationhouse.

"You could have told me how Mrs. Cleary died."

"And do myself out of a few minutes' peace?"

"Could Howard have connived with the truck driver?"

Hen put down the paper he was holding, removed his reading glasses, and said, "No."

"Did anybody test her to see if she was drugged when it happened?"

He picked up the paper again, replaced his reading glasses, and said, "No."

"Anybody check to see if her car had been tampered with?"

"No. And before you ask, she was cremated and scattered to the winds and her car was totaled and hauled away and compacted and buried in a landfill under what is now a high-end shopping mall up near Atlanta."

"Well—"

"Go look up her death certificate."

I did. It took a few minutes for the clerk to find it, gaining Hen that much more peace, but it had no more light to shed on the woman's death. Maybe it had been suicide, to get away from Howard. When I presented myself to Hen shortly thereafter, before I could even frame a question about the existence and current status-of-health of any siblings Howard Cleary might have had, Hen said, "I want you to go out to the high school and get Clearance Widdicome and bring him in for a talk. Somebody turned him in for having drugs in his car, and he says it's his daddy's car and he don't know nuthin' about no drugs and why are we always pickin' on him, anyhow."

"You're not making that up, are you?"

He waved me away.

"Clearance?" I asked from the doorway.

"Jerome called in a little while ago, while you were over pesterin' Mama and the probate judge's clerk. He's bringing in Clearance, Senior."

"Clearance?" I asked again.

"They spell it the way they say it," he said. "Not the worst name I ever heard. I nominate Draino Barnhart or Captain Crunch Richie for that honor. Go get him."

The interview with Clearance and Clearance was just about as lively as you would expect, with Clearance the Elder claiming he was just keeping the car for a friend and had no idea the friend was messin' around with anything illegal and he didn't much appreciate the man putting him (Clearance the Elder) and his son (Clearance the Younger) in bad with the po-lice,

239

after all he'd been doing to be a good father and manly role model and keep his son away from drugs.

Hen, himself, went to talk to Lloyd Tatum again and came back with Dixon's deer rifle, a Winchester. "So if we do get a bullet to compare something to, we've got the obvious contender."

"You don't believe he killed himself," I said.

"Guns don't kill people," Hen said. "People kill people. If this is the gun, we won't know what or who made it go off, but we'll know that much."

All of which did not bring us any nearer closure on what I was now thinking of, for simplicity, as the Cleary case, but it did pass the time.

Chapter 26

When the lab let us know they'd successfully performed a bullet-ectomy on the cross-section of Conrad Tatum's pine tree and would be happy to compare the rifling to any likely candidates, Hen set about collecting likely candidates. He sweet-talked the Tatums into volunteering their guns for comparison testing. Guessing that Howard Cleary would instinctively be less co-operative, even if he didn't have anything to hide (which we thought he did), he applied for a warrant to search for and take possession of any guns in Howard Cleary's possession that might have fired the bullet.

Armed with the warrant, we found Howard, as I had found him when I visited earlier in the investigation, in his workshop. He didn't look especially happy to see us, but I've noticed, oddly enough, that people often do not look happy to see uniformed police officers at their door. On the other hand, neither did he look nervous or guilty. If news of our poking around in this cold case and collecting firearms had unsettled him, he concealed it well.

He was cleaning some gardening tools and did not pause in his work, merely nodded and waited for us to declare ourselves. Hen started out slowly.

"We're still trying to clear up some questions in the Josh Easterling investigation," Hen said, puffing up a little, adjusting his gunbelt. "Got a minute?"

"Just about a minute," Howard said, hands still busy, eyes

watchful. "Got to go see a man about a dog here in a little while. Anyway, I told you everything I know about that, which I'm sure you remember wasn't much, down at the church and again when Officer Roundtree came by."

"Sometimes people remember things later," I said. I tried to look hopeful and optimistic. Hen was taking his time looking around the shop.

With a look of satisfaction on his face, pride in his workspace, Howard gave Hen a moment to admire and envy before he spoke. "Heard you had a bunch combing through Conrad Tatum's woods," he said, acting like a man who had the leisure to chat instead of a man who had business elsewhere, now that he'd made the point that he wasn't necessarily available at the whim of the police. "What was all that about?"

"Gotta give those fellers a little something interestin' to do every now and then," Hen said with every appearance of making absent-minded chit-chat. His attention had settled on the gun rack by the door. "That's a good-looking weapon there, the Winchester. Mind if I take a look at it?"

"There's nothing special about that gun, and you know it, Hen. What did you think you'd find out in the woods?"

Hen grinned at Howard. "Chiggers. Ticks. Squirrels. No tellin' what-all. So you don't want me looking at your Winchester?"

Howard shook his head but reached under the counter for the key ring, which he tossed to Hen. Hen studied the keys, chose one, and unlocked the cabinet. Howard was now burnishing the tines of a pitchfork, but his eyes were on Hen.

"Nice collection you got here," Hen said. "Where'd you get this Kalashnikov?"

"Souvenir of my holiday in Vietnam."

Hen took the gun down, hefted it, and pointed it high through the open door, squinting through the sight. "Ever use it?"

"Ammo's a little hard to come by."

"Does that mean you don't use it?"

"Not much."

Howard didn't bother to ask again why Hen was interested in his guns.

Our goals, Hen's and mine, were two: Show up with a warrant and take away any firearms likely to match the bullet the posse recovered, and, just to see what it might shake loose, to see if we could rattle Howard. I started on the rattling.

"Look at that knife, Chief. Ever see anything like it? Howard, didn't you tell me it was one of a kind?"

"I did."

"Well, I saw one just like it the other day," I said.

"Couldn'ta been just like it," he said, but he must have seen something in my face to make him hedge. "Handmade. That automatically makes it one of a kind. Means it's not mass produced."

Now Hen was handling the knife, to Howard's evident annoyance.

"It was enough like it I thought it was this one," I said. "I even have a photo of it." I handed him a carefully selected photo from Deena's collection.

Howard studied the photo before he spoke.

"Why'd you take a picture of that knife?" he asked.

"I didn't take the picture," I told him.

"That's got to be my son's knife. We had them made to order. You can tell them apart by the initials etched up near the handle. Mine's got an H."

Hen squinted at the knife, then nodded.

"Who has Mitch's knife? Who took this picture?" Howard asked. He put the photo down on the counter top.

I picked it up and tried to flick it menacingly. "I was talking to some friends of Crys's mother. It turned out they still had some of Sandra's things."

"It was Mitch's, not hers. Don't y'all have enough goin' on to keep you busy without crawling around in the woods and meddling into my family?"

"No," Hen said, handing the knife to me and returning to his menacing handling of Howard's guns.

Howard started to say something else, but thought better of it. He smiled a tight little smile. No doubt he had come to understand why we were there. I smiled back, unable to hide my elation at noticing that Howard had realized we had made a connection between Dixon Tatum's death and Sandra Cleary's. Hen continued to examine the guns, picking them up one by one, taking his time to run his hands up and down the stock, take aim. Howard picked up a screwdriver and began cleaning it. How would a screwdriver get dirty, anyway, and who could care if it did?

"Mind if we take this one with us?" Hen said, holding up the Winchester. "I'd like to run some tests."

"I don't know what you're up to," Howard said. "The ballistics experts need some make-work like the sheriff's men?"

Hen waggled the gun, urging a straight answer.

The straight answer didn't come. "I've been hunting in those woods with Lloyd and Conrad and their boys more times than you've had murder cases to solve, Huckabee. Be a big surprise if I haven't left some ordnance out there."

"Well, we found a particular bullet we want to compare to your rifles." With a flourish he produced the search warrant.

"Knock yourself out," Howard said.

"This your whole arsenal, Howard?" Hen asked.

"Yep. You want to search the place?"

"Might as well, just so nobody can accuse us of being sloppy in the execution of our duty," Hen said.

Howard put down the cleaning rag and the spotless screwdriver. "Come on, then, but I'll keep my eyes on you. Don't think you can plant incriminating evidence."

As we poked around through the small house, looking for more guns, I made conversation.

"Did you ever take Crys over to Macon to see her mother?"

Howard gave his head a slow shake. "Wanted to see if that woman could get herself together before I let her and Crys get back together."

"Did you ever go to see her by yourself, without taking Crys?"

He slowly turned and gave me the full force of his glare.

"Why would I?"

"I don't know," I said. "Could be any number of reasons for you to pay your daughter-in-law a visit. To talk about what would be best for Crys. To take her something. To get something."

He didn't bother answering.

"Looks like we've done our duty here, Officer Roundtree," Hen said, "unless you can think of anything else."

"Not right now," I said.

"Let's go get that Winchester, then," Hen said, leading the way back to the workshop.

"Be nice if I could have Mitch's knife back. For Crys," Howard said. He glowered when Hen picked up the Winchester but channeled his energy by applying his oily rag to a pair of hedge clippers.

"We'll see about it," Hen said. "Far as we know, that knife ain't evidence of anything."

"Where you keepin' her?" Howard asked.

"Crys?" I asked, not really confused by the abrupt change of subject.

"She's safe," Hen said.

"She better be," Howard said. "But where is she?"

"That's a deep dark secret," Hen said. "That why I'm so sure she's safe."

Howard's admirable control finally slipped. "You want me to do a column on the police state? CIA, OSS, KGB, FBI, GBI, OPD—it's all the same. Tap our phones, read our mail, take a man's family away from him—give people like you some authority and a gun and you think you can do anything you want to do. Good thing those bleeding heart gun-control freaks haven't been able to take away our constitutional means of taking care of ourselves yet."

I was about to try to explain that Crys was staying somewhere else for her own protection, which was more or less the truth, given her state of mind, but Hen wasn't on board for an appeasement policy. He smiled "You threatening us, Howard?"

I sensed something sinister in the way Howard kept wiping his cleaning rag over the hedge clippers, but, after all, none of his alleged victims had died from mis-application of a garden implement. All he said was, "Crys belongs right here with me. This is her home. I don't see why hiding her somewhere has anything to do with what you're supposed to be doing. Josh Easterling is dead and gone. He's not a threat."

He didn't say "anymore," but it was in the air.

"You saying he *was* some kind of a threat?" Hen asked, resting the stock of the Winchester against his hip.

"Something has been making her run away from home, from you, Howard," I said, before Hen could stop me. "Maybe she knows something that has her scared."

Howard looked at me in a calculating way. "Like what? Wherever she is, they won't be taking better care of her than I would." He jerked his head toward the gun Hen was holding. "Even if you are violating my constitutional right to bear arms by carrying off some of my arsenal."

"We'll talk about it later, Howard," Hen said, waving the

search warrant in one hand and the Winchester in the other.

"That was about as much fun as the time I got a cat tangled in my hair," I said when we finally decided we were satisfied and Howard was sufficiently irritated.

"Shook him up some, though, didn't we?" Hen asked, rhetorically, clearly pleased with himself.

And that's where we were at the end of the workday.

CHAPTER 27

Later, sitting with Phil in my back yard, enjoying a glass of iced tea and the soothing sound of a bug zapper, which should have been delightfully relaxing, with an assortment of cats chasing an assortment of lizards and other cats in and out of the bushes, I realized I hadn't been able to relax. I was still fuming because I wasn't confident all the shaking and rattling Hen and I had done on Howard had dislodged anything.

"Now we've got to wait and see if they can match that bullet to one of his guns. I just can't stand the idea that he might get away with it! With all those murders! Nobody will be safe, not anybody. If we're right, he's getting loonier and loonier. It's getting easier and easier to fit his idea of who deserves to die. Maybe Miz—I mean the person who's taking care of her right now—will be next because she's letting Crys stay there with her."

"Crys's whereabouts is—are—a secret, aren't they?" Phil was relaxed.

"Do you suppose it really is a secret?"

"Of course it is. You haven't even told me, and if you were going to leak the information, you'd leak it to me, wouldn't you? From what you've told me, Crys is really afraid of what will happen if she has to go back home."

"She's not worried about the right thing, if you ask me. She'd be safe and Howard would be safe, but nobody else who ever

248

came in contact with her would be." I tried for a lighter note, afraid that even Phil, for all his steadfast virtues, might get tired of hearing me whine. "But if we can't prove anything, he'll get away with murder, and we'll have to keep on reading his columns."

Phil laughed. "Last I heard, he's workin' on one about the evils of brainwashing, hero worship, fandom, and personality cults."

"That one might be worth reading. A lot of people don't know how to think for themselves or even know when they're being manipulated."

"You're probably right about that. If he comes through with it, you'll have to let me know what you think. I don't read most of what he gives us. He e-mails his column in, and we set it from that."

"Phil! I'm appalled—appalled and disappointed—appalled and disappointed and annoyed—to learn you don't read his columns. I read every single word of *The Beacon* every single week, and sometimes it takes all my self-control to be so loyal, and now I find out you—."

"Loyalty. That's a really good quality, Trudy. To show the depth of my love and my total lack of principles, and to cure your appalledness and disappointment and annoyance, I'll fire him if you want me to."

While I was considering the offer, he continued. "But if I fired him, then I might be on his hit list. Or you would."

"You leave me no alternative, Phil. We've got to nail him."

"I have no doubt you'll succeed. Even without Hen and the rest of the guys to help, you have wit, intelligence, dedication, perseverance, know-how, beauty, and God on your side." He beamed at me.

"Aw shucks," I said, trying to hide how pleased I was by

ducking down to pick up the nearest cat. But I did feel better about the whole thing. I began to relax.

Later, when Phil had gone, and I was unaccountably unable to sleep, I remembered the photographs Deena had given me on my return visit to Macon, photos I'd once again been too distracted to pay any attention to at the time. I began looking at the photos now, comparing them with what I remembered of the few Macon police photos of Sandra Cleary's death scene I'd reviewed earlier.

For lack of any inspiration for a more promising approach, I tried to imagine myself right there in Sandra Cleary's apartment, at those two scenes, to get into the mood and feel of what had happened. I was hoping for a message from the dead, I suppose, a true message, not corrupted by the point of view of whoever was serving as interpreter—not Howard, who blamed Sandra for all his family's woes; not Thom Sawyer, who saw only a poor depressed drunk; not even Marlene and Deena, her friends, people who might have been willing to cut her more slack than she deserved.

The few police photos had told me nothing I hadn't already known. They were clear, stark, documentary, as they were intended to be. They showed the glass, vodka bottle, and pill containers on the coffee table, handily on display in case the police were too dimwitted to find them on their own, and the peacefully dead Sandra Cleary, lying on her side, back curled into the cushions of the sofa. I couldn't help thinking of it as a display, since I was sure it was composed intentionally, for the benefit of the police, composed not by Sandra herself, poor woman, but by a killer, still to be named and nabbed.

The party pictures Deena had taken were more interesting because they were more confused and somehow seemed more real, not staged. Although it pained me to see the hunting knife

I'd been so sure would link Howard Cleary to the crime, I forced myself to consider the party scene again, the women's loving attempts to celebrate their children's birthdays.

And there it was, after all, against all sense: my message from the dead. The picture Marlene and Deena liked so much, the one they'd framed because Ray looked so cute hidden behind a balloon, had also hidden most of the birthday present Sandra had bought for Crys. Some of these other pictures showed it more clearly. It was younger and cleaner, but there was no doubt it was Crys's ever-present companion, the ever-present present, the dilapidated unicorn.

Was this our breakthrough? I fell asleep hoping that when I woke up in the morning I still thought so. I was sleeping the sleep of the righteous, with one cat on my chest and another on my feet, when my phone rang, long before the light of morning, upsetting all three of us.

"What?" I hoped the caller could hear me over the squalling cats, but I couldn't be sure I'd heard her. I made her repeat herself, assured her I'd be there immediately, and called Hen while I was struggling into my uniform.

"What?" he asked.

I spoke slowly, enunciating carefully, so as not to have to re-repeat myself. "Crys Cleary just called me. Something or somebody has the dogs stirred up, and she and Mrs. Peyton think they've got a prowler. Or worse. They're scared. But Mrs. Peyton has a gun."

"Good God Almighty!" he said. "I'll meet you there."

CHAPTER 28

When we got to Mrs. Peyton's place, we found her in control of the situation. She had neutralized Howard by letting off one barrel of her shotgun in his general direction, close enough to convince him she knew what she was doing. Crys identified Howard and vouched for him, but Mrs. Peyton still wouldn't put her gun down or let Howard in the house. Even if I hadn't already been an admirer, this demonstration of her good sense and ability to take care of herself would have impressed me.

When backup sufficient to her assessment of the situation arrived, in the person of the Chief of Police and another armed officer, she sensibly relinquished her shotgun to Hen, and we all had a conversation about what had been going on.

"One at a time, now," Hen instructed. "Miz Peyton, you want to go first?"

"I certainly do! We heard a commotion outside with the dogs. They don't get stirred up for no reason. It's always something. Sometimes it's just deer, but this time it wasn't. They were really agitated, yelping and squealing enough to make me think somebody was hurtin' them. I took a look and saw him out there sneaking around. 'Course I didn't know who it was then, but nobody law-abidin' comes visitin' in the middle of the night without callin' first, so I went for my gun. I don't want anybody out there poisoning my dogs or breaking in here up to no tellin' what, and me with a girl to protect."

After that spate of remarkably coherent storytelling, she

stopped, seemed to be thinking it over, then nodded in satisfaction. "That's it. You gonna take me in for puttin' a gun on him?"

"For protecting your home and yourself against an intruder? I don't think so," Hen told her. "And I doubt Howard's going to want to press charges." He turned to Howard. "Now, you want to tell us why you were out there botherin' Miz Peyton's dogs?"

The look on Howard's face made it plain that he did not want to tell us that or anything else.

"Howard?" Hen said. "It don't make much difference to me whether you say anything or not, because I am about to haul your sorry self off to the jailhouse for trespassing, cruelty to animals—"

"I didn't hurt those dogs!"

Hen might not have heard. "Menacing, and . . . you think of anything else, Officer Roundtree?"

I hitched my gunbelt in as threatening a manner as I could muster and shook my head sorrowfully.

"I was looking for Crys." Howard was dressed in dark camouflage. What in the world had he been thinking?

"What were you planning to do when you found her?" Hen asked mildly.

"Take her home. You got no legal standing to keep her from home."

"Add attempted kidnapping to the list of charges, Officer Roundtree."

"Yes, sir," I said smartly.

"You're the ones kidnapped her," Howard said.

"How'd you know where to find her, anyway?" Hen asked.

Howard smirked. "Followed that Saddler boy. Figured he'd know where she was and if I watched him long enough, he'd lead me to her."

"But he didn't know where she was," I protested.

"I saw Evan out here geocaching," Crys said. "I saw him over there at his geocache. But I didn't talk to him. I didn't tell him I was here."

"I had my field glasses," Howard said. "I saw you through the window."

"Howard, for a man with a lot of smarts and a lot of know-how, you are sure one heckuva screw-up," Hen informed him. "Let's go, now, and let these women get back to sleep. We'll talk some more in the morning, but right now I'm putting you to bed in a place where you will not ramble, and I'm going home to my own soft bed."

As Hen reached for Howard and Crys reached for her unicorn, my late-night revelation came back to me. My last revelation, concerning what turned out to be a look-alike knife, had been wrong, but I was sure about this. Now was the time to stick my neck out.

"Chief?"

Hen looked at me, no doubt startled by the formality and unhappy at being pulled back from his thoughts of his own soft bed. "Officer Roundtree?"

"I need to talk to you."

He nodded and took his time looking at Mrs. Peyton, Crys, and Howard. "We're gonna walk over here and have a quiet little conference," he told them, "but I'll be keeping an eye on you, and I swear, Howard, if you make a move, I'll shoot you."

I led the way back toward the kitchen and stepped through the door so that I could talk without risking being overheard or having my lips read. Hen stopped in the doorway, where he could watch the living room.

"What in the world is going on?" he asked without looking at me.

This was neither the time nor the place to enjoy spinning out the story like I wanted to, nor the time to shout in triumph, so I whispered. "We've got him!"

"Uh-huh," he encouraged. "Talk fast."

"It's the unicorn, that mangy stuffed toy Crys always has with her. It was in Sandra Cleary's apartment the night she died. I've got pictures Sandra's friends took that prove it."

"That's good," Hen said, like the Lord God on the sixth day of creation. "That's very good." Unlike the Lord God, he added, "keep talkin'."

"I know," I whispered. "It might just *look like* the same animal, not *be* the same animal, but it's a pretty big coincidence, and there's no way Sandra Cleary could have brought it to her or mailed it to her. No way Crys went to get it. Howard says he never went to see Sandra in Macon. He lied. He brought that unicorn to Crys."

"Bringing it from the murder scene would have been pretty stupid," Hen said out of the corner of his mouth.

"He wouldn't have thought so. He never expected anybody to pay any attention. We can settle this right now."

"What you got in mind?"

"We ask Crys about it, where she got it, when. That will clinch it."

"In front of Howard? I don't think so."

"You're right. Why don't you go lock him up, and I'll talk to her."

He thought that over, thought about how long it would take to get Howard processed into the jail, thought about what he'd be missing if he wasn't there to hear what Crys had to say, first hand. Then, to my immense surprise, he paid me a great compliment by agreeing. Or maybe it wasn't a compliment. Maybe he thought I was wrong again, and this would be less embarrassing to the OPD. Whatever he was thinking, he sighed, then pushed himself away from the doorway. "Let's go, Howard." To Mrs.

Peyton and Crys he said, "Officer Roundtree will finish getting your statements. We'll all sleep better if we take care of this tonight."

To be on the safe side, I went outside with Hen and Howard and saw Howard safely confined in the back of the cruiser and the cruiser on its way. The world would be safe from Howard Cleary tonight at least, for much longer than that unless I was mistaken.

I took a moment to stretch, breathe deeply, and enjoy the starshine, moonshine, and gentle breeze blowing. It was by then not too long before sunrise, and I had that great exuberant feeling that goes with the dawning of a new day.

Back inside, I had the impression that neither Mrs. Peyton nor Crys had moved. I was glad to see they both looked awake, alert.

"He wouldn't have hurt anything," Crys said.

"You're probably right," I said. "But he might have got himself hurt, prowling around like that. Mrs. Peyton might have accidentally shot him."

"I never accidentally shot anything in my life," Mrs. Peyton said. "I'da shot him on purpose in another minute, though. What now?"

"We've got a few more things to wrap up." I stretched and yawned and tried to look sleepy and vague and purposeless. "The Chief wanted me to make sure y'all are okay, that Miz Peyton isn't about to go berserk."

"I'm fine," Mrs. Peyton said.

"Me, too," Crys said, hugging her unicorn, which gave me my opportunity to try what I hoped would pass as a casual change of topic.

I smiled, stretched, yawned, doing my best to look like somebody who was tired and making conversation merely to pass the time. "Your unicorn must be special," I said.

She held it out as though she'd never seen it before and looked at me with a puzzled frown.

"I've noticed it before," I said.

"Yeah."

"Do you always have it with you?"

"Pretty much."

Mrs. Peyton must have wondered what was going on, but she was gamely listening, maybe even understood that I was not as sleepy as I was trying to appear. She helped out with my pretense that this was nothing more significant than the casual conversation of three girls at a slumber party. With a glance at me she asked, "Was it from somebody special, Crys? A boyfriend?"

"No." A pause. "It was from Gramp."

"It looks like it's been around a while," I said. "How long have you had it? Do you remember?"

She eyed me with suspicion. "You're thinking I'm too old for it?"

"No." I shrugged and yawned again.

She humored me. "It was a birthday present."

"On your last birthday?"

"No. Why? You want one?"

"Just wondering."

"It was on my birthday three years ago."

"Was that a special birthday?"

She nodded. "Not the way you think. It was the last birthday my mother was alive. It reminds me of her."

"You like keepsakes," I said. "I remember you asked Mrs. Peyton for that clothespin holder, for a keepsake of her."

"I thought it was pretty lame when he gave it to me," Crys said. "I mean, I was thirteen, and it looked like something for a six-year-old. But he's an old man, so I guess he wouldn't know. I didn't like it and didn't want it, but I didn't want to hurt his feelings, so I acted like I liked it, and then that same day, I heard about my mother, about her dying, I mean, and then I felt like a six-year-old, and it was something warm to hold on to, and it sort of got connected to her in my mind. It still makes me feel a little closer to her, you know?"

I did think I knew how she felt, but I couldn't tell her I thought the unicorn was more than "sort of" connected to her mother. I wondered how she'd feel if she knew her mother had picked out that lame present for a thirteen-year-old. It made me sad. It showed how separated they were. But maybe if Crys had known it came from her mother, it wouldn't have seemed lame.

I left, after letting them assure me one more time that they were fine. I felt like a hypocrite as I reassured Crys that everything was going to be fine. If things turned out the way I expected them to, the way I was working to make them turn out, with her losing Howard, too, even if the cause of truth and justice demanded it, she would not feel like I had helped her. There wouldn't be a stuffed animal in the world large enough to help her through that.

I was satisfied that we'd managed to separate enough of the crossed wires to put Howard Cleary away for murder, but it didn't hurt that we had objective evidence to support my belief.

The lab matched the bullet from the pine tree—a bullet out of reasonable trajectory for aiming at a deer but just about right if it had gone through a person of Dixon Tatum's stature—to Howard Cleary's Winchester. We were elated. "Explains the two shots Lloyd talked about," Hen said. "Howard wouldn't have been reckless enough to try to get the boy's gun and kill him with that, so he killed him with his own, from close enough to be pretty sure it would go through him, and then fired off Dixon's gun so there'd be a casing."

"Still pretty risky," I observed. "What if it hadn't gone through?"

"He'da thought of something," Hen said with certainty. "It's Howard Cleary we're talking about here. He mighta claimed it was an accident. Who could prove it wasn't? If the shot hadn't killed the boy, Howard would have had another kind of problem." Hen pursed his lips. "How would you solve a problem like that?"

"Shoot him again in the same place, with his own gun," Jerome said. "Hope it would mess up the evidence enough."

None of that really mattered, though, since Howard's one shot had gone through Dixon in a vital place as he had intended, and since, even after all that, we felt we had stronger evidence in the Sandra Cleary case: that bedraggled unicorn. We had Crys's statement about where the unicorn came from. We had Marlene and Deena's testimony, backed up by photographs, and the fact that Howard had lied about being in Macon and lied to Crys about where the unicorn had come from. We had enough.

"Too bad Miz Peyton didn't go ahead and shoot him, though," Hen said. "Woulda been the perfect solution to this oddball case, not to mention saving us all the hassle and expense of a trial and his extended incarceration."

"Funny that what started us out on his track isn't what we can get him for," I said.

"Yeah, funny. If Raynell Harden still has doubts about the real target in Josh Easterling's death, assuming she ever really did, she'll have to work them out for herself. I'm plumb satisfied, but I'm sure glad we don't have to try build a case that would stand up in court based on Howard's skill as an electrician and his aversion to churches and church people."

CHAPTER 29

Hen likes to say that most criminals are so stupid law enforcement doesn't have to be particularly smart to catch them. Don't get him started providing supportive evidence, or you might be late for supper. There was the couple who claimed somebody stole their truck with the baby in it, and then, after disposing of the baby's body in the county landfill in a dim-witted effort to conceal their ongoing abuse of the poor child, parked the truck in their own garage. Yeah, they locked the garage, and put blankets over the truck, but still.

Then there's the aspiring bank robber who got so excited he put his gun down on the counter while he stuffed the swag into his bag—stupid enough if it had been a real gun, really stupid since it allowed the savvy clerk to recognize it as a plastic water pistol, which brought that particular foray into a life of crime to a halt. He's probably stupid enough to try again, though, as soon as he's able.

A local favorite is the woman who called the police to lodge a complaint against her drug dealer, who, she claimed, had sold her some sub-standard crack. Jerome and Miguel followed up on that one, controlling their guffaws.

And so on.

A special sub-brand of stupid is loose-lips stupid, the kind that makes a man tell his girlfriend if she doesn't do what he wants her to, he'll kill her like he did that other whore, or the kid who gives his mother his bloodstained clothing to clean up, or the airhead who brags to her friends about how easy it was to hit the pedestrian at the dark intersection with the new car her daddy bought her, never realizing that her confidantes might have issues of their own and might tell the police.

Some people in law enforcement would admit that the actual in-practice stupidity of the first kind and the can't-help-bragging stupidity of the second kind account for the greatest percentage of their solved cases.

Howard Cleary wasn't any kind of stupid. His downfall was arrogance. He seriously underestimated the capabilities of modern forensic science in general and the Ogeechee Police Department in particular. He was so sure of himself it simply never occurred to him that anybody would question the face he put on the deaths he engineered. It almost worked for him. Sadly, arrogance does work a lot of the time.

"What will become of Crys now?" Aunt Lulu asked one evening, waving a sepia-toned photograph of a girl in a lace dress and bows in her sausage curls, who bore a resemblance to Crys. Although a bribe hadn't been necessary, I'd offered peach ice cream and pound cake to my nearest and dearest if they'd come help me sort through a pile of old photographs I'd discovered in the back of a cupboard and see if they could help me identify the people. Aunt Lulu, of course, was likely to be more helpful than anybody else, but Hen can still surprise me. I'd invited Teri and Delcie to be polite and Phil to make the ice cream. I don't know all Phil's emotional issues, of course, but I'm pretty sure he likes it that I never doubt he'll be there when I need him. I think it makes him feel secure. And I do make a point of letting him know how much I appreciate him.

We'd finished the ice cream and cake and cleared the dishes. Delcie was sprawled on the floor, adding flourishes to an already elaborate drawing of some of the cats she was making with chalk pastels, and the rest of us were gathered at the table passing around pictures of interest.

"I think this is my great-aunt Angela's daughter, Caroline. We called her Carrie," Aunt Lulu said, waving a picture of a pretty blonde-haired girl. "What about Crys? Will she have to go to an institution or to those relatives that don't care a whit about her?"

"Miz Peyton's stepped up," Hen said. "Turns out she used to do a lot of short-term foster care. Been cutting back on that lately, but she and Crys hit it off, and I don't think it's just that Miz Peyton likes the way Crys keeps house. That'll work out well for Crys, with her so near finishing high school. Then they'll have to take a look. Won't be too long before Crys could be on her own, anyway."

"How's Crys taking all this?" Aunt Lulu asked.

"That girl's had so many hard blows it's like she's grown scar tissue over her feelings," Hen said.

"One thing that will help is Kyle Simpson," I said. "He's the Boy Scout who helped us with the fingerprinting at the church," I explained to the civilians. "According to my sources, he's been showing an interest in Crys. If he can be patient, patient enough to wait while she realizes it will be okay for her to get attached to somebody, that interest could turn out to be good for both of them. I mean, he's a Boy Scout, after all, which means he likes to do good deeds and help people. Right?"

Teri smiled. "It could help them both enjoy their senior year."

"Mrs. Peyton will be good for Crys, too," I said. "She really likes Crys. Poor Crys is bound to be in an emotional mess, not even counting the fact that she's lost the only person left in her life that she loved and that she knew loved her. She's got to be missing him. No matter what he did, I think he was always good to her. Mrs. Peyton is doing what she can to help. She got in touch with Sandra's friends in Macon, Marlene Booth and her daughter, and they're going to get together."

"It'll be a good thing for Crys to know some people who liked her mother and get Howard's poison out of her system," Teri said. We observed a moment of silence, and then Teri spoke up again, eyeing Phil in a way that made me think Hen had put her up to it. "I'll miss Howard's column in *The Beacon*. Will he keep writing it from prison?"

Phil dropped a stack of photos and took his time collecting and arranging them before he answered. "I hadn't thought of that. It would give Howard a whole new subject matter, but I believe it's time I took *The Beacon* in a new direction. Maybe find somebody to do a column on cooking or gardening or seniors. We've got a growing senior population. Miz Huckabee, you want to do that?"

Both Teri and Aunt Lulu are, of course, "Miz Huckabee," but Phil calls Teri "Teri."

"Not that I'm not flattered, Phil," Aunt Lulu said, almost concealing her annoyance at being considered an insider on the senior scene at a mere sixty-something, "but I don't see where I'd ever find the time."

"How about me?" Teri asked, possibly annoyed at being overlooked. "I might enjoy doing something like that. If you're looking for a senior angle, I could profile seniors with interesting hobbies, like that man with the walking stick collection, or maybe talk to people about how things have changed here in Ogeechee or wherever they grew up—but most people who live here have lived here for a long time, so it would be Ogeechee history—or maybe a series on some of the old buildings around town. I could start with this house, couldn't I, Trudy? Or maybe organizations that attract seniors. Maybe one column about the Geezerettes."

I was stunned at the ideas she threw out so easily. Phil, too, was struck silent. Not Aunt Lulu.

"Oh, no, you don't," Aunt Lulu said. "You leave the Geezerettes alone. People would be wanting to get in, and you know we're choosy."

"Just what are the membership requirements?" Hen asked. "I've always wondered."

"You know perfectly well it has to be people we like and can get along with, people who're willing to go along with our ideas. We don't like wet blankets."

"What's your latest idea?" I asked. They've had some doozies in the past, but I wasn't prepared for this one.

"We're thinking of doing a calendar, we'd call it the Un-Calendar, one of those photographic ones, for a fundraiser, since Hen wouldn't let us do the football pool we wanted to do for the Super Bowl last year."

"It was the laws of the State of Georgia that stopped that godless gambling," Hen said. "Don't blame me."

"Photos of what?" Phil asked.

Aunt Lulu fluffed up her already fluffy Cosmopolitan-colored curls and said, "Us."

"Us?" Delcie looked up from her drawing, clearly taken with the idea. She struck several undeniably photogenic poses before her grandmother burst her bubble.

"The Geezerettes," Aunt Lulu said. Then, turning her face away from Delcie, she mouthed the word "nude."

"How's your picture coming, Delcie?" Teri asked.

"Just about done, but these cats won't be still."

Aunt Lulu watched until Delcie, that devious child, apparently turned her attention back to choosing the right color pastel, then said, "I want to be Ms. December. I have a couple of really nice poinsettias, but naturally Della Stubbs thinks she should be December, just because it's her birthday month. I see her more as Ms. January. Bleak. Two-faced."

So much for the Geezerettes' membership requirement that it be people "we" can get along with. Even Aunt Lulu can't always have her way.

"And the timing is right," she chattered on, since everybody else had been struck dumb. "We'd need to have it out well before the end of the year, before everybody already has their calendars for next year, don't you think?"

"Who's doing the photography," Phil managed to ask, although his voice did sound a bit strangled. Naturally, as a photographer himself, he'd be interested.

"We haven't decided yet," Aunt Lulu said. "You think you'd want to do it?"

Before Phil could summon an answer to this, Hen stepped in. "I don't want to hurt your feelings, Mama, but who'd want to buy this calendar?"

A gleam in her eye told us there was something tricky afoot. Geezerettes. "I didn't say anything about selling them, did I?"

"You did say 'fundraiser.' "

"Well, yes. I probably shouldn't say so right here in front of the Chief of Police, but we were thinking of blackmail. The State of Georgia probably has laws against that, too."

"You taking notes, Officer Roundtree?" Hen asked.

"Should I be?"

"Probably not. Anyway, it's not likely we'll forget this. Go on, Mama."

"Well, most of us are pretty sure our families would be happy to make a donation to the charity of our choice instead of us having to go to the actual expense and trouble of producing the thing. That's why we're calling it the un-calendar—un-dressed, un-published. I'm the one who thought of that."

"Sounds simple enough," Phil said, safe in the knowledge that he had no relative who was a Geezerette. "I suppose each of you could discreetly—if that's the word—have one picture taken that you could flash—I mean show—to certain people.

Will you be making suggested donations or just taking what's offered?"

Aunt Lulu beamed at him. "We haven't decided about that. What do you think, Hen?"

"I'll have to check my bank account and get back to you."

We went back to the pile of old photos.

"What do you think of me as a columnist, Phil," Teri asked in a moment.

"You're hired."

"Don't you even want to see a sample column?" Hen asked.

"No. I can tell from her enthusiasm that the columns would be worth reading."

"When do I start?"

"The day you give me five to seven hundred words."

"Can I do my first one on the Un-Calendar?" Teri looked, wide-eyed and innocent, from Hen to Phil and back, skipping Aunt Lulu.

"I'll have to check with my, uh, board of advisors, and get back to you on that," Phil said, with a quick glance around the table.

"Look! Here's one of Mama and me when I was just a baby!" Aunt Lulu said brightly.

"Do you have any clothes on?" Hen asked, leaning closer.

Delcie's quickly suppressed grin might have had something to do with the fact that she was cleaning the chalk off her hands by stroking the cats, but I didn't think so.

All the Un-Calendar talk upstaged what Phil and I had agreed would be our big announcement. It didn't matter, though. We could enjoy keeping our secret for a while longer, and when the time was right maybe we'd turn Aunt Lulu and Teri loose and see what they could plan around an Un-Wedding wedding theme.

ABOUT THE AUTHOR

Linda Berry lives with her husband in Aurora, Colorado, but her Trudy Roundtree Mysteries grow out of her small-town Georgia roots and an extended family that keeps her in material—specifically her cousin Johnny Shuman, now Chief of Police in Swainsboro, Georgia. Her published credits include poetry, plays, craft articles, short fiction for children and adults, preschool curriculum, and a newspaper entertainment column, in addition to her six Trudy Roundtree Mysteries. She's a member of the Denver Woman's Press Club, Rocky Mountain Fiction Writers, and Sisters in Crime. She describes herself as a community arts activist and an insatiable theatre-goer.